SAVIOR

A Novel By:

Jessica Gadziala

DEDICATION

To my mother. Who I pray never reads this with all its smutty deliciousness. She bought me the laptop I use to write all of these stories and listens to me prattle on endlessly about this indie writer thing.

I promise to show at least two-thirds the same enthusiasm when she talks about embroidery.

SAVIOR

-

ONE

Elsie

Thank God for charity 5ks and the heavy layer of guilt people slathered on to get you to agree to do such a thing in the first place.

Those were thoughts I never thought I would think. See, I hated running. I hated running the way most people hated clowns. Meaning with a fiery passion. People who thought sweating through their makeup and clothes and chafing in unmentionable areas would be a jolly good time were seriously whacked.

That being said, thank God for all those pre-dawn mornings I was dragged out of bed to train before my mind was awake enough to object to the absurdity of it all. After all, anyone with a fully functioning brain would know sleep was much more preferable to going out in the freezing cold and running along the empty streets.

Because, well, that training was paying off.

In the way that I was running for my life. Sort-of. I was pretty sure anyway. See, I was being chased by two men. Now perhaps all they wanted was to tell me I had a pretty smile. But I seriously doubted it seeing as A) I didn't smile at them and B) they just caught me snooping around some kind of warehouse they were obviously in charge of protecting and C) men didn't chase you down street after street to compliment you. So yeah, I was sticking with the 'running for my life' idea.

My lungs were burning no matter how much I tried to control my breathing and my leg muscles were screaming in objection. And, well, running in jeans wasn't fun. Then there were my feet. Ballet flats were cute and all, but they weren't meant for running and the ones I was wearing had been rubbing at the backs of my heels well before the running started. I half-expected, when I took them off later, assuming I lived, that there would be some nice cuts that would ensure there would be nothing I could put on my feet for a week that wouldn't hurt except for flip flops. It was January.

But, if I got out of this, I figured cold feet were a relatively small price to pay.

Behind me, the guys were keeping pace, but not gaining on me. I said a silent 'thank you' to my dead mother for the long legs I inherited from her.

I was out of the slums. Crap. 'Slum' was probably not the P.C. way to phrase it. But every other word that came to mind seemed even worse: projects, ghetto. Okay. I was sticking with slum. It was a slum, meaning it was a really really crummy part of town that there was no way that I should have been in at twelve o'clock at night, alone, ever. But I had my reasons. I had to be there. I had to see if I could figure out what happened...

"Give it up, Barbie, you ain't getting away!" one of them called behind me, annoyingly in control of his breath. I'd caught one good glance of him before I started running and didn't look back. He was the kind of built that came from endless hours in a gym and a very likely heavy use of steroids. He put my thrice-weekly normal workouts and my once weekly hot yoga classes to shame.

The road split ahead and I heard one tell the other to go up some other street to head me off. I needed to lose the guy behind me. Even if it was just for a couple seconds, a couple seconds to find a place to dip into and hide, call the cops, call my father, call someone.

When I heard only one set of feet behind me and, judging by the huffing, it was not the gym rat, I threw everything I had into it and sprang forward, turning the corner with every bit of strength and determination I had in me.

I had just barely made it around the corner when I found myself snagged around the waist. A hand clamped down over my mouth as the arm around my waist held tight and hauled me off my feet, pulling me backward and inside some building.

I felt hysteria flood my system, making me flail out wildly, having no clue what I was actually doing, but knowing I needed to do something.

"Shh," a voice hissed into my ear as I was pulled deeper into the store.

I was pretty sure quiet wasn't something I should be either. I was pretty sure I was supposed to scream. But seeing as there was a very strong hand across my mouth, that was pointless anyway.

"How many of them are there?" the voice asked and I noticed two things at once: it was a very nice voice, smooth, sexy and it was not the voice of one of the guys who had been following me for the past ten or fifteen minutes. I made some kind of noise, muffled by the hand. "Don't scream. You scream, babygirl, and they'll find you. Got it?"

I felt like some chick in a movie. Like one of those cheesy B-action movies. I was the girl who was going to blindly trust the guy whose face she hadn't even seen, whose motives I had no idea of. Because, well, what choice did I really have?

I nodded and his hand moved off my mouth. "Two," I said, sucking in a desperate breath.

His arm released my middle and he moved out from behind me and toward the front of the store. It was dark, but I could make out some things that made it unmistakable. There were tables and chairs, desks with locked drawers, big framed flash art on the walls. It was a tattoo shop. For some reason, I felt marginally better at least knowing that fact.

My savior's back was to me as he opened the front door and stood in the opening, looking out at the street. The streetlights out front gave me a slightly better look at him. From what I could tell, he was tall. Meaning tall. See, I was tall 'for a girl' at my five-foot-nine. He was just plain tall for a human being. My best guess was somewhere around six-three or four. And it seemed like every inch of that six-three or four was made of solid muscle. He had one of those bodies that only some guys managed to get where he had massive shoulders and a strong looking back that tapered into a slim waist. He had on slate gray heavy sweatpants that were slung low on his hips and showed nothing of what was underneath, though if I had to place a bet, my money was on a fine looking backside and muscular legs. His top was clad in a black wifebeater that fit him like a second skin and, therefore, let me make out the strong back and shoulders I mentioned before. His arms were bare, and what (very little) skin I could see underneath all the tattoos, was a really envy-inspiring shade of caramel.

I heard footsteps on the street and felt the panic well up strong and almost crippling. Was he going to sell me out after all? Did he actually work with those guys? I pressed hard into the wall then silently slid down it, wedging myself into the corner behind a tattoo table, knees tight to my chest, arms around my legs, not so much as breathing in some insane fear that it could be audible.

"Paine," the fit guy who chased me said, making my face scrunch up. Pain? What about pain? "See a girl around here? Looks like a Barbie? Blond hair, blue eyes, nice tits and ass, blow job lips?"

I felt my lip curl at that particular description. I wasn't unaccustomed to the 'Barbie' nickname. There was a little bit of truth in it. I was tall; I had blond hair (it was actually a balayage

9

I paid way too much money for); I had long legs. That part, I could live with even if it was getting old. But the tits, ass, and blow job lips comment? Yeah, that was just messed up. Did all guys think things like that when they saw women?

Hey look, it's a chick. Quick- we need to objectify her before we realize she's a human being!

"The fuck would I tell you shit for, D? This isn't your part of town. Enzo know you're out causing problems on Henchmen turf?"

"Ain't afraid of no pussy fucking bikers," the other guy, the one who was huffing and puffing, said.

So, if you were from Navesink Bank, you knew about The Henchmen. Even if you didn't know much about them, you knew they existed. You probably saw them driving around on their bikes in town on any given day or night. If you went to the only decent local bar, Chaz's, you ran into them there. That was their hangout. As a somewhat informed citizen, I knew The Henchmen Motor Cycle Club wasn't one of those 'weekend warrior' type organizations. They were actual criminals. If the papers were to be believed, which I was generally raised not to trust, they were some kind of arms dealers. As a woman, however, I also knew that it seemed like every last one of them was really good looking. Not that I would date a biker, let alone a criminal biker, but still... they were nice to look at.

I also knew that pretty much no one would call The Henchmen "pussy fucking bikers". Or, at least, if they did and word got around, they would live to regret it.

"I'll pass along your opinions, Trick. Now I suggest you get the fuck out of my part of town before you really start to piss me off."

"Know you think you're some badass mother fuck..." D, the muscle-y one, started. The rest of his sentence got cut off. This was mostly because his breath got cut off. Meaning the guy who sort-of saved me grabbed him by the throat and slammed him into the side of the doorway, almost lifting him off his feet.

"Don't forget who the fuck you're talking to D. Now it's late and I'd rather be in front of my TV with a beer than out here talking to you dipshits. But I am always up for handing out an ass kicking to dumb ass mother fuckers who forget who used to own them."

Own them?

How the heck did someone own someone else?

And, also, what had I gotten myself into?

"Hey hey," Trick started, waving his hands. "He's got a big mouth. Always has. You know how he is. You're gonna kill him. Put him down. We'll get back to Third Street and out of your hair."

My savior let D's throat go, but he did it all rough, somehow turning him and tossing him into the street by it.

"Don't want to see your faces around my shop again. Got it?"

"Got it. Got it," Trick, obviously the one with more brains, said, moving backward until I couldn't see them anymore.

The shop owner slash badass stood in the doorway for another couple of minutes, I assumed, watching the guys disappear, before he moved back into the store, locking the door, flicking the lights, then turning to me.

Yeah. Okay.

He was good looking. Seriously good looking. He legitimately could have been a model. He had that perfect mixed-race skin tone, light-skinned black with a chiseled face, buzzed short black hair, and the most hypnotic hazel eyes I had ever seen in my life. Those eyes were looking around the shop.

"Babygirl, come out. You don't have to hide. You coulda been standing right behind me and they wouldn't have touched you."

Yeah, well, I seriously doubted that. What an ego. But I slowly unfolded my body and stood up, staying close to the wall, away from him.

"I'm Paine," he said, head tilted slightly as he looked at me. He did the typical male inspection, but he had the decency to make it short and sweet and focused all of his attention on my face after.

"Paine?" I asked, feeling a smile pull at my lips despite the night I was having. I looked around the shop real quickly before looking at him again. "A tattoo artist... named Paine?" The smile was no longer tugging, but full.

"Yeah yeah yeah," he said, rolling his eyes.

"Heard that before, huh?"

"Only every day for years."

"Oh, gee, sorry I couldn't be more original. I was just running for my life for the past fifteen minutes."

"Yeah, about that... what the fuck did you get yourself into? 'Cause I gotta tell ya, babygirl, don't know if I have it in me to have another damsel in distress situation 'round here. Things have finally calmed down."

"I'm not a damsel in distress," I objected immediately. "I would have lost them eventually. You just happened to stop me before I could."

"Sure," he agreed in that voice that implied he didn't believe a word I said. "Why are guys from the Third Street gang chasing money like you?"

"Money like me?" I repeated, not understanding the turn of phrase.

"Babe, eighty dollar jeans, one-twenty on your feet and you're bleeding all over them, hair like that must have cost a mint. And if I'm not mistaken, those are diamonds on your ears. Real ones. Money like you."

"My hair is real," I bristled.

"Not that color."

"What are you a hairdresser on the side too? Tattooing doesn't bring in enough money?"

"Cute, but you're not throwing me. What is a girl like you doing in the ghetto?"

Ghetto. Maybe slum was the worse way to put it. "I don't see how that is any of your business."

"You looking for smack?"

"Smack?" I asked, my nose scrunching up. I knew that was a slang for a drug. I wasn't stupid. But I also had no idea what that drug was. There were too many names for all of that stuff: smack, angel dust, ice, crank, speed, rock, chalk. It was amazing that a person who did said drugs could keep all those names straight.

"Heroin. Guessing if you don't even know what it's called that you ain't shooting that stuff into your veins or sniffing it into that pretty nose of yours."

"I don't do drugs."

"Babe, it's late. Work with me here."

"Actually, if you don't mind... I am just going to make a quick phone call," I said, reaching into my pocket and pulling out my cell, "then I will be out of your hair as soon as a ride comes for me."

"Limo?" he asked with a smirk. "Town car?"

Okay. So maybe I did have a town car at my disposal if I wanted it. But that wasn't who I was calling. And the mocking way he said it made me feel almost guilty.

"Name."

"Excuse me?" I asked, pausing in scrolling through my contacts.

"Your name, babygirl. What is it?"

Oh.

Well. I guess it was fair enough to give him my name. My first name. No way was he getting any more than that. It wouldn't be hard to find me if he had my full name. And I didn't want to be found. I didn't want anyone to know what I was up to.

"Elsie," I told him then went back to scrolling, finding the only name in my contacts who would come get me at this hour in the part of town I was in.

"Alright, Elsie. You have any idea how dangerous those men out there were?"

"Really? Because I was sure they were just chasing me to tell me they hoped I made it home safely."

"Okay, smartass," he said, smiling a little as I lifted my phone to my ear, "you got secrets. I get it. But I'm trying to make sure you know what you're getting yourself into by messing with Third Street guys..."

"Elsie, it's late. Everything okay?" Roman's voice asked, sounding like he had been sleeping.

I ignored the stab of guilt I felt at waking him up. "Roman, can you give me a ride?"

"A ride?" Roman asked and I could hear him shuffling. "Sure, Else. Give me an address. I'll be there in ten tops."

I muttered off the address I could see printed on the business cards on the desk. "Thanks Rome. I really appreciate it. Sorry for dragging you out of bed so late."

"Your boyfriend's name is Roman?" Paine asked, lips twitching.

"I don't think someone by the name of Paine can judge," I said, putting my phone away. "And he's not my boyfriend." Shoot. Maybe that wasn't something I should have said. I was pretty sure it was smart for scary dudes to believe you had the protection of some man, even if said man wasn't exactly a scary dude.

My response was knee-jerk. Roman and I had been friends since infancy. I mean that literally. Our mothers were best friends. There wasn't one memory of my childhood that didn't have Roman in it. When my mom died and my father had no interest in keeping friendship with Roman's family, we still managed to spend most of our time together. It was a friendship that somehow managed to stand strong despite his four years of university on the West coast while I stayed in Jersey for college.

Everywhere we went from puberty on, everyone assumed we were a couple. It was an assumption I was so used to correcting that I hardly even noticed I did it anymore.

"Sure he knows that?" Paine asked, sitting down on one of the two rolling stools in the shop.

"Yes, I'm sure."

"He's coming to get you in the middle of the night without asking you why you're in this part of town..."

"So? He's a friend. Friends do that for each other." Why was I discussing Roman with the random tattoo shop guy? Well, I guess it was better than talking about what I was doing getting the attentions of a dangerous gang.

"Poor guy aware he's got no shot with you?"

"I don't see how that is any of your business."

Paine didn't seem riled, if anything, he just smiled a little wider, showing off some pretty perfect white teeth. "You want some coffee?" he asked, standing before I even gave him an answer and moving through the back of the shop where there was an open door.

"Ah, sure. Thank you," I said, leaning around the corner to see where he disappeared to.

"You can come through. I'm not gonna hurt you." Yeah, well, he'd have to forgive me for not being entirely trusting of that fact given that those guys that were chasing me seemed to be, at least a little bit, afraid of him. I didn't know a lot about bad guys, but I was pretty sure that if the bad guys were scared of someone, that made him an even bigger bad guy. Even if he did have really nice teeth and pretty eyes. "Your non-boyfriend is on his way right now. Even if my intention was to hurt you, think I'd do it knowing that?"

Well, he had a point.

I glanced at the desk, grabbed the pair of scissors sticking out of a pen holder and tucked them into my pocket, making sure my shirt was down to cover them. You know... just in case. Not that I believed I was actually capable of stabbing someone, but who knew what they were capable when push came to shove. Then I walked down the short hall through an open door to... an apartment.

Well, I wasn't expecting that. I thought storefronts with apartments usually had the apartments upstairs. But Paine had one behind it. I understood why his tattoo shop was on the small side, because his apartment was rather large. It was a loft, a completely open floor plan with dark blue walls and floors that had been finished in the darkest shade possible, just shy of black. The large California King bed was to the left with a plush white comforter; a living space was toward the center in the back of the room with a big sectional that looked like I could sink into and never come out and was in front of a massive television. The kitchen was u-shaped and looked pretty state-of-the-art with white subway tiles, white cabinets and white marble counter tops. I found myself wondering if he cooked. I also wondered why he lived behind his shop when he obviously had the money to afford a better place in a better part of town.

Maybe he just liked being close to work.

"How do you take it?" he asked, back to me, pouring coffee into mugs.

"Milk if you have it." To that, he turned, brow quirked up. "What?"

"No fancy shit?"

"Didn't imagine you had sugar-free caramel syrup just laying around."

"Not caramel, but I got..." he reached up into a cabinet, shuffling things around before coming back with two bottles, "toasted almond and... fuck... blueberry?" he declared with a weird inflection, face scrunched up.

"I'll take blueberry," I said on a smile.

"Seriously?"

"Yeah."

"In coffee?"

"No, in my soup. Yes, in my coffee. That's what we're talking about, right?"

"Caramel, mocha, almond... get that. Fruit in coffee? That's some weird chick shit," he said as put a few drips into my coffee with the milk I requested, stirred, then handed it to me.

"Why do you have it if you don't drink it?" I asked, taking a sip.

"Sisters," he said, shrugging as he leaned against the counter, holding his mug by the top despite the steam coming out of it. "They come over, drop off food shit like they live here so they can have what they like when they visit."

"Is that frequent?" I asked, not wanting to fall into awkward silence.

"A little too."

"How many sisters?"

"Two."

"They're younger, right?" I asked.

"How'd you know?"

"You have that... tone people use about little sisters... like you're both annoyed but charmed by them."

"Do you have little sisters?"

"No," I said, inwardly cringing at the finality of my tone.

He picked it up too, brows drawing slightly together. "So, Elsie with no little sisters, you going to tell me what you were doing out on the street at this hour, pissing off Third Street guys?"

"Who said I pissed them off? Maybe they're just jerks who chase girls down the street."

"Maybe, but the way you're evading answering me says otherwise."

"How do you know those guys?" I countered, lifting my chin a little.

His smile was at once devilish and charming and I felt the tiniest twinge of desire spark through my system. "Smart girl," he said, shaking his head.

"How so?" I mean, I was smart, but he couldn't possibly know that.

"You picked up on the fact that I don't want to talk about that particular connection like you don't want to talk about your involvement with them, so you brought it up."

"So we're agreed- we can both keep our secrets."

"Sure, but babygirl, a little advice..." he paused, crossing the kitchen toward me, completely taking up all my space as we came almost toe-to-toe. "Whatever you are doing involving them, stop. Immediately. You're pretty. You're smart. It would be a shame for you to end up in a casket."

Well hell. I had been sort-of trying to convince myself that the guys weren't that dangerous. Stupid, I know. But I needed to believe I could deal with them, that I could fix things. And to believe that, I needed to think there was a way to reason with them or, at the very least, work around them without getting into too much trouble. Being chased, well, I could have maybe convinced myself that they wanted to stop me and figure out what I was doing. They might figure out I wasn't a threat and just let me go.

But with Paine telling me that they would apparently have no qualms about killing me, well, it made it impossible to pretend ignorance of the danger.

"Elsie," his smooth voice said, making my head snap up automatically. "Whatever it is, get out of it," he said, his hand raising and snagging some of the large amount of hair that had fallen out of my ponytail whilst running. He tucked it behind my ear, brushing the lobe and trailing his fingers down my neck slightly in doing so. And I totally shivered. Visibly, not just on the inside.

"I..."

My mouth clamped shut as his hand dropped, both of us looking out toward the door to the shop when there was banging.

"Your not-boyfriend," Paine surmised as my hand automatically reached for my cell. It wasn't like him not to text when he arrived somewhere.

But, he had. Three times. I must have been too distracted to hear the ding.

"Must be," I agreed, slipping my phone into my pocket again and moving out toward the shop, taking a long, greedy sip of my coffee before placing it down on one of the desks. "Hey, Paine..." I said, turning back toward him, "thanks for, um, letting me in and for the coffee. I really appreciate it."

"Don't mention it," he said, shrugging. But he was also advancing at me in an almost predatory way that made me go back a foot before his arm went around me.

No, not just around me.

His hand settled hard on my ass, squeezing for a second.

My entire body froze, shocked, unsure how to respond. But the whole thing only lasted a total of maybe five seconds before his arm pulled back and I saw the scissors in his hand.

"Like I said," he said, placing them on the desk, "smart girl. Now go out there to your not-boyfriend, go back to your safe little life and forget all about the Third Street guys. And me," he added as he brushed past me, unlocked the front door, and pulled it open to reveal Roman.

Now, just because he was my not-boyfriend didn't mean I couldn't appreciate how good looking he was. Roman was a good six foot- maybe six-one. He was thin, but strong in a non-aggressive sort of way. Maybe it was fair to call it a swimmer's body. His chestnut-colored hair was slightly long on top, and brushed back then cropped close at the sides which only succeeded in making his classically handsome face even more striking. He had a straight nose, strong brow ridge, and very endearing brown eyes framed in thick lashes. He kept his face clean-shaven and he dressed well. Even after being woken up in the middle of the night, he was put together. He had on dark wash jeans that fit well and a white, thick-knit sweater with two buttons near the throat, which he left undone.

"Christ, Else, you scared me," he said, gesturing with his phone in his hand.

"I'm sorry. I didn't hear the ding," I shrugged, brushing it off. Though, in general, I was hyper aware of my cell. It was completely out of character of me to not answer right away, let alone at all.

"Are you alright, you look a little..." he trailed off, giving me a smile I always found myself smiling back at, warm, teasing. "You're a mess, Else."

"It's a long story."

"That ends in a tattoo shop," he commented, jerking his chin toward the building I was standing in the doorway of. "Planning on getting some work done? Or have you already? Somewhere naughty? If so, can I see?" he teased and I found myself laughing as I stepped out into the street. I wasn't aware Paine had followed behind until Roman's eyes went behind me and almost... darkened. "Who is this?" he asked me, giving me a look I can only describe as probing before turning his attention back to Paine.

"Oh, um... Roman... this is Paine. Paine, Roman. Paine is..."

"A friend," Paine supplied, offering his hand which Roman took and shook hard before dropping like it burned him.

"Well, Paine... thanks for keeping an eye on Else for me," Roman said, reaching for my hand and tugging a bit roughly as he turned toward his car parked right by the sidewalk, opening the door for me.

When I chanced a look back at Paine, his lip twitching said a hundred different things at once. Not the least of which was: it sure doesn't look like he knows he's not your boyfriend. But then I was pressed into Roman's car and the door slammed, the blackout windows making it hard to see him anymore at all.

Then Roman was in his seat and the car turned over and he shot off.

TWO

Elsie

"Whoa, slow down," I said, pressing hard into my seat with one of my hands on the dash. He had to be going sixty on the main drag, thirty above the speed limit. My stomach felt like it took up residence on the floor. "Roman, slow down!" I shouted when he didn't immediately take his foot off the pedal.

"Else, what the fuck?" he asked, glancing over at me, his features looking tight like he was... angry? Why would he be angry?

"I know. I'm sorry. I shouldn't have called. I should have gotten a cab. You have work in the..."

"No, Else. Always, always call if you need a ride. That wasn't what I meant."

"Then what did you mean?"

Roman pulled the car off onto a side street, throwing it into park while somehow simultaneously un-belting and turning to face me fully. "I'm not being a snob..." he started.

"Okay," I said, head tilting to the side a little.

21

"You want to be in this part of town on a Friday or Saturday night, having drinks with the girls, having fun. No problem. All for it. But what the fuck are you doing at this hour in that part of town... alone?"

I forced my lips to tip upward. "Not being a snob, huh?" I teased.

"Elsie," he said, his tone firmer.

"Don't dad-voice me, Rome," I scolded. We'd never had that kind of friendship. If anything, we always encouraged each other to do wild things, to push the boundaries, to do things that would cause raised eyebrows. But, then again, we generally did those things together. I couldn't think of anything, aside from losing my virginity at the tender age of fifteen, that I had ever done without him at my side. Maybe that was what this was about. He was feeling left out, excluded.

And, in a weird kind of way, I was pushing the boundaries without him. But I wasn't doing it for the raised eyebrows or even the rush of adrenaline. I was doing it because I had to. And I was keeping it from him because I had to do that to. So, for the first time in probably our entire friendship, I had to lie to him too.

"I'm not dad-voicing you. I'm trying to understand what is up with you lately."

Of course he had picked up on that too.

I'd been off.

I knew that. It was something that couldn't be avoided. I was more scatterbrained, less easy to get in touch with, secretive. All things that had never been qualities I had before.

"Fine!" I said, throwing my hands up in mock frustration. "I was looking into tattoo shops for us. You ruined it!"

Roman's head tilted, his brows drawing together slightly. "Tattoos? For us?" He said it in a way that implied I might as well have suggested we get septum piercings and wear them with huge bull rings every day.

"For our friend anniversary. Twenty-eight years next month," I said, thinking of my birthday. That was the first time we met. We have pictures of us lying side-by-side on the hospital bed the afternoon of my birth, Roman a mere ten weeks older.

To that, Rome's face softened. A sweet smile pulled at his lips. "What did you have planned?"

"Honestly? I hadn't gotten that far." I hadn't gotten that far because I had just come up with the idea. "I was just looking around."

"Else... why after midnight? That shop didn't even look open."

"Paine's, ah, he's very busy. Popular. He couldn't fit me in any other time. I don't know a lot about tattoos so I had a bunch of questions."

"Where was your car?"

Crap. Of course he would ask that. It was a good question. I loved my car. I drove it whenever possible. It was a recent purchase and I was proud of myself for being able to get that kind of financing on that kind of car without a co-signer, without having to involve my father. That being said, it was the kind of car that stood out. It was last year's Porsche 718 Boxster S in Miami Blue paint. It was more than a down payment on most people's houses. It was not the kind of car you drove into the slums when you were trying to not be seen. Or, you know, have it stolen.

And that was exactly what I was going to go with, even if it made slightly less sense to use it when talking about the industrial part of town. It was believable enough.

"I didn't want to bring him into that part of town. You know how I feel about that car. I took a cab. But um... the driver was really creepy. I didn't want to get stuck with him again on the way home..."

"Aw, Else, glad you called then," he said, satisfied as he moved back into his seat, pulling his belt, and putting the car back into drive. "Let's get you home. You have work in the morning too."

So then we were driving, me flicking impatiently through the radio stations while Roman tried to fight for the songs he liked and I largely ignored him.

There were two sets of townhouse developments in Navesink Bank, one was a typical middle-class sprawling development full of families and the occasional single man or woman. They were perfectly nice and I had done a walk-through of three different units before my father got wind and threw a fit. And, see, that sounds pathetic given my age, but then again... you don't know my father. Edward Bay was intimidating, if not downright terrifying, when he was in a good mood. So when he was ticked off, or personally offended like he was when I wanted to get a middle-class townhouse, he was wet-your-pants scary. Why was he personally offended, you ask? My father was a successful businessman. By that I mean he made the kind of money that bordered on obscene and he liked to live like he did. He liked to flash his wealth around. So he was insulted when I refused to dip into my trust fund and drop half a million dollars on a house way too big for one person to live in.

From there, I put up a valiant effort to profess my independence and stick to my guns. But, well, my father made a career of browbeating men and women far greater than me.

So I had a townhouse that cost half a million dollars that had two extra bedrooms I had no need for, a state of the art kitchen I had no skills to cook inside of, and a HOA fee that was the cost of a nice two-bedroom apartment in pretty much any town surrounding Navesink Bank.

I'm not saying it wasn't nice to live in a beautiful townhouse. I wasn't a fan of falling into the 'poor little rich girl' trope. I was lucky; I knew that; I had always known that. That being said, some gifts came with clauses and mine was feeling forever under the thumb of a man who I had spent my entire life trying to free myself from. It meant that he would always feel he had a say in my life decisions, my career decisions, and pretty much anything else I did that he felt might reflect back on him.

Roman parked in the driveway in front of my garage where my car was stashed away. Each townhouse in the neighborhood was two stories and part of a three-home section. The two on the ends had pitched roofs and shutters, the one in the center with a flat roof and a extended picture window. The bricks on the fronts were also in a pattern in colors: Regency brick, Dover, then Orleans. I had a house on the left with the pitched roof, the shutters, and the Regency brick. I might have resented the money coming from my trust fund, but it was a gorgeous house.

"Do you want to crash here instead of driving home?" I asked as the car idled. We each had stuff stashed at each other's houses for the occasions when one of us got too tired or too drunk to drive home. He had an entire dresser in one of my guest rooms. I had half a closet in one of his.

"You don't mind?" he asked, facing me and I noticed how tired he looked for the first time.

"No, of course not," I said, shaking my head. "You can always stay."

With that, I climbed out of his car and made my way over to the stairs that led to my front door, reaching under my shirt for the key I kept around my neck before Roman came up behind me. It was another thing that he would find out of character. I had a janitor's key chain I usually carried, fifteen different keys on it that I considered everyday essentials to have on me. So just having the key to my door, not even the deadbolt key, around my neck was weird. But I was worried about the keys jingling while I was looking around in the slums.

I hit the code for the security and stepped inside. "Haul it, Rome. I don't want to call the security company again," I called, flicking on the lights as Rome came inside and closed the door. He hit the code for me as I moved to kick out of my flats before I remembered Paine's comments about me bleeding all over my shoes.

The entryway was wide with a white staircase leading upstairs and crown molding. To the left was a large living room painted in a soft blue-gray and decorated with gray sofas and chairs and white accent furniture. There was a television mounted over a fireplace I had never used. The living room led into a small enclosed sun room off the back of the house. To the right was a dining room in a slightly darker shade of blue with a white dining set and sideboard. The dining room led into the kitchen off the back, white cabinetry and walls with stainless steel appliances and a massive island.

"Coming up?" Roman asked, gesturing toward the stairs.

"You go ahead. I think I am going to have a cup of tea before I tuck in."

"Goodnight, Else," he said, running a hand down my arm before moving up the stairs.

I waited ten minutes, standing right in my doorway like a weirdo, listening to him move around and settle down in bed before I dashed up the stairs as silently as I could and made my way into my room, going straight through to the bathroom and slipping off the shoes.

Adrenaline and fear gone, the pain was settling in. The backs of my heels were cut open and, as Paine said, there was a fair amount of blood smeared onto the once-expensive ballet flats. I reached into the shower and turned on the heads as I stripped out of my clothes.

Even though he wasn't exactly a scary guy, I was glad to have Rome in the house that night. It was silly to feel unsafe locked into a gated community with a full time staff of guards and a state of the art security system, but after the events of the night, I did. It was nice to have a man around. If for nothing other than my peace of mind.

Rome's house, if you could believe it, was a step up from mine. He had a much better relationship with his father than I did with mine. This was evidenced by the fact that he worked at his father's tech company, one of many businesses he owned and the only one that wasn't medical or pharmaceutical. Rome and his father, Rhett, were in no way nerdy or even all that up-to-date on technological advances, but they were shrewd businessmen who knew that technology was where the money was. So after college, Roman came back to Navesink Bank and got a job making high six-figures and had something I called a mini-mansion one street over from where I grew up. In an actual mansion, like he had grown up in as well.

That being said, his house was big and lonely and, when given the option, he always chose to stay with me.

I dressed, slathered on some triple antibiotic and big band-aids on my heels, then climbed into bed. It was well on its way to two in the morning and I knew sleep wasn't going to come easy, despite having to get up for work at seven.

My job was another thing my father hated.

See, my dad worked in energy. As in, the not-so-green kinds: coal, oil, gas.

I also worked in energy, but in the green kind: wind and solar.

My father made tens of millions a year. I made the mid-low six figures.

His gripe was not necessarily in the kind of energy I worked in. Even he knew that green was going to be the way of the future. His issue was with the fact that I worked for his competitor. In public, he would just throw an arm around me and claim I had inherited his enterprising spirit. In private, I got lectures.

Yeah, twenty-eight years old and being lectured by my father.

It made it really hard to feel like the adult I was at times.

But, aside from the townhouse, I made my own way in life. My trust fund sat and didn't get touched and I worked to pay for my utilities, my car, my hair, my nights out on occasion, my wardrobe. I took care of myself. Before my mother passed away when I was twelve, she told me that that was what she wanted more than anything for me- independence. She begged me to never let myself be dependent on a man. Being her dying wish, and perhaps an insight into the kind of life my mother lived being dependent on my father, I threw myself into that mission with every bit of determination I possessed. I got good grades at school, never settling for a B when I could get an A. It was the same attitude that got me through college, then got me a good job at a Fortune 250 company despite being one of the youngest and most inexperienced candidates.

I never settled. I got what I set my mind to. I never gave up.

So, even given the minor setback that was being chased by two gang members through the streets of Navesink Bank, I was not done. I was not settling for non-answers. I was not giving up.

I just had to come up with a new strategy.

The problem there being, I was obviously no kind of detective. And, good stamina aside, I had no real skills to help me in this particular mission. I couldn't involve Rome. I didn't want to involve my father. But I obviously needed some kind of help.

Top of the next day's agenda was to go online and find out what kind of PI or whatever I could hire or bend the ear of in the area. Even if all they could do was point me in the right direction, it would be well worth whatever fee I would need to pay. I couldn't keep snooping around and putting my life in jeopardy to find answers.

I needed to find someone who could just... give some to me.

THREE

Elsie

I had two calls out to two different PIs I had come across when I searched around on my lunch break. One, to a man named Sawyer who boasted a resume that made me slightly uncomfortable to even think about, full of information on his time in the military and the extensive training he had done afterward. The second was to someone who, if his website was anything to go by, seemed younger, a bit more in touch with millennial generations and their penchant for broadcasting their lives online. His name was Barrett and he claimed he could find answers to any questions you might have.

Call me crazy, but I was leaning toward the latter of the two. Maybe it was for the sole reason that the Sawyer guy sounded intimidating and I had a tendency to feel nervous around men who reminded me of my father. So the Barrett guy seemed more approachable and, therefore, the more likely candidate for the job.

I drove home feeling productive and hopeful. I needed to get some answers. I needed to know what was really going on. I couldn't just go on with my life and pretend that things weren't seriously messed up and my father and everyone around me was largely ignoring it.

I pulled into my garage and parked, grabbing my purse, closing the garage door, and going up toward my front steps. It was a habit Roman picked on me about, telling me it was safer for me to enter my house from the door through the garage. I tended to call him a worrywart and blow it off. It was stupid to go through the garage when I needed to pick up my mail in the box by my front door.

But when a shadow stepped out from beside my steps, sending my pulse into a frantic stammering and my heart up into my throat, I maybe finally understood his point.

My mouth immediately opened to scream as I gripped my keys hard, trying to slip them between my fingers like I had heard some guy on the news tell women to do when they were walking home or something.

"Don't scream," a somewhat familiar voice, a smooth and sexy voice, said as its owner stepped out of the shadows.

"Jesus, Paine!" I hissed, my hand moving over my pounding heart. "Do you always hide in the shadows at women's houses?" I asked, then looked down the road where a black Challenger was parked. "How did you even get in here? This neighborhood is gated."

"Yeah, it is," he agreed, tucking his hands into his pockets.

"Care to explain?"

"I know the night guard, babygirl. Just a bit of luck that when I showed up, planning to wait for you at the gate, he was on. Let me in."

Well, that was seriously messed up. Friend or not, the guard had no idea if Paine's intentions were to rape and murder me in my own home.

"How did you even know who I am, let alone where I lived?"

"Babygirl," he said, giving me a charming smile.

"That's not an answer."

"Money like you, name like yours, name like your not-boyfriend's, all I had to do was ask around and I got a name. Elsie Bay, daughter of Edward Bay, the biggest schmuck this side of the city."

I felt myself laugh, caught off guard. It was something me and my close friends might have said about my father in secret, in whispers, but no one else ever had the balls to say something like that in a loud, confident voice. "It's still really creepy, Paine. Why are you here?"

"Invite me in for coffee," he suggested, his breath hanging in the cold air for a second.

"No."

"No?" he asked, head tilting, brows drawing together, like maybe he didn't understand the word.

"No. It's a complete sentence," I clarified and his lips tipped up.

"Smart."

"Yes, I am. Now tell me why you're here before I call the owner of this complex and have you escorted off the premises and your friend fired."

His smile spread, showing me his perfect white teeth again. He really was ridiculously good looking. I wasn't unaffected either. I was a bit of a workaholic since I started at my company, wanting to prove myself. And when I wasn't working, I was hanging with Rome or girlfriends and having my weekly Sunday dinners at my father's. I wasn't even sure the last time I had made time for a man. So, to put it perfectly frankly, I was horny. I was horny and Paine was attractive and charming and he had this tiny little hint of danger that made my lady bits clench in what I was convinced was a prehistoric, biological impulse to mate with an alpha male to pass on good genes to a new generation.

Yeah, well. That wouldn't be happening. First, because I had an IUD. Second, because I had absolutely no intentions of giving in to some primal drive and having sex with Paine. No matter how much my belly fluttered when he called me babygirl or how nice of arms he had. So my body needed to chill the eff out.

"Elsie, we need to talk about why you were being chased by drug dealing pimps last night."

Well, that was blunt.

I cringed inwardly at the words 'drug dealers' and 'pimps' even though I knew that was what they were. A part of me flinched away from those... professions on principle. But, more than that, there was more of a personal reason I didn't like to be reminded of that. A personal reason I was praying to all hell that the Barrett guy could help me with.

"I don't see how it is any of your concern. You did a nice thing. If you do things solely because you want something out of it, even something as simple as an explanation, then maybe you shouldn't be doing nice things in the first place."

"You'd rather I didn't help you?"

"I'd rather you didn't ask around about me, find out where I lived, then hide in the dark waiting for me to get home so you could badger me. That is what I would rather."

"Badger you?" he asked, taking slow steps toward me. "Is that what I'm doing?" he asked, his voice soft. It was soft in a way that was meant to be sexy. And, well, it was. It was sexy and I felt myself retreating, knowing it was only going to lead to somewhere not good (but, oh, so good) if he got too close to me. My back hit the railing to my staircase, stopping me. Paine closed the last step between us. "Babygirl, if I was badgering you, you would know it," he said, his hand raising and tucking my hair behind my ear. His fingers brushed down my bare neck in a way that made me do a small, involuntary shiver before they trailed over my shoulder and down my arm. His fingers brushed over the back of my hand as my eyes held his, my mouth parting slightly and even I knew it was an invitation. But a second later, it fell open wider when I felt his hand tug my keys out of my palm.

"Hey!" I yelped as he jingled them and moved from me, jogging up my stairs and stopping in front of my door before I even fully realized what just happened. He stole my keys! He stole my keys and was using them to get into my house. "That's it, I'm calling the cops," I said, reaching for my phone as I looked up at him.

"Jesus, you finance that Porsche working as a fucking janitor, baby?" he asked, smiling over at me as he sifted through my keys, apparently completely unconcerned about me calling the police. "Ah, here it is," he said and, sure enough, slipped the right key into the lock.

What, was he some kind of burglar when he was younger? How did he know what key would work?

"Better get up here and punch in this code, Elsie, or the cops will be here in under five minutes."

"That was the plan," I said, waving my phone around where I had dialed in the nine and one, but hadn't added the last one or hit send.

"We both know you're not calling the cops so get your pretty ass up here and punch the code."

I looked down at my feet for a second, stuck inside clogs that made my lip curl anytime I looked at them, but were the only shoes I could wear that didn't have backs to rub on my cut heels.

He was right; I wasn't going to call the cops.

Why? I had no idea. But I wasn't.

I hauled it up the staircase and gave him a pointed brow lift until he turned away as I punched in the code and the warning beeping finally stopped. When I looked back at Paine, he was casually looking around my house. I couldn't tell from his impassive expression if he was impressed or disgusted or simply unaffected.

"How're your feet?" he asked, nodding down at my clogs that I was in the process of kicking out of.

"Fine," I said, lifting my chin slightly. "Now, say what you want to say and get gone. I need to get dinner and make a few calls."

"You cook?" he asked, craning his head into the doorway to the dining room.

"No," I said and, for the first time, felt a little embarrassed by that fact. In my normal friend group, everyone grew up privileged like me and Rome, with maids and cooks on the payroll, so it wasn't weird that none of us knew a whisk from a monkey wrench.

"So let's order in," he said, moving into my dining room, making his way toward my kitchen, leaving me to follow behind like a little lost puppy, not the actual owner of the house.

"Um, excuse me but I didn't invite you in, let alone invite you for dinner."

"I know. Who taught you your manners? They should be ashamed of themselves."

A strange snorting sound burst out of me, making my hand slap down over my mouth in embarrassment. I didn't... snort. That wasn't like me at all. Paine hauled himself up onto my island, giving me a warm smile as I struggled to get my composure back. "You do understand why I don't want a strange man in my house when I live alone, right?"

"I do," he nodded.

"And yet you're barging in here and inviting yourself to dinner."

"Baby, we aren't strangers."

"Ah, yeah we are."

"Really? We are? How weird that I know your name, your best friend/not-boyfriend's name, that you like your coffee sweet but without actual sugar because, I'm assuming, you like to keep that tight body tight. I know you have good, but understated taste. And I know that you're into something. As in, way in. As in, over your head. In turn, you know where I live, what I do, that I have two sisters and that I have better manners

34

than you. I'd say strangers don't know that much about each other."

On a sigh, I dropped my purse down on the counter. "You're impossible."

"And you're headstrong as fuck."

"I'm not headstrong, I'm cautious."

"Cautious about me, who saved you. And headstrong about not sharing why you're involved with a street gang."

"Because it's none of your business! You're not my boyfriend. You're not my father. You're not even my friend. So why the hell do you care what I am involved in?"

"Because," he said, his voice still as calm and soothing and, yes, sexy (damn it) as ever while mine kept getting increasingly frustrated, "babygirl, I don't think you have the slightest clue how dangerous those guys are."

"Really? It wasn't me that they were chasing last night? Weird. It totally felt like me. And it felt pretty scary and dangerous. Huh. Guess that was all my imagination."

"Cute," he said, hopping off the island and moving toward where I was leaned against the counter, planting his hands on either side of my body, his thumbs pressing into my hips, forcing me to crane my neck up to keep eye contact as my body urged me to wiggle my hips against his. Christ, I needed to have a serious session with my vibrator when he left. "Baby, they kill people. They kill people without thinking, without blinking."

I swallowed hard, believing him. It certainly seemed like they were capable of that. I nodded tightly. "Okay. I got it. Thank you for your concern. You can go."

The side of his lips tipped up as his head ducked down slightly, our foreheads almost touching as his hands left the counter and rested on my hips. "Is that what you really want?"

At this point, my nether regions were seriously threatening to get up and detach themselves from my body if I didn't inform him that, no, that wasn't what I wanted. That, in fact, what I wanted was for him to grab me and give it to me hot and hard right there in my kitchen.

I wet my lips and fought to clear my mind. "No."

"No?" he asked, ducking his head lower and I could feel his warm breath on my neck, making my head tilt the other way slightly to invite more of the sensation.

I closed my eyes and took a deep breath. "No."

"What do you want then, babygirl?" he asked, his lips close to my ear, his words making my sex clench hard.

God, I needed to pull it together.

"I want you to order dinner while I go get out of my work clothes. Then I want you to tell me everything you know about the Third Street gang."

Whoa. Where the hell did that come from? That was not, was absolutely not what I wanted. That was like the last thing I wanted. First, I wanted some good, hot sex. Then I wanted him to get the hell out of my business.

Paine moved backward, brows furrowed slightly, like he was just as surprised as I was. God, was I that obvious about my sexual frustration? I felt like a dog in heat for chrissakes. "Chinese or Italian?"

"What?" I asked, my brain somehow taking that dog in heat thought and turning it into a doggy style against the kitchen island thought.

"For dinner," he clarified, smiling in a way that made me think that maybe, just maybe, he knew exactly what my dirty brain was thinking.

"Oh, um... Italian," I decided, finding my common sense enough to plant my hands on his very solid, very nice chest and push him back a foot. Space, I needed it. A few feet, yards, miles. "There's, ah, a menu for Famiglia on top of the microwave. Order whatever you want. Everything is good. I'll, ah, be right back," I said, not chancing a look at him as I all but ran from the room and stormed up the stairs.

Collapsing against the inside of my bedroom door, I took a couple deep breaths.

"What is wrong with me?" I demanded in a whisper as I pushed off the door and pulled off my shirt.

It wasn't that I was unused to arousal or even frustration. I was a grown woman who had a healthy sex life when I wasn't being a workaholic like I had been for the better part of the last six months. But this felt different, stronger, all consuming. I couldn't be within five feet of him without feeling like a puddle of need. And true, it had been a while. I had a reasonably high sex drive and my body was humming with a need I had denied it for a long time. That being said, I had gone a six month stretch before without my imagination making me picture all the ways some random hot guy could screw me on the surfaces of my kitchen.

I finally understood all the nights when my girlfriends would tell me with a small amount of guilt about going home with a one-night stand because they just 'couldn't help themselves'. It didn't make sense to me then, control being an important part of my life. But it made sense then as I stripped out of my clothes that felt like they were chafing my over-sensitive skin, my breasts heavy, nipples half-hardened, my panties damp. And I wasn't even in the room with him anymore.

I threw myself backward onto my bed in my underwear, running my hand down my belly and slipping it inside my panties. I wasn't that girl. I wasn't some kind of exhibitionist who got off on touching herself while a clueless man stood one floor below her ordered dinner for her. But that being said, if I didn't get some relief, ease some of the need, I was going to go back down in that kitchen and let him take me any way he wanted me. And that, well, that could not happen.

I closed my eyes tight as I ran my fingers over my clit, already feeling halfway to an orgasm. I couldn't come without a story, without a fantasy playing out before my eyes. So, despite knowing it would only complicate things, an image of Paine popped into my brain, opening my bedroom door, seeing me touching myself and knowing it was about him. Then he would pull off his shirt in that sexy way that only men did, reaching behind their back and pulling it forward then off, discarding it to the floor as he reached for his button and zip as my eyes took in his strong chest, the deep indentations of his abdominal muscles. Then my eyes would dip lower as his pants fell to the floor, eyes roaming over every glorious inch of his hard dick. Then he would cross the room to me, his body vibrating with alpha male certainty, with primal promise of a pleasure I had never experienced before. He would kneel at the edge of the bed, knees on either side of my thighs, keeping me a willing captive.

His hands would move upward, nothing tentative, nothing uncertain, as his hands grabbed the cups of my bra and yanked them down, covering my throbbing breasts with his large palms and squeezing hard. Then they would be off my breasts, ripping off my panties. Then as he pushed off the bed, grabbing my hips and turning me, throwing me face down on the bed, he would haul my ass in the air, and shove in hard and deep.

I came on that thought, groaning out my release as my body shuddered hard.

I got up, threw on jeans so tight they in no way invited the idea of someone trying to peel them off, and Roman's old baggy red and white Stanford sweatshirt that I stole when he visited the first time he came back home for winter break, marking the longest we had ever gone without seeing each other since birth.

"Pull it together," I murmured to myself, finding a hair band and tying my hair into a messy knot at the top of my head. For good measure, I walked into the bathroom, slipped out my contacts and put on my huge hipster glasses, nodding at my reflection. It had a certain nerdy appeal, but it was in no way a sexy look. I considered it another guard against ill-advised sex with with the hot guy in my kitchen. Nothing about how I looked right that minute screamed 'take me now'. If anything, it said 'hey can you hold my library books while I look for my retainer'.

So then I flicked off my lights and went back downstairs, hoping for some answers.

And not sex.

Nope.

Not at all.

Totally didn't want that anymore.

FOUR

Paine

One year.

I hadn't even needed to so much as lay eyes on one of the Third Street guys in a full year. The last time I did, one of my best friend's girlfriend's lives was at risk. It was probably the only situation I would have dealt with them again. I had fought my way out of that life; I had done things that would wake me up in a cold sweat even now, years later.

So having to so much as speak to a member of Third Street didn't exactly make my week.

But having to do it to save another chick? Yeah, I guess that made it worth it.

Unfortunately for me, she wasn't just some chick who got caught on the wrong side of town at night and caught some unwanted attention. No, she was up to something. She was up to something and she had no idea how much danger she was in. Things had changed in Third Street over the years under different leaders. Five years alone had three separate faces. As such, the men were wild, unpredictable, sometimes calling their own shots instead of following orders.

That meant whatever the pretty blond Elsie was involved in could have any number of unforeseeable results. Oh, and she was pretty too. Fucking gorgeous actually. D wasn't wrong calling her Barbie. She definitely had that look- tall and lean, a body that was testament to either pilates or yoga and a strict diet: all shapely legs, a nice rack, and an ass that could make a man cry. While whatever color she was sporting wasn't natural, if her brows and lashes were anything to go by, she was a natural blond. Regardless, it was nice hair and she had a fuckuva lot of it, just begging for a man to take a good handful of it while he fucked her from behind and yank it hard. The blowjob lips comment, yeah, that wasn't that far off either. They were full and pink and just begging to be kissed. And, if what I had seen in those blue eyes of hers were anything to go by, she was due for a good makeout session that led to a good fucking session.

I had every intention of letting her walk out of my life with her hand wrapped up with her not-boyfriend's. I had no reason to get involved. But I had a mostly sleepless night tossing and turning and wondering what the hell she could possibly want with a gang that sold H and pimped out whores. So I called around, dropped the names Elsie and Roman, and I got an answer pretty fucking quick.

Apparently I was one of the very few people in the area who didn't know who Elsie Bay and Roman Matthewson were. First, because they had been hellions as teens, a couple of rich kids getting themselves into all kinds of trouble. Second, because they were well-off in the way that they went to charity functions and art openings. And, third, because they were the children of some of the biggest businessmen in the state. Elsie's dad was in energy, apparently a very loud-mouthed, abrasive man who was hell to work for and, I imagined, hell to grow up with. Which made her teen rebellion less obnoxious and more understandable. And Roman's father, Rhett, had a huge tech company, but they had their hands in many different areas: medicine, military, and security.

"How the fuck you never see her at Chaz's?" Shooter, one of my best friends and also a contract killer, one of the best in the country, asked the next morning as I stuck a needle into the back of his neck, working on some rose tattoo with huge ass thorns he got it in his mind to get done.

"Dunno." And I didn't. She was the kind of woman who stood out. There was an air about her that screamed class, but with a bit of rebellion any man in his right mind would be drawn to. "You never had her?" I asked, knowing that Shooter's reputation was one of the worst around before he finally settled down with his woman a year before.

"Nah. Felt bad as fuck for that Roman guy. Didn't want to make his life any more miserable than it was."

I snorted. "She seemed completely clueless about him wanting her."

"Sees what she wants to see," Shoot shrugged. "Why are you so interested in her all of a sudden?"

"D and Trick were chasing her last night, man. I grabbed her and pulled her in, covered for her."

"D and Trick?" Shoot asked, sitting up straight. He was rightfully worried to hear those names again. "The hell could she have gotten herself into involving them?"

"I don't know."

But I had every intention of finding out.

So I got into her neighborhood and I waited outside her house for her to get home from work. It was almost seven when she finally pulled up in that sweet light blue Porsche of hers.

I hadn't exactly expected full cooperation from her, full disclosure, but I didn't expect to be butting my head against a wall either. Whatever she was hiding, it was something she really didn't want people to know about.

I listened to her go up the stairs and looked over the menu for Famiglia for a minute. I ordered tortellini and a chicken parm then went up the stairs when she still hadn't come down, needing the number to the front gate so I could tell the guard, Al, to let the delivery guy in.

As soon as I got into the hall outside her closed door, I heard her.

I heard her and it was like a shot of white hot desire to my dick.

Because what I heard was the sound of her throaty whimpers. And there was only one thing that made a woman make sounds like that. She was behind that door touching herself, giving herself some relief from the desire I had seen in her eyes down in the kitchen.

My balls felt like they were in a vice grip as her whimpers became groans that culminated in one drawn out moan as she came.

She wasn't quiet.

Even believing I was one floor below her, almost in the exact spot she was, she hadn't bit her lip or buried her face. Or, if she had, then all it did was suggest that she was even louder when she wasn't concerned about being overheard.

Fuck if I didn't want to know what she sounded like uninhibited, riding my cock as hard as she pleased, watching what I could only imagine were perfect pink-tipped tits bouncing as she did so.

I shook my head, ignoring the chafing in my jeans as I turned to go back down the stairs as quietly as I could.

I might have been a man who had the very strong urge to tell her I heard her and that I would be all too happy to give her the kind of orgasm that would make her scream until her lungs hurt. But that was a private moment. I had no right to hear it in the first place, let alone comment on it. So I took my ass back down to the kitchen and rummaged around to make coffee. If the ten minutes before she went up to change were anything to go by, I was going to need a gallon of it.

"I forgot to tell you the number for the gate..." she said, sounding a little less flustered than it had been before she went upstairs.

43

I turned, expecting the typical chick 'lounge around' outfit of yoga pants and a tank, but saw instead an image that was going to be playing at the forefront of my brain when I jacked off later. Because gone was the cool, calm, collected rich girl persona she usually had. In its place was the sexiest fucking nerd I'd ever seen in my life. "Oh babygirl, if you were going for unappealing, you missed by a long shot," I smiled, taking in the messy hair, the glasses, the baggy sweatshirt and the skinny jeans.

Her feet faltered a second before she forced them forward. "I wasn't trying for anything. My contacts were bothering me."

"And the hair?"

"It was getting messy. I wanted it out of my face."

"And that sweatshirt?"

"It's Rome's," she said, shrugging as she reached for the phone to, presumably, call the gate.

"Stealing his comfy hoodie and he ain't your boyfriend?" I smiled, thinking about the endless hoodies women had lifted from me over the years.

She ignored me as she talked to Al at the gate, telling him to let in the guy from Famiglia, then hanging up. "Did you make coffee?" she asked, brows drawing together.

"Yeah."

"Jeez. Just make yourself at home why don't you?" she asked, smiling a little.

"Someone's got to. Your coffee grinder still had a factory seal on it."

She gave me a small smile. "It's easier to get coffee in the lobby at the office."

"Your stove front still has that protective plastic on it," I pointed out and she laughed.

"I don't cook or bake and even if I did cook or bake, it seems pointless to just cook for myself."

"Your not-boyfriend isn't over here all the time?"

"Jesus. What is your obsession with Roman?" she asked, waving a hand out like I was being unreasonable.

"He stayed here last night, didn't he?"

"Yes."

"In your bed?"

"In the guest room!" she yelped out, frustrated. "Alright enough about Rome. You're here to give me answers."

"Actually, baby, I'm here to get answers," I countered, watching as she moved past me and went toward the coffee pot, fumbling for a second as she looked at her cabinets, like she couldn't remember where the coffee mugs were. Back to me, I got to see her fan-fucking-tastic ass in those second-skin jeans she had on.

"Well I have no answers for you. So you can just get that out of your head. What do you know about the Third Street gang?" she asked, going into her fridge for milk.

"Babygirl..." I groaned slightly, not wanting to go there, but knowing there was no way she was going to give in. She turned, brow lifted behind her giant glasses and fuck if it wasn't the cutest God damn thing. "Fine," I sighed. "What do you want to know about them?"

"Well, you've told me they sell slam..."

"Smack," I corrected, grinning.

"Smack, whatever. And that they are pimps."

"Yeah, babe."

"So what are they doing at that huge warehouse on Kennedy?"

The warehouse on Kennedy? I didn't know shit about a warehouse on Kennedy, let alone one connected to the Third Street gang. "Is that where you were last night?"

She waved out a hand on a huff. "Yes. Okay, fine. Yes, that's where I was last night."

"Why?"

"That's my business," she said in a firm tone, her chin lifted, her brow arched in a haughty way that had my lips

45

twitching. "What could the Third Street gang be doing in a factory that big? Making heroin?"

"No, baby," I said, trying not to laugh.

"How do you know that?"

"You know nothing about drugs, do you?"

"It wasn't exactly in my curriculum at school, no."

Guess that made sense. Sad thing was, I knew everything there was to know about drugs by the time I finished grade school. Despite my mom's, grandma's, and aunts' best efforts, there was no shielding me from all that shit growing up in the area I grew up in.

"Heroin is an opiate, but it's part synthetic so you can't just extract it from poppy. It's made from morphine. So first you need to extract the insides from the poppy, dry the morphine so you can ship it, then chemically extract the heroin from the morphine."

"And you know that they aren't doing this because..."

"Because it's too much fucking work, Elsie. The biggest supplier of opium and morphine is Afghanistan. Do you know how hard it is to ship shit in from Afghanistan to the United States right now? Third Street isn't big enough to grease the palms they would need to to get that shit in here. And why bother when you can get a contact from Mexico or Columbia, fuck, even fucking Burma or Laos, to do the dirty work for you? You lower your overhead and your risk of getting found out. So, no, they're absolutely not making heroin in that warehouse on Kennedy."

She was silent for a moment, tapping her nails on her mug as she thought. They weren't fake nails, either, I noticed with a bit of surprise. They were short and shaped and painted a pale pink, but they were her own nails.

"Could it have something to do with the prostitutes?" she asked a minute later with a shrug that suggested she already knew the answer.

"Can't think of a reason why it would."

"All you are doing is nixing my ideas," she shrugged. "Got any of your own to throw around?"

"Babygirl, I don't know what you want from..." I trailed off as the doorbell chimed.

"Say 'saved by the bell' and I'll throw my coffee at you," she warned, clicking it down on the counter and moving over toward where she dropped her purse. I bypassed her, going to the door, taking the food and paying the delivery guy before she could even get her wallet out of her purse. "Hey what are you doing?" she asked as she walked up to me closing the door.

"Getting dinner."

"Yeah, but this is my house."

"And?"

"And that means I pay for the food."

"You have a dick?"

"I'm sorry?" she asked, her eyes almost going comically wide. Talk about how to make heroin and she doesn't even blink, use the word 'dick' and she gets the face of a school girl.

"Dick. You got one?"

She shook her head slightly as if to clear it. "Not the last time I checked."

I bit the inside of my cheek to keep from commenting on just how long it had been since she checked. "Right. I got one. So I pay for the food," I said, brushing past her toward the kitchen.

I was putting the bag on the island when she came in, arms crossed over her chest. "That's incredibly sexist of you."

"My mother calls it chivalrous," I said, pulling out the takeaway containers and putting them on the counter. "You got plates?"

"Only if you want to wash them after you use them. I'm eating out of the containers," she said, going to a sliding drawer and pulling out utensils.

"You're eating out of the containers?" I asked, watching as she pried open the lids to the food.

"What?" she asked, leaning down and sniffing the chicken parm. "You've never eaten out of a takeaway container?"

"Yeah, baby, just didn't think you would have."

"Right," she snorted, rolling her eyes. "Money like me couldn't possibly know how to eat out of plastic. It's been all fine China and silver spoons for me. I hope you didn't order either of these exclusively for yourself, because we're sharing."

As if to prove her point, she stabbed some tortellini and started cutting up the chicken. "Knock yourself out," I said as she did just that, diving into the food like she hadn't eaten in a month.

"Don't look at me like that," she said, lowering her eyes at me. "I eat fatty stuff like this maybe once every two or three months. It's here in front of me and I have every intention of pigging out."

I held my hands up, palms out. "Babygirl, you stuff your face. Something sexy about a woman enjoying her food." To that, she choked on her mouthful, bringing her hand up so she didn't spit it out. "Drink?" I asked.

She waved me toward the wine rack and I moved to it, not bothering to hide my smirk. It was no secret I had enjoyed my fair share of women. More than, if I were being perfectly honest. It was rare that one genuinely surprised me. After growing up surrounded by women then spending my teens and adulthood successfully chasing them, it was hard to find one who threw me.

Elsie threw me.

She was simply a mess of contradictions. Rich girl who liked to eat out of takeaway containers, who had the money to get lasik but wore huge dorky glasses instead, who gave me bedroom eyes then went upstairs and eased her sexual tension then practically blushed when I used the word 'dick' or said it was sexy to watch a woman eat, who seemed straight up and down in every way that mattered but was getting herself involved with a fucking street gang.

I picked a bottle at random, opened it, and poured into glasses that were beside her sink like she used them recently and rinsed them out and left them to dry. Unlike her coffee mugs, her wine glasses apparently got used.

"Gonna save any for me?" I asked, pulling up a stool and sitting down next to where she was leaning over the counter steadily devouring both meals somehow simultaneously.

"Darwin," was her mouth-filled answer, her hand up masking her lips.

"What?" I asked as she reached for her wineglass and took a long sip.

"Survival of the fittest. It isn't my fault you're weak," she said, putting her wineglass down with a clink and diving back in.

Not more than ten minutes and maybe six bites later, the food was gone, mostly into Elsie's body. She finally reached out for a stool and pulled it up to sit on as she topped off her wine.

"So you have no clue what the warehouse is for, aside from telling me it's not to make heroin or store prostitutes."

"Right," I agreed. "And you're not going to tell me why the fuck you're sticking your pretty little nose in street gang business."

"Right," she agreed with a small nod.

"So that's it?" I guessed, at a loss for how I could get her to tell me anything more than what she had already.

"That's it," she agreed, standing, making it clear dinner was over. "I'll walk you out," she said, turning and walking off toward the front room, leaving me very little choice but to follow behind. She had pulled the door open and was standing off to the side. "Thanks for the chemistry lesson and dinner."

I felt my lips tip up and nodded, moving out onto the front step before I changed my mind and swung back around, pushed inside, and pressed her up against the door in her entryway. My hands went to her hips, my thumbs spanning across her stomach as my head dipped down.

"Listen, Elsie. I get it if you have some shit you're in and you think you need to handle it on your own. But don't get yourself in too deep without back-up. If things look like shit and you need some help, find me, okay? I don't want to read it in the society pages that you got yourself killed because you were too fucking stubborn to ask for help." My fingers dug in, pressing her harder against the wall as her mouth fell slightly open. "Got me, babygirl?"

Her lips pressed together and she swallowed hard. "Ah, yeah. I got you, Paine," she agreed with a small nod.

"Good," I said, trying to force my hands to let her go, but all they did was sink in harder as they lifted upward, bringing her up onto her tiptoes as she gasped. My lips crashed onto hers hard and fast before I tore myself away and threw myself outside, slamming the door behind me before I turned around, stormed back in and fucked her right there in the open doorway.

FIVE

Elsie

The next day went as follows: got up, didn't think about the kiss, got dressed, didn't think about it in the shower, got to work, didn't think about it during coffee breaks, set up an appointment with the Barrett guy, didn't think about it while stopped at the god damn red lights on the way to said appointment...

Yeah, so Paine kissed me.

One minute, I was walking him out the door. Everything was chaste, calm, somewhat normal. The next second, he had me pinned against the wall, his strong hands on my belly and holding on tight, pulling me almost off my feet. And, let me tell ya, for a tall girl, that was quite a feat. Then he was offering me backup if I needed it.

And then his lips were on mine.

Hard.

Crushing.

SAVIOR

I felt it down to my freaking toes. My toes. Like a middle-school girl getting a kiss from the most popular boy in school. It went through my whole system, pinging rather intensely at the nerve endings between my legs before it journeyed down.

Then not more than five seconds later, I was collapsing against the wall without his hands holding me up. The door slammed and my hand moved up to press into my lips that felt electric from the contact.

That was just what my under-utilized sex drive needed.

It goes without saying that I did a really bad job not thinking about that kiss. Never mind that it was barely even a kiss, just a meeting of lips. No motion, no tongues, no nothing. But, regardless, it was effective. And it was impossible to not think about.

So as I parked my car across from the police station and climbed out, I was thinking about it. Which was why it didn't immediately strike me as odd that the PI had his office across from the NBPD. But as I beeped my locks and rounded my car to look at the building, well, the strangeness started to settle in. Because not only was it across the street from the police station, but it was completely windowless and the door was a simple white wooden one. I use the term 'white' loosely here. It had, at one time, presumably, been white. In current times, it was more... brown thanks to what looked like mud smatterings all up the front of it. The only way you'd know there was an office there was a small plaque under one of the windows that said Barrett Anderson Investigates.

On a loud exhale that sounded a lot like second-guessing, I reached up to knock on the cleanest part of the door that was well above eye-level as I reminded myself that there was always the Sawyer guy to fall back on if the Barrett guy turned out to be a flop.

I waited, shifting my feet for a second as I looked over my shoulder toward the eerie alley to the side between Barrett's 'office' and the Chinese food place next door, the smell of

52

broccoli, garlic, and soy sauce making my stomach growl in anger.

There was shuffling inside the office, the sound of several things crashing to the floor and sliding across it, a soft curse, then the door flew open.

And there was Barrett Anderson.

And I was pretty sure I needed to put out a call back to the Sawyer guy.

Because Barrett looked like a mess. He was in his late twenties, tall and lean in an almost underfed kind of way, with shaggy brown hair, warm brown eyes behind glasses that looked eerily similar to the ones I wore the night before around Paine, pants that were a shade roomy and a thick gray sweater with brown elbow patches. Yes, elbow patches. And a dark blue beanie.

Okay. I was being a snob.

Maybe he looked homeless because he was an uber-genius or something. You know, smart people were known for being rather absentminded about normal, every day tasks like haircuts and... eating proper meals. The clothes, well, some guys just genuinely didn't know anything about what did and did not go together, let alone what was and was not in fashion.

All the awful clothing aside, he was actually pretty good looking. A good couple square meals to get some meat on his bones, he would actually be really attractive in a sort-of hipster kind of way.

"You ready?" he asked, giving me quick eye contact before turning away and disappearing behind his office door.

Alright. Not having great social skills wasn't unusual either if he was smart.

I took a deep breath, shook my head slightly, and followed him inside, closing the door at my back.

Yeah, well. If you ever stopped to consider what the office of some of the great writers in the twentieth century before computers were a thing looked like, offices like Bukowski or Salinger might have inhabited, yeah, that was what Barrett Anderson's office was like. Meaning it was a small room with a simple black office desk and chair with a chair for visitors and a hip-level office cabinet on the side. But every single surface was stacked with books, with paperwork, folders. The walls had newspaper clippings, online printouts, pictures, and handwritten notes pinned with colorful thumbtacks to above my personal eye level.

Barrett was already behind his desk, shuffling papers that made the five or six discarded coffee cups sitting on top of some of said stacks of paper wobble ominously.

As I walked toward the guest chair, I immediately rethought my impression that Barrett was the tech-savvy guy his website implied. Because, well, he didn't even have a computer in his office. No computer, laptop, fax, phone... nothing. How the hell had he even made the website in the first place?

"Not what you were expecting?" he asked, reading my expression with a small smirk.

"Where's your computer?" I blurted out as I sat down.

"What do most you think is the most valuable thing in your house?" he asked, but it was rhetorical because he went on with barely a pause. "High-end jewelry, the TV, stereo system... no. It's your computer and laptop. If I broke in, I wouldn't even have to steal it. I could just use a zip drive with some specific malware on it, stick it in the USB port, let it do its thing, pull it back out, and I have access to every password to every bank website, investment website, 401K website you have ever visited. I also have all the dirt on everything you've ever looked at online. A computer should never be left out where someone else could access it for even a couple of seconds."

Well. Didn't I kind of feel like an idiot?

"But the paper trail you have here?" I asked, waving a hand around.

"Take a closer look," he invited, nodding toward the paperwork on his desk.

Curious, I reached for the closest stack and picked it up to read. It was some kind of mathematical papers and while there were words, they weren't in English. "Is this... Russian?"

"Polish," he said, taking them back from me. "They're also in code."

"Quite fastidious," I nodded, feeling a bit more secure in my choice, and also making a mental note to start storing my laptop in my safe when I wasn't in the house.

"What do you need help with, Miss..."

"Elsie is fine. And I guess, for right now, I need help figuring out what is going on at the warehouse on Kennedy."

"The warehouse on Kennedy," he repeated, brows drawing together.

"Yes."

"That's all you're gonna give me."

"Does knowing my motivations somehow change the information of what is going on inside the warehouse?"

"See your point," he said, reaching for a drawer and pulling out a fresh piece of loose leaf paper, scribbling notes in, I imagined, coded Polish. "So you want information of the people coming and going, items being brought in or out," he kept babbling as he grabbed his coffee with his left hand, brought it to his lips, took a long sip, then settled it back down. "Do you want full workups on every person?"

"Full workups?"

"Jobs, past jobs, habits, financial records..." he trailed off, looking up at me from behind his glasses, the expression there very much intimating that he thought I was an idiot for making him explain.

"Ah, sure," I said, shrugging. "Whatever you can find."

"Anything else?"

I pressed my lips together to keep them from twitching. I'd been on more than my share of consultations with various professionals over the years: attorneys, accountants, doctors, etc. Never had I been in a meeting as clipped as this one with the strange, sloppy, hungry-looking Barrett Anderson.

"A word of advice?" I offered and his head snapped up, one brow raised. "I think whatever is going on at that warehouse involves the Third Street gang. So you might want to be... careful."

"Right," he said in a rough voice, the way his lips had thinned out implying he was angry or insulted. "Is that all?"

"Do we need to fill out any paperwork?"

"What for, Miss Bay? If I need you, I know right where to find you. Word of advice?" he threw my own words back at me. "Stop checking in on social media every time you go somewhere. From your Facebook alone, I know: you go to Shane Mallick's gym over on Willow; you have dinner at your father's every Sunday; you get to work early and stay late; you go to Chaz's with your girlfriends; you go out to eat way too often with Roman Matthewson; you get your hair done over at that expensive salon on Monroe; you..."

"Okay. I get it. I am making myself a perfect target for a stalker," I bristled, annoyed. I mean, I had privacy settings for God's sake. I wasn't an idiot. Only friends were supposed to see things like that. But apparently, Barrett had found a way around all that. "Sorry I bruised your pride with the warning. Excuse the heck out of me for thinking you look more like a future college professor than some badass who can take on a street gang. No need to be an ass."

I stood abruptly, slinging my purse back up on my shoulder.

"I'm good at my job, Miss Bay," he said, standing as well, but fisting his hands onto the surface of his desk, hunching slightly forward.

"Good. Then prove it," I demanded, turning and walking out of his office.

Sometimes leaving on a bitch-note was the best bet. It sounds counter-intuitive, but it was one of the few things my father taught me that I felt actually did have practical applications in daily life. Yes, sometimes it was good to kill people with kindness, but something was telling me that Barrett Anderson was too smart to fall for the honey trap.

--

I didn't hear from Barrett for two days. I had six unreturned phone calls and emails out to him. Now, I can be patient in that I will put the work in and I am willing to wait for the results to come in. However, when all control is taken out of my hands and I have nothing to do but think and stress about said situation that I have no control over, well, I get decidedly less patient.

I tried taking a couple extra nights at the gym, thinking to sweat out the anxiety. I went out with Roman and one of my girlfriends for dinners, I stayed late at work to keep myself busy.

But, well, I was done just waiting.

So, on my way home from work around seven-thirty, I detoured back into the industrial part of town and parked out front of the police station for added security. What can I say? It was dark; I loved my car; I didn't want to come out to find parts of it missing.

There was no way to tell if Barrett was in his office given that there were no windows to see if the lights were on or not through them. I clutched my keys a little tighter as I ran across the street toward his door.

My feet faltered right outside, hearing shuffling and feeling a tiny bit of anger rise up. So he was in his office. He was just ignoring my calls. That ass...

But then the shuffling sounded decidedly unlike actual shuffling and a lot more like an altercation.

Okay, so I'm no hero. When it came to fight or flight instincts, mine leaned quite heavily toward flight. Whenever danger seemed evident, I got that weird swirly feeling in my belly and instinctively shrank away from whatever the perceived danger was. Personally. But when there seemed like something bad was happening to someone else, then something protective welled up in me. Like the time I had been walking out of Chaz's bar to get some air and I had seen some musclebound jerk grab his girlfriend's face and shove her back against a wall, something protective in me welled up and I flew at him, screaming like a banshee loud enough to draw a crowd that ensured that I wasn't going to get my ass handed to me too.

So as I stood outside Barrett's office and heard what was undoubtedly the sound of someone getting hurt, and that person very likely being skinny, underfed, nerdy Barrett Anderson, well, I didn't think. I didn't run back across the street and get a cop. I just did what my gut told me to do. I grabbed the handle and threw the door open.

Barrett was already on the floor, the front of one of his old man sweaters held in the giant fist of the man towering over him, his other arm cocked back. I couldn't even draw a breath to yell before he swung forward toward Barrett's face, a face that was already so bloodied and swollen that if it weren't for the shaggy hair, I wouldn't have recognized him, and smashed into some sweet spot that made Barrett's skinny body go boneless, suspended in air by the front of his shirt only.

"No!" I gasped, my heart slamming in my chest as I watched Barrett's, looking for the telltale rising and falling. It took a long second before I saw him draw breath.

But by that point, I was already screwed.

I knew this because suddenly Barrett was no longer suspended, but crashed down to the floor in a weighted way that made me cringe. I also knew this because suddenly the back of Barrett's attacker wasn't toward me anymore. He had stood fully and swiveled, a small smirk toying at his lips.

All I could think at that point was: run.

See, my good old flight instinct kicked in.

I turned back toward the door and was all of one foot outside before I was tagged from behind, one strong arm going around my throat, pulling me up and off my feet, the other going tight around my middle, anchoring me back against him. With his forearm pressing into my throat, I couldn't even draw a breath to scream. I was pulled back a few feet, the door slamming behind me, cutting off the chance of someone seeing in. Seconds. It was just seconds, but I was starting to feel light-headed from the pressure on my neck and had the horrifying realization that I was going to pass out. God only knew what kind of things could be done to me while unconscious. My nails clawed at his arm as I tried to wrench my body out of his hold.

Then I was dropped.

Surprised, my legs didn't react fast enough to lock and hold my weight and I went down on my knees, sucking in a greedy breath. My hair was grabbed from the crown of my head and yanked viciously back. "What do we have here? You his girlfriend?" he asked, jerking his chin toward Barrett's awkwardly twisted body. "Came in at the wrong time, bitch," he said, yanking my hair back harder. His other hand snaked out and grabbed me at the throat hard, using it to haul me back up on my feet. "Ain't gonna kill you. Stop giving me the big eyes," he said, rolling his eyes as he slammed me back against a wall.

Of course the dying thing crossed my mind, but it was more the before-dying thing I was worried about. You know... the likely beating, the possible rape, the definite strangulation. Yeah, that stuff was what was giving me the so-called big-eyes.

That and the fact that it felt like my esophagus was being crushed.

"I need you alive to give your boyfriend a message," he said, leaning in close and, even with most my air supply being cut off, the scent of stale cigarettes on his breath made my nose crinkle up. "You tell him to keep his fucking..."

The rest of his sentence got cut off when he was suddenly grabbed from the back of his neck and hauled backward, thrown so hard he crashed to the floor and slid several feet across it. My hand rose to my throat, holding there loosely, as I watched another man reach down to my attacker, grab his shirt, and pull him back onto his feet where he proceeded to beat the ever loving hell out of him, his hands moving faster than my eyes could follow.

The new guy's back was to me and all I could see was dark brown hair, a tall, lean, strong body clad in dark wash jeans and a somewhat tight dark blue tee.

I watched, horrified and fascinated, as the new guy decimated the guy who had choked me and knocked Barrett unconscious.

Barrett.

I flew toward his body, dropping down on my knees, and reaching my hands out toward his neck and chest simultaneously, feeling for how strong his breath was and his pulse. His face was hard to even look at, swollen and bloodied to nonrecognition. His breathing was shallow, but steady. I reached down for his sweater, hauling it upward to expose his chest and stomach. There were huge pools of red and purple bruises at his ribs. While I was no expert, I was pretty sure that meant they were broken.

"Oh, God. Shit. Okay," I mumbled to myself, frantically patting at my pockets, looking for my cell.

"Relax," A deep voice said from behind me, making me yelp and fall back onto my ass. My head tilted up to find the random good (or very, very bad) guy towering over me, looking down at me with deep green eyes that were eerily familiar. It was in the bone structure too: the strong jaw, the straight, almost perfect nose, the brow ridge. Whatever his name might be, there was no mistaking it. Random hot good or bad guy was Barrett Anderson's brother.

"Relax?" I ground out, cringing at the razor blade sensation in my throat. "He's unconscious," I objected, noting that the office was empty save for the splatters of blood all over the floor. Whoever the other guy was, he was bleeding and long gone.

To this, I got a tight nod as he took a step to the side and crouched down next to me, doing a similar, but faster, check of his breathing and pulse. "It looks worse than it is."

"It looks like he was attacked by an entire gang."

"You his?" the guy asked, turning his head to look down at me and there was such an intensity in his gaze that I almost shrank away. I was pretty sure right then that he was very likely a bad, bad guy.

"His?" I repeated, not understanding.

"His. Girlfriend, side piece, fuck buddy..."

"What? No!" I exploded, cringing as my throat did the razor blade thing again.

"Yeah you're too rich-bitch for his taste."

Okay. I was getting pretty freaking sick of people commenting on me being well off. And, well, whoever this guy was, he was obviously bad. And an asshole. Completely.

"Are you planning on sitting here insulting me or getting your brother some help?" I asked with a haughty chin lift that totally screamed 'rich bitch', but I didn't care.

"He never should have gone off on his own," he said, reaching into his pocket for his phone. "Tig, it's Sawyer. Need help getting Barrett to the hospital. Right. His office. Thanks."

I was only half-listening after I heard his name.

Sawyer.

His name was Sawyer.

No way was it some kind of coincidence that the other PI that I had looked into and contacted, then ultimately decided against because I thought he was intimidating, was also named Sawyer. Looking at him now, 'intimidating' was definitely the right word to describe him. There had been no last name on Sawyer's website, just the name Sawyer Investigations. There was no way I could have known.

"Sawyer Investigations!" I blurted as I watched his profile, a muscle ticking in his jaw which I found almost sexy.

His head jerked, his eyes pinning me. "Yeah, babe."

"You're brothers and you're both PIs?"

"He used to work for me," he confided.

"Used to?" I prompted when the silence drug on and he just kept staring at me, like he was seeing something, like he knew my secrets.

Sawyer's lips tipped up then, but it wasn't a smile. I was pretty sure he wasn't the kind of man capable of smiling. It was more like a sneer. "He's a smart kid. Great with digging up leads. Fucking fantastic with computers. Can find shit that none of my other guys can. But he's a kid. He's soft. No training. He belongs in the guts of the office, not on the streets getting his fucking ass handed to him. He didn't like that. He split. Got his own game. And..." he waved his hand to Barrett's body in a way that would have seemed callous and unfeeling if there hadn't been pain in his eyes.

"And got his ass handed to him," I finished for him, feeling the guilt settle in low in my belly. While there was certainly a chance that Barrett was handling other cases while working on mine, cases that might have been dangerous, my instinct was telling me that whoever the guy was before, he belonged to Third Street. So if he belonged to Third Street, it was my fault that he got his ass handed to him. It was my fault, and Sawyer was sitting there looking like he felt the guilt. "You couldn't have prevented this. He's not a kid. He's a grown man."

"Do I look like the kind of man who can't prevent something if he really wanted to?"

Yeah, well. He had a point.

"Then why didn't you?"

"Does Barrett really seem like the kind of guy who likes being told what to do? I might have wanted to prevent this from happening, babe, but my brother would never forgive me chopping off his balls like that."

"Yo," a deep voice said, no... boomed, from behind me, making me jolt violently, my heart going into overdrive.

"Tig," Sawyer said to him but at me as he took his feet.

I sucked in a breath and followed suit, turning toward the voice and finding the largest man I'd ever seen in my life. Literally. He was six and a half feet easy with shoulders that were so wide that I was pretty sure he needed to turn sideways to fit through the doorway. He was solid muscle with a slight beer gut underneath his tight black exercise shirt. He was good looking in a giant kind of way, with strong masculine features, light brown eyes, and a deep mahogany color to his skin.

Tig and Sawyer were talking in hushed tones but my movement drew Tig's attention. His eyes did a slow inspection, but it was almost clinical, not sexual.

Sawyer waved a hand. "This is Barrett's not-fuck-buddy."

My arms folded over my chest, my eyes lowering. "That's rude."

"So is not introducing yourself, babe."

"You didn't introduce yourself either," I snapped. "I put two and two together."

"Sawyer Anderson," he said with an exaggerated bow, then waved a hand at Tig. "Tig you-don't-need-to-know-his-last-name. Happy?"

"Somehow I doubt you have the capability to make anyone happy," I said before I could stop myself. Tig's laugh was a sound that filled the small space, making it feel like it vibrated up into your skin from the walls and floors and reverberated through all your cells in your body. I felt my lips tip up in reaction to the sound. My eyes slid over toward Sawyer to find that he had really nice, straight, white teeth. I knew this because he was actually smiling.

"Like it when a kitten shows her claws," Sawyer said, his eyes warm. "You got a name?"

"Obviously."

"Gonna tell me or make me run your plates on that sweet Porsche?"

Of course he would know that was my car. I sighed. "Elsie Bay."

Tig, who had started across the room toward Barrett, froze mid-stride. "Of Edward Bay?"

"The one and only," I said and even I could hear the bitterness in my voice.

"You called my office," Sawyer said as Tig moved behind me toward Barrett. It almost sounded like an accusation.

"Yes. I was looking for a PI."

"And you picked Barrett over me? Babe, I've got ten years of experience on him. What the fuck were you thinking?"

"Arrogant much? If you must know, Barrett seemed really tech-savvy and less intimidating."

"Don't you think that maybe having a intimidating private investigator is the way to go? Especially if you got yourself wrapped up with that piece of shit that had you up against the wall when I first got here?" Yeah, well, hindsight was twenty-twenty and all that cliche stuff. Though I was still convinced I made the right choice seeing as Sawyer was not only intimidating, but a cocksure asshole. At my stubborn silence, Sawyer sighed, shaking his head like I was an idiot. "Well, like it or not, I'm tapping out Barrett and stepping in. Don't know what the fuck you got yourself involved in, but make damn sure I will find out. I'm gonna be visiting my brother in a hospital room for a good three days and I want to know why. So you can go ahead and try to hide in a gated community behind security guards, but mark my words, babe, I'll get in and I'll get my answers."

I was just opening my mouth to snap when Tig was suddenly beside me, Barrett in one of his arms like he weighed nothing. Which, well, was somewhat true. His other huge hand lifted and moved out toward my neck. I felt myself stiffen, unsure, but all he did was brush the hair away and run a finger down the column of my throat gently, way too gently for someone so massive. "Ice and ibuprofen," he said, dropped his hand, and moved with Barrett toward, then out, the door.

I watched him go before looking back at Sawyer whose piercing eyes were on me, looking right into my soul. Then he

64

wasn't by the door, he was stalking across the room toward me in such a predatory way that I took a few steps back before Barrett's desk stopped me. He kept coming until the toes of his shoes touched mine, his face mere inches from mine.

"Keep your head down until I can figure your shit out. Get your nails done. Have twenty dollar cocktails with your girlfriends. Don't poke your fucking nose in any more of this. I don't have the time to be visiting your clueless ass in the hospital too."

With that, he was gone.

I sank down onto the desk for a second, my heart thumping against my ribcage so hard it was almost painful. My hand rose to the lowest point of my neck and settled there and I realized for the first time that there must have been a bruise there. That was how Tig knew I needed to ice and take pain medicine. Great. That was just great. I would need...

"Get your tight ass in your sweet fucking car and get home," Sawyer's voice barked at me from the doorway. I yelped and jumped to see him standing there, looking decidedly displeased.

"Jesus," I gasped, putting a hand over my heart.

"Now Elsie. I don't have all night to stand here and watch you get all hysterical. Do that shit at home."

"You're such an asshole," I snapped, getting off the desk, snagging my purse off the floor and looking around for my keys.

"Under the pile of shit in the corner."

My brows scrunched together as I moved across the room to where he indicated, not seeing a single key sticking out. But lo and behold, when I moved the papers, there they were. "What, you have x-ray vision too?" I asked, storming over toward the door and slamming him hard in the shoulder to get him out of my way so I could step outside.

"I don't want you involved in my case at all."

"Too fucking bad."

"Fine. Then you're fired and so is Barrett."

"Porsche. Now," he growled, advancing toward me again and damn if I didn't retreat. Again. "I'll be in contact like it or fucking not." When I didn't immediately move, he took another, more threatening, step forward. "You don't get in the fucking car, I'll throw your ass in it."

Somehow, I believed him.

"Fine," I snapped and turned to storm across the street. I turned back suddenly to find he was still standing there, watching me. "I hope he's alright," I said and watched as his hard face softened.

"He'll be fine," he said in a voice that was almost... reassuring.

Before I could rethink my idea that he was just a heartless, arrogant, dickhead, I ran across the street, threw myself into my car, and got home like I was told to.

Then I iced my neck and took some ibuprofen, also like I was told to.

And then I decided that Sawyer was right; I needed to keep my head down. I needed to get my nails done and sip overpriced drinks and let people who knew what they were doing handle things for me from now on.

I might have been stubborn and determined, but two run-ins with very dangerous guys and an innocent guy getting caught in the cross hairs, yeah, I wasn't stupid. I needed to step back.

So that was what I was planning to do.

SIX

Elsie

So the next night, I did what was expected of me. I came home from work; I ate a light meal of yogurt and almonds (pretty much the only food I kept in the house in case of a late night snack craving); I showered; I slipped into a skintight deep purple dress with lots of leg and a fair amount of cleavage; I got my hair extra dolled up; I made my eyes smoky and my lips tinted; after I sprayed on some liquid bandage, I slipped into sky-high silver heels.

I tried my hand at covering up the bruises on my neck. After a night of sleep, I woke up to a room temperature icepack on my neck and really vivid purple and blue bands and fingerprints on my throat. Problem was, I didn't have the kind of makeup one needed to cover bruises like I had. I had a little greenish concealer for when I was hormonal and got a breakthrough pimple or something that I needed to mask the redness of. But I didn't have the yellow tones I would need to cover what I had going on. Besides, if my teen experiences with trying to cover up hickeys was anything to go by, I knew makeup was rather useless on bruises anyway. So for work, I tied a funky scarf on and called it a day. It looked appropriate with work attire.

The silver and purple scarf I tied around my throat that night, yeah, well... it didn't exactly look right. Who wore a scarf with a club dress? No one. No one did anything that stupid. But what choice did I have? I couldn't cover it with makeup and I couldn't leave the house with strangulation bruises on my throat either. I thanked my lucky stars that it was a long scarf, tied it tight at the throat, then left the ends to dangle, one down the front, one down the back.

It would just have to do.

On a sigh, I walked through a mist of perfume, grabbed my clutch and cell, and headed out the door.

Chaz's wasn't the kind of place you expected to see a bunch of silver-spoon men and women. In all honesty, it looked like and usually was, a biker bar. That being said, it was about all Navesink Bank boasted that had a genuine bar atmosphere. There were upscale restaurants we could head to that had a bar area, but it just wasn't the same. When we all turned twenty-one, we started going to Chaz's just because we knew it would piss off our parents that we were slumming it. But, in the end, it was somewhere we genuinely liked to go.

The outside was nothing to write home about, just a brick building with a simple sign. The inside had been redone, all the woods stained dark, the walls painted a deep color, the back bar boasting a whole plethora of unique looking bottles. They added a cocktail menu that, while not twenty dollars a round, was still overpriced. I guess that was the pink tax seeing as the beer was cheaper than you'd find almost anywhere else.

The clientele was a unique mix of bikers, middle class men and women, college kids, and well, me and my friends.

The music was always of the top-forty variety on the weekends and there was plenty of room to dance or scope guys.

"What's with the scarf?" Bea, a friend who was really not a friend at all, asked as I walked up and air kissed two of the other girls who were actual friend-friends. Bea was thin to the point of concern, making me wonder since adolescence if her "vacations" she took every year or so were actually vacations at all or trips to eating disorder clinics. She had a crop of short dark hair that worked with her pixie-face and huge gray eyes. To put it mildly, bones sticking out aside, Bea was freaking gorgeous. She was gorgeous and rich and she really liked the things that came with being gorgeous and rich, like gorgeous and rich boyfriends that she constantly cheated on with 'downtown strange' as she called them. Meaning, guys she met at Chaz's, fucked in bathrooms or cars, and never thought of again.

She was a real peach, let me tell you.

"Oh, just something different I'm trying out. Hey Rome," I said, quickly trying to turn my attention away from her. "I didn't know you were coming."

I didn't know because for the past couple of days, I had been really hit or miss about answering his texts. It was something he was too cool of a guy to comment on, but the flash of hurt on his face said it hadn't gone unnoticed. I sidled into his side and rested my chin on his shoulder for a second.

"Sorry I suck. I've been crazy at work this week." My stomach twisted painfully at the lie and I tried hard to ignore it.

His arm went around my waist, hand settling into my hipbone and squeezing. "No worries. Got some stuff going on at work too."

"Maybe we can get together and dish. Not tomorrow though," I said, curling my lip and he laughed, dropping his arm as I moved a step away, somehow feeling less comfortable with being too touchy-feely with Roman after all the comments Paine had made about him and me. It had honestly never crossed my mind before that what I had been doing was inappropriate at all, because it was nothing out of character for me. I was touchy-feely with friends. But I had also never even stopped to consider that maybe Roman didn't see it the way I did.

"Your dad isn't that bad," Rome said, giving me a head shake.

"My company had a better last quarter than his did. The numbers just came in."

"Alcohol!" Rome called out. "Get this poor woman some alcohol!"

I threw my head back and laughed, the movement making my throat hurt, but it felt good to feel good for a minute. Things had been crazy for weeks. I had been so determined to get answers, to figure out the truth, that I had only really been half-living, half-involved in everything around me. Right then, standing in Chaz's in my ridiculous outfit, with three good friends and one not-good, but familiar friend, I felt present. I felt present and okay for a change.

When I reached out for the very blue-looking drink in a stem glass the waitress brought over, I felt my smile falter and fall slightly as I made perfect eye contact with a very unamused looking Paine. My hand closed around the stem of the glass and the waitress moved away, seemingly unconcerned that I hadn't thanked her. But then again, the bar was packed. The bar was packed and I somehow made immediate eye-contact with someone I had been trying not to think about for the past several days. I say trying because, well, there were times when he would pop up. Like... in bed at night. And... in the shower.

See, that one session the night he was in my house seemed to unlock a long-buried need for constant sexual satisfaction. And because that session involved me thinking about Paine, anytime I got the urge to spend some time with my vibrator, his image immediately popped into my head.

It was a problem.

It was especially a problem because the second our eyes locked, I felt a flush overtake my entire body. I felt my sex clench and my breasts get heavy. I felt every shift of the fabric

of my dress on my suddenly hypersensitive skin. I felt the sense
memory of his lips press into mine.

To put it simply, our eyes locked and I was turned on.

I was starting to feel like some kind of freaking
nymphomaniac. It was unsettling.

But not quite as unsettling as the way Paine's eyes
looked me over, lingering a minute on my legs which sent a
thrill through my body. I liked my legs. They were a testament
to the weekly hot yoga sessions and three-times weekly cardio
sessions at the gym that kept them looking like they did. They
lingered again at my chest, but more briefly, then at my scarf. It
was then that his brows drew together like he was confused.
Which was understandable. He had sisters and word was that he
got around, so he knew women didn't wear freaking scarves
with dresses, but whatever. For all he knew, it was the hot new
thing in Milan. But by the time his eyes got back to my face,
they looked tight and angry.

Confused, turned on, but confused, I looked quickly
away.

"Else, you okay?" Rome asked, his breath warming my
ear in a way that felt oddly too intimate.

"What?" I asked, jerking back slightly. "Oh, yeah. I'm
fine. Sorry. Scatterbrained," I explained, waving my free hand
while bringing the one holding my drink up to my lips for a
long sip.

"Gotta leave the office at the office," he advised. "You're
gonna be here, be here, right? Have a couple drinks, unwind,
forget about all that shit."

"You're right," I agreed, silently thanking the foresight to
call a cab and not drive to the bar. I needed booze and I needed
a lot of it if I was going to be in the same bar with Paine.

Twenty minutes and two and a half drinks later, I was
laughing at something Rome said, loving the fact that once he
got a couple drinks in him, he loosened up and actually had a
rather risque sense of humor. My arm was up and out at my side
with my almost empty drink, my head thrown back, my laugh

71

loud and uninhibited, when suddenly my aloft wrist was tagged in a firm grip and I was being pulled.

"I'm borrowing her for a minute," Paine's tense voice informed Rome whose face fell as his eyes landed on me.

"Um, Paine, I'm here with my friends..." I started, wanting to wipe that look off Roman's face as I realized for the first time that Paine was right; he wasn't fully aware that he was not and would never be my boyfriend.

"Two minutes," he said, pulling my wrist harder as he pried the drink out of my hand and passed it off to a Bea who was too surprised to do anything but take it from him.

"Oh, um, I'll be right back," I told Rome, eyes begging him to understand as Paine turned and started walking, dragging me behind.

"Paine what is your proble..." I started to ask as he pulled me outside and walked down the small alley between the buildings. He pushed me up against the wall, hard enough to make me stiffen, wondering how safe I was with him after all.

Before I could open my mouth to try to either diffuse the situation or start yelling about his treatment of me, his hand was at the side of my neck, yanking at the knot I had tied there and whipping off the scarf so fast that I couldn't bring my hands up to stop him. "Jesus fuck," he growled, balling up the scarf in one hand as his other raised toward my neck. I felt myself flinch; I wasn't sure if it was just a knee-jerk response after being choked or because I genuinely felt fear right then, but I flinched. Hard. And Paine noticed. His eyes flew up to my face, the tightness around his eyes softening. "Babygirl, never. I'd never put my hands on you that way," he said and punctuated the statement as his hand closed the space and gently stroked up the side column of my neck. The whisper-soft touch sent a shiver through my body, seeming to end in a strong tightening at my sex. His hand flattened around the side and back of my neck and he leaned forward, resting his forehead against mine. "Who did this?"

"I don't know," I said honestly, my voice sounding almost shaky to my ears.

"What'd he look like?"

How the hell did he expect me to recall something like that when he was all up in my personal space, causing all kinds of chaos in my system that had gotten used to fantasizing about him while I self-completed over the past few days? I took a slow breath, pulling in the slight spicy scent of his cologne and his skin and knowing nothing else had ever smelled quite so erotic before.

I pushed the thoughts away, drawing up the image of the night before. "Um. Tall, but not as tall as you. Dark hair. Dark eyes. Built but not as big as that other guy who chased me the other night. He wasn't too distinctive. Except he had... a scar..."

"Scar?" he repeated, pulling back just far enough so that our foreheads weren't touching and his eyes could look into mine.

"Yeah, here," I said, my hand raising and touching the space above his upper lip, resting there as I spoke. "Like maybe it was a cleft lip repair?" I surmised, but my eyes were suddenly on his lips. I felt my own part slightly, like an invitation.

"Keep looking at my mouth like that and I'm gonna have to kiss you," he said, calling me on my staring and making my eyes snap up. "And, babygirl, it won't be no lame ass two second meeting of lips this time," he said, referencing the kiss that had still managed to make me tingle for hours afterward. "No, this time," he went on, hand curling slightly into my skin, his other hand with my scarf in it raising and cupping my jaw at the other side of my face, "it will be long and deep and you'll feel my lips on yours for a fucking week afterward."

I swallowed hard, my lady bits thrilling at the notion, trying to convince myself to tell him to step away. But, in the end, my hand dropped from above his lip and onto his bicep, curling in. "All talk," I said, giving him a small smile.

"You sure you want this? Babygirl, I kiss you, I'm gonna have to fuck you. Maybe not tonight, but it's definitely happening. I get another taste, I'm gonna want more. I'm gonna want it all."

"Paine..." I said, need clear in my voice and I was too far gone to care.

"Warned you," he said, hands tightening on the back of my neck and jaw as he tilted my face up and dipped his down, pausing slightly before our lips met, making my belly swirl in anticipation as my eyes fluttered closed. Then his mouth pressed into mine and my legs felt instantly wobbly, making my hand curl harder into his bicep and the other go around his waist and pull him against me. His head slanted, a hint of his teeth grazed my lower lip and I felt my mouth open slightly. That was all he needed. His tongue slipped inside and claimed mine, moving over it with exquisite precision, making a small whimper escape my lips. His hand left my jaw and snaked around my hips, hauling me upward and against him, making my heels lift up out of my shoes.

His tongue released mine and his teeth sank into my lower lip hard, drawing out something that was in no way a whimper, but a full-blown moan. Paine made a growling sound deep in his chest that made my sex clench as a rush of wet rushed to dampen my panties. As if sensing this, he twisted our positions so his back was to the alley opening and his hand released my neck and moved between our bodies and up my skirt to cup my sex over my panties, fingers crooking in and making my lips pull from his on a gasp.

His eyes were already open and on me, looking as heavy lidded as mine felt. "No one can see," he said in a sexy, rough voice that made my stomach flutter as his forefinger moved to press between my folds and find my clit, pulsing against it in a fast, unrelenting pace. I bit into my lip to keep my sounds in, leaning forward to bury my face in his neck as he kept up the perfect torment. "Knew you'd be wet for me," he said, his lips to my hair.

"Paine," I whimpered into his skin as I felt myself tightening, getting close.

"Not yet. Not like this," he said, pressing in hard for a moment before I lost his hand completely as he yanked my skirt back down, shifted so my back was against the wall, and wrapped the scarf back around my neck.

"What?" I asked, my body feeling too frazzled from the interruption of an orgasm that was going to make my world splinter apart to fully understand what had just happened.

"Not here. Not like this," he said, his eyes on his task as he knotted the scarf and pulled it tighter.

My sex was pulsing in a way that was just shy of painful, begging for the orgasm it was denied. And, to my complete and utter horror, I felt tears sting at the back of my eyes. It was just the final straw. I had a shitty freaking week and the last thing I needed was to be toyed with sexually by the guy I had been fantasizing about for days. It was all just too much.

Paine shifted the scarf to how I had it before he pulled me out of the bar and his eyes went to my face again, his eyes taking in the pools in my eyes threatening to spill over. His mouth parted as if on a silent gasp, brows drawing together. "Babygirl..." he said, his hand resting on my cheek just as a stupid tear slipped out and slid down, catching on his skin.

"Don't," I barked, jerking my head to the side.

"Elsie, if you need me to finish..."

I jerked away, shoving hard at his chest as I moved into the mouth of the alley. "I'm not crying because you're a tease. I'm crying because I've had a shitty week that has involved being chased by thugs, being scared half to death by you showing up uninvited to my house, watching someone I know get beat half to death, and then had my hair yanked out of my head and was strangled. I don't need your pity orgasm. I need you to leave me the hell alone," I said, realizing I was yelling at that point and turning to flee back into the bar.

I swatted at my cheeks to get rid of the tears before Bea could see as I made my way back toward the group.

"Else..." Rome said as soon as he saw me, mid-sentence talking to someone I didn't know, his smile instantly falling.

"Alcohol," I barked at him as he walked toward me. "Rome, I want this entire night to be a vodka-soaked blurry memory."

Rome took a deep breath, like he didn't agree with my method of coping, but snagged the closest waitress and ordered a round of shots and another cocktail for me.

Three rounds later, I watched as Paine caught my eye, shook his head, tossed money on the bar, clapped his hand on a young, attractive guy with a scar down his cheek and a Henchmen emblem on his leather jacket, turned and left.

Another two rounds after that, everything was a swirling, happy, numb nothing.

And I almost, but not quite, managed to forget about Paine and the kiss and the... everything else in the alley.

There were some moments in life that not even vodka could erase.

Damn it.

SEVEN

Elsie

Sunday morning brought the hangover to end all hangovers. I rolled over in bed, still in my dress and scarf, sans shoes and jewelry, and vaguely aware of the memory of Roman half-carrying me up to my room, laughing as I recalled a couple particularly stupid adventures he and I had embarked on as teens, doing so with the grandeur and giggle fits only a true drunk could. I even blearily recalled him rolling me onto my back and pulling out my earrings and gently slipping my ring off my finger. I closed my eyes as I remembered his hand closing around mine for a second and squeezing.

I sat up in bed, cradling my head.

God, I was so stupid.

Poor Roman.

How long had he been showing obvious signs that he had more than friendly interest in me? As I made my way toward the bathroom, I ventured a guess that it was most likely since he came back from college. It was then that his gaze seemed to linger and his touches felt less like the brotherly jabs I had known all my life.

Years, I had been unwittingly leading him around for years.

"Oh that's lovely," I groaned at my reflection, my eye makeup smeared half down my face, my hair a tangled puffy mess. I washed my hands and pulled out my too-dry contacts, then threw myself in the shower with every ounce of admittedly small energy I had.

I chugged water, but forewent the over the counter pain medicine because, well, if I was going to do the crime, I was going to do the time. Meaning, I was going to suffer my way through a hangover. I got into light wash skinny jeans, tan bootie wedge heels, and a tan heavy knit sweater, tying a scarf around my neck, then heading out.

I stopped at a coffeehouse and a florist, unsure what the hell I was supposed to bring a near stranger to the hospital after they took a beating because they were working for you.

Barrett was on a normal hospital floor in a room by himself at the end of a hall. I felt a swirling of anxiety in my stomach as I stepped into the open doorway and saw a very sunken, bruised, and sutured Barrett Anderson lying in a hospital bed. Sitting on the windowsill, leg up, back against the window, looking somehow casually arrogant in jeans and a black long-sleeve tee, was Sawyer.

I felt my eyes roll at the smirk he gave me.

"See you met my brother," Barrett's voice called to me, sounding at once resigned and amused.

"I didn't think it was possible given how anti-social you are, but you seemed to inherit all the charm genes in your family," I said, giving him a small smile as I placed the vase on the nightstand beside his bed.

Sawyer's laugh followed me as I moved to hand Barrett his coffee. I realized this because he was suddenly at my side, taking my coffee out of the tray. "You shouldn't have," he said, bringing it up to his mouth and taking a long swig.

"I didn't. That was mine."

"Yeah, bet it would really help that hangover you got going on. Too bad it's mine now."

I turned back to Barrett who gave me a 'what can you do?" shrug. "Have I mentioned how glad I am that I hired you and not him?"

"Babe," Sawyer snorted, reaching out and snagging the side of my scarf, pulling it down to look at and show his brother my bruises. "Sure about that?"

I saw Barrett wince and felt double guilty. "I'd take getting strangled over dealing with you any day."

"Too bad I'm gonna be the one you're working with. At least until Barrett is out of here," he conceded and it was the first hint of kindness I'd seen in him.

"No. That's actually why I came. Just forget it. The case is over."

It wasn't over, not really. I mean I was going to take a step back and make sure I kept myself out of actual danger, but I wasn't done trying to find some answers. I would never be done, not until I found them. But I wasn't involving other people who could get hurt. Of course, common sense said I should probably let Sawyer get involved. He'd quickly dispatched of the guy who had attacked his brother and me. And while he was a dick, he definitely was intimidating. But, well, I didn't want to have to be in a room with him ever again if it was possible.

"Ever hear that phrase about trying to bullshit a bullshit artist?" Sawyer asked, sipping the full fat, sugar-filled coffee I bought myself as a treat. "You aren't over this case and I ain't letting you wade into the Third Street gang on your own."

"Third Street gang?" I asked, feigning innocence.

"Cory is one of their enforcers."

"Cory?" I asked, not able to help the laugh that escaped me. What kind of thug enforcer guy was named Cory? That was the name of a five year old boy, not some muscled, mean-spirited bully.

"Yeah, babe. Cory. And you can take that innocent act and shove it. You know damn well that what you're wrapped up with involves the Third Street gang. And don't think it's escaped my notice that you sent my brother on a job without giving him the information he needed to keep himself safe. That shit won't play. So real soon, you and me, we're having a sit down and you're spilling."

"Sawyer, enough," Barrett said, moving the bed to sit up straighter.

"Show up at my house or my work, I will call the cops. Stay the hell away from me if you value your freedom," I snapped, turning back to Barrett. "I'm sorry I got you beat up. I will have a check sent to you for your services. I hope you feel better soon." I turned and stormed out of the room, my heart slamming so hard in my chest I felt like I was choking on it.

It really was a lousy freaking week.

And it was only about to get worse.

--

"You're seriously not going to talk to me about it?" I asked, crossing my arms over my chest at my father's massive dining table, having just finished the last course and waiting for the coffee to be served. Coffee meant another fifteen minutes of tense conversation before I could finally hightail it the hell out of there and curl back into bed like I had been wanting to do since the moment I woke up that morning.

"There's nothing to talk about, Elsie. The matter is closed."

My father was intimidating in all ways. He was tall and kept up his body, despite most men his age deciding to 'let themselves go'. Those weren't words he even understood. He wore expensive suits from waking until sleep, only ever changing to get into gym clothes. His hair was cut expertly and was an attractive salt and pepper color that gave him the silver fox, not old man, look.

"How can the matter be closed, Dad? We can't just act like..."

"That is exactly what we will do. Is this all you have going on in your life? Get a hobby, Elsie. Work more hours. Get yourself a husband already. Stop harping on non-issues."

Anger for me was an extremely uncomfortable sensation of bugs under my skin, like I wanted to claw them out, like if I didn't, I would go insane. Very few people were capable of bringing out that feeling. My father, unfortunately, was one of those people.

"It's not a non-issue!" I shrieked as my dad's butler brought out the coffee on a cart and poured us each a cup.

"No need for the hysterics, Elsie," he said in a calm voice that made me want to reach across the table and slap him. That was his MO. He got all firm and demanding, got his opponent riled beyond reason, then accused them of being irrational. It worked every God damn time.

"You know what... fuck this," I said, standing so fast that my chair turned back and knocked into the coffee cart, splashing the liquid everywhere.

"Sit down," he said, his voice low and clipped.

I felt my body jolt, wanting me to do what it was told, what I was trained to do my entire life. But, for once, I wasn't going to give him the satisfaction.

"No. When you decide to find that shriveled little heart of yours and inflate it back to an acceptable human-size, then we can talk. Until then, you can take these Sunday dinners and shove them up your ass, Dad," I yelled, moving toward the door.

"Just like her," his voice followed me and I felt myself freeze.

81

I knew what he was doing. He was trying to rile me. He knew exactly how to push my buttons. But if I went back at him, if I lost my cool again, in his eyes, he would win. I was done losing to him. I curled my hands into tight fists at my sides and turned. It took an effort to make my voice calm, almost hollow.

"I know you like to think you control everything. I know that's your thing. But you don't control me anymore. And you never will again. What could you possibly do now, Dad? Ground me? Take my trust away. Have at it. I don't need anything from you. I hope you enjoy your big, empty house. And I pray to God nothing truly awful happened because there is no coming back from that. That guilt will follow you to your grave and into hell afterward."

With that, I grabbed my purse and jacket and exited with an exaggerated calm I most definitely did not feel.

Again as I rounded my car, I felt the tears stinging my eyes.

I was not a particularly overly-emotional person. But everything was screwed up. Nothing was going to plan. I'd had a week from hell that culminated in an argument with my father that was a lifetime overdue. My entire world felt like it was holding on by a thread and I had no one to turn to.

I couldn't go to Rome for two reasons. One, he would be absolutely infuriated and devastated that I had kept it from him for so long. And two, because I felt weird leaning on him now that I realized he had different intentions than I did.

And, well, there was no one else in my life that I was close enough with to involve.

Never, not once in my life, had I ever felt truly alone like I did as I drove back home, swatting at my cheeks, cursing the tears and everything that had taken place to make them appear.

I went in through the garage that brought me into my kitchen, yanking off the scarf that felt like it had been strangling me the entire day. I flicked on the light and went straight for the coffee machine, despite the fact that all I wanted to do was curl up in bed and sleep away the traces of my hangover and all the emotions I didn't want to face.

"Barrett and Sawyer Anderson, babygirl?" Paine's smooth voice asked from my side, making me screech and fly back several feet, the stainless steel coffee carafe raised like I planned to strike with it. I guess the couple of close encounters I'd had over the past week was altering my fight or flight response.

"Jesus Christ, Paine," I gasped, slamming the carafe down as I spotted him leaning against the counter. "How the hell did you get in here?"

"When you punch in your code, Elsie, make sure no one is watching."

"How about you don't be a creepy stalker who looks over my shoulder, how about that? What is it about our society that teaches 'don't be a victim' rather than 'don't be a criminal'?"

"Not here to debate society with you. I'm here to figure out why you are involved with the Anderson brothers."

I lifted my chin, grabbing the carafe and going back to making the coffee just to have an excuse to not look at him. He was looking way too good in dark jeans and a black sweater. "The night we met, you advised me to get out of what I was in. I'm not stupid. I got out. I got someone else involved for me."

"Barrett Anderson? Seriously, babe?"

"In his defense, I didn't exactly tell him what I was wrapped up in. He went in blind. It was my fault he got put in the hospital."

"No, Elsie. Don't take that shit on. He should have gotten answers out of you before he took the case. Sawyer was right in thinking he didn't belong in the field. It's not your fault he got cocky. It's not your fault you got choked either. So stop thinking that way."

I stood facing the coffee machine, listening to it drip as I took a couple deep breaths. I wasn't in any kind of shape to deal with him right then. Not after the day I had, with my emotions raw and all over the place. I just needed to be alone.

"Babygirl," Paine's voice said in my ear as his body cozied up behind me, his arm snaking around my lower belly and holding me against him.

"Please don't. I can't do this right now," I said, not caring how desperate my voice sounded.

"Talk to me," he urged, leaning down and resting his chin on my shoulder. I felt my head start to shake and his arm tightened around me. And damn if being in a man's arms, held back against his strong chest, didn't feel like exactly what I needed right that minute. "You need to get that shit out. It's eating you up. I'll listen."

"And get angry. And judge. And lecture me."

"No anger or judgment or lectures," he said, using his hand at my hip to turn me so I was against his chest, and wrapping me up tight. "Just an ear."

And, well, that just melted what was left of my puny defenses.

"My sister is missing," I said aloud for the first time ever.

Against me, I could feel him stiffen and his hold loosened slightly so he could push me back and look down at me. "Your sister is missing?"

I felt myself nod tightly. "Not officially seeing as there is no report of it."

"Why not?"

"Because my father is convinced she's not missing. She... was acting off for a long time before she disappeared. She was secretive and distant. She and I used to be best friends, then suddenly, she was like a stranger. And then she was gone. But she cashed out her trust fund first. Everything else, though, was left. Her house, her car, all her jewelry and clothes and, God, even her freaking parrot..."

"Her parrot," he repeated when I trailed off.

"He's fine. Living large in a bird sanctuary in Florida thanks to a nice donation from my father. But she left him. In his cage. For God knew how long. There was no food or water left when I finally went over to check on her when she hadn't returned my calls for three days. She never would have just... left him to starve to death in her empty house. No way."

"So why haven't you filed a report if you're convinced she's missing?"

"The detective I talked to agreed with my father. He said to give it a few weeks to see if she just got a wild hair and took off to Boca with a new guy or something."

"Was she a big dater?"

I felt the side of my lips turn up. "I tried that angle. She wasn't exactly a relationship girl. She had men in and out of her life, but no one serious. I couldn't see her just taking off with a guy. Not by choice anyway."

He nodded, pressing a quick kiss to my forehead in an offhand way that made my belly flip flop with the casual intimacy of it all. "Why are you working the Third Street angle?"

My hands went up, squeezing his sides and pushing until he let me go. I moved out into the living room, clicking the hidden latch inside the fireplace that unlocked the picture beside it and pulled it open to reveal the safe.

"Ain't looking," he said as I turned to check, his words of caution definitely making me more cautious about my codes.

I punched in the code and pulled the safe open, reaching inside and pulling out the small jewel-encrusted jewelry box that belonged to my sister, and holding it out toward Paine.

His brows drew together as he took it, pulling off the top. His breath hissed out of his mouth as he grabbed one of the small baggies and pulled it out. There were at least a dozen of them inside, clear zip-lock drug bags with a large blue three printed on the front and a fluffy brownish powder inside it. "She was using heroin," he surmised, putting the baggie back, but not handing it back to me.

"Seems the most likely explanation. Why else would she have drugs hidden in her bedroom? It also explains her weird behavior for the weeks before she went missing. I've never

85

really known anyone on drugs; I didn't know what to look for, so I didn't see it."

"It happens," he shrugged. "Can't beat yourself up about it. So you thought... what? She cashed in her trust to buy more drugs?"

"Maybe."

"Babygirl, H is cheap. I don't know, and don't need to know, what was in her trust, but no way did she need to cash it all out to fund her drug habit."

"Maybe she got herself... involved with one of the guys in the gang. Maybe he got her trust, conned her into giving him the money? I mean... why all of a sudden can a measly street gang afford a huge warehouse like the one on Kennedy?"

"Got a point," he said. When I reached for the jewelry box, he shook his head and pulled it back. "I have to get rid of this, Elsie. You can't keep drugs in your house. Or evidence like the baggies even if you flushed the H."

Well, that was true enough. I felt uncomfortable having it in my house, even locked up in the safe. "Okay."

"Are you worried your sister is dead?" he asked bluntly, making me start.

I reached up and ran a hand through my hair. "I don't know. Maybe. I guess I'm kind of hoping she's just holed up with some gang banger, too in love or too high, or both, to care about her old life."

"It's possible," he said in a guarded voice.

"But not likely," I said, interpreting his tone.

"Not likely. So you want answers."

"Yes."

Paine looked away for a long minute, staring out my front window before he turned back. "I can get you answers."

"How?" I asked, thinking he was going to start bashing heads together until he got them.

"Babygirl, I used to run the Third Street gang," he admitted in an empty voice. And damn if it was the absolute last thing I had expected him to say. I would have been more accepting of him telling me he was an alien from Mars who spent his free time training poodles to dance while he dressed in women's clothing.

"I'm sorry... what?"

"That gang... I ran it for years. And the man who is in charge now? He's my brother."

"Brother?" I repeated dumbly. "You said you had sisters," I said, knowing my face was a mask of confusion.

"I do. And we're tight. I also have a half brother. Same father, different mother. His name is Enzo and he is in charge of Third street and the drugs and the whores."

I flinched inwardly at that word, but was too preoccupied trying to reconcile the image of Paine, the drug and whore lord, and the Paine I thought I was beginning to get to know, the one who saved a girl off the street and asked for nothing in return, who loved his sisters, who kissed like no one I had ever come across before, who was willing to be an ear when I needed one and get rid of illicit drugs I had no business having in the first place.

"Are you and Enzo... close?"

To that, Paine let out a humorless snort and shook his head.

"No."

EIGHT

Paine

If you looked into me, if you pulled up my records, I was as clean as the fresh fallen fucking snow. No arrests, no holds for questioning, not even a damn parking ticket.

That being said, looks could be deceiving.

I grew up in the ghetto with a mom who had enough of the lying, cheating, drug-addicted shithead who sired me and my sisters. I distinctly remember a few days after my fifth birthday walking out into the hall with my mother, one sister on her hip, the other in a cheap umbrella stroller, and almost walking right into a kid who could have been my twin. Tall for his age, solid, same color skin, same color eyes. The baby bag my mother had been trying to get onto her shoulder fell to the ground and the contents flew across the dirty hall as she looked down at the little boy with understanding, then at the kid's mother with horror.

"That mother fucker," the other mother said, shaking her head. I remembered Annie as being too upper class to live in the crummy apartment building. I don't know where my young mind got the idea. Maybe it was her clothes that seemed nicer than my mom's and my aunts'. Maybe it was the way her short cap of blond hair was always perfectly styled and shiny. Something about her screamed 'money' to me. "He's five?" she asked my mother who gave me a tight smile.

"Yep."

"Wow," Annie said.

"Yeah," my mother agreed, shaking her head.

From that day on, those two were as tight as two women could be. I guess it came from sharing a lying, cheating, drug-addicted shithead unwittingly then both dumping him and trying to move on with their lives. Annie, I would learn later, had just divorced from her husband, the couple being an upper-middle-class childless family who just couldn't make it work. She had a nice apartment in a nicer town where she met my father who had been working at a repair shop she brought her car into for a tune up. The rest, as they say, was history. He saw dollar signs; he latched on; he pulled at her heartstrings and sucked her dry. She wisened up and kicked his sorry ass to the curb and about three weeks later found out she was pregnant. So fast forward to her working two jobs to support a kid in a roach-infested apartment.

Because our mothers got tight, Enzo and I became brothers in all the ways that counted. We walked to and from school with each other, we had each other's and my sisters' backs. We raised hell together. We chased girls together when we were old enough.

And, being so close, we grew into similar young men: driven, ambitious, wanting nothing more than to rise up out of our shit beginnings. Living in the slums, that meant one of two things: you got good at a sport and got a college scholarship the hell out of there, or you sought a way to run the streets. Enzo could shoot hoops, but busted a kneecap his senior year, killing his chances of any kind of sports career.

I had never had any skill in any sport, so by sophomore year, I was already learning the ways of street corner politics. I made myself available. I carried product because I was underage with no priors, making myself the fall guy for whatever hustler that knew that if he went back inside, the only way he'd be leaving was through the back door.

Back then, it was weed or rocks.

Before long, I was doing the actual dealing with some other banger watching over me to make sure I didn't fuck up deals or take a cut that I wasn't entitled to. It wasn't more than a couple months before I was having a meeting with the shot-caller, a tall, skinny dude in his late twenties with eye teeth so pointy they looked like fangs named Terrell. It didn't take much for me to realize he wasn't long for the leadership position. First, he smoked rock himself. Second, aside from somewhat crazy eyes, there wasn't a fucking scary thing about him.

"Ain't got no time for no fucking pussies workin' for me. You want in, you get beat in. You survive, you're in. You follow orders. You don't run your fucking mouth. And we have a reputation to uphold. Don't be selling no wolf tickets. You calling someone out, you better back that shit up. Got it?"

"Got it."

That night, in the empty parking lot of an abandoned department store, a circle of Third Street boys closed in on me. Within minutes, I was unconscious. When I woke back up, I was in.

It was that easy. Fifteen years old and I was bringing in several G's a month, easing the burden on my mother and dropping way too much cash on bullshit like shoes and watches and shit. Young and stupid, that was me.

Terrell caught a charge for possession with intention to distribute and was put away for a dime. It didn't take more than an afternoon for someone else to step into his place, a much bigger guy by the name Darius with a rap sheet longer than my forearm. By all accounts, he was a better leader. As such, he was much more violent, much more paranoid and ruthless. You scuffed his shoes, you were eating through a straw for the next three months. You took a cut you didn't earn, you weren't heard from again.

So when someone started roughing up the whores, thereby stealing money from him 'cause no one wanted to pay to fuck a chick with a busted face, he was itching for some bloodshed. And who did he choose to go mete out that punishment? Yeah, just-turned sixteen year old me. With very little choice, that was exactly what I did.

I was never a violent person by nature. If you fucked with me or mine, I handled it. When pushing came to shoving, I was a mother fucking fighter. But I didn't enjoy it. I didn't get off on it like some of the other guys did. Maybe that was why I was picked, for my control. And as addicted as I was to the money lining my pockets, there was no way I was fucking up my standing in the gang by refusing an order. That and, well, roughing up a woman who had very little control over her own safety in the first place, that was some pussy-ass shit and the fuck deserved what he got. Which included eight stab wounds and a busted jaw. He lived, just barely. But he never went anywhere near one of our women again.

I moved up in favor, given power over the new bloods on the street, despite being the same age or even younger than some of them.

During this time, me and Enzo, we started drifting. He was the good kid. He kept up his grades; he kept his head down and his nose clean; he respected his mother's wish that he never fall into the streets. He had his jock friends and wanted nothing to do with his drug-dealing, pimping, fist-fighting, knife-wielding half brother. It was a wish I understood, even as young and cocky and money-hungry as I was, I got it.

I graduated at eighteen, just barely. Enzo recovered from his surgery and went to work at some pathetic nine-to-five that was eating away at his soul little by little. Each time I saw him, he seemed just a little bit more run down and hopeless.

I had a top of the line Mustang and a five-thousand dollar watch on my wrist. I also had a reputation and a squeaky clean rap sheet.

When Darius took three to the chest during a drive-by and bled out right at my feet, I decided it was my time. I was stepping up. I was calling the shots.

It didn't happen as effortlessly as it had for Darius. I was young. I wasn't as experienced as some of the other guys in the gang. But I was power hungry and still headstrong enough to think I was untouchable. Anyone who questioned me got a reminder of why Darius used me to handle his problems. If they didn't bend, they were broken.

Older, wiser, I didn't look back on those days fondly. I didn't look at the things I had to do to hold my power for as long as I had with a smile. It was cold, brutal, and lonely at the top. I understood why Darius was so paranoid, why Terrell turned to the drugs. You lived your life under the weight of the constant realization that you were always one backstabber or one police raid away from a coffin or a cell.

So I became hard.

I ran shit with an iron fist and a loaded gun. My women were kept clean and safe. I traded in crack for heroin when the time came and the demand switched. I got contacts from South America. I brought the operation to a whole other level. My men were smart, discreet, and ruthless. No one stepped in on our turf. All things considered, it was one of the bloodiest reigns the Third Street gang had since the early nineties. The power struggle in Navesink Bank was a delicate balance of respecting the right organizations: The Henchmen, The Grassi family, The Mallicks, and Richard Lyon. Later, Hailstorm, V, and Lex Keith; but also knowing who needed to be tamped down before they got too powerful. The Mexicans, the small time MCs, the Irish. They weren't full blown wars, but only because I got wind of something I didn't like the smell of, I attacked hard and early. No one got the chance to dig in their roots and threaten our control of the streets.

Ten years. Ten years I called the shots. Ten years I spent lining my pockets, tagging women, growing my empire, listening to my mother and aunts and sisters and grandmother lecture me about not wanting to bury me or visit me at the penn.

Eventually, they all moved in together, pooling their money, and refusing one cent of my 'bloody money'.

Just shy of our twenty-ninth birthdays, an old shadow darkened my door. I wasn't sure how long it had been since I'd seen Enzo. Annie had died of cancer three years before and I had covered the cost of the arrangements and been present at the funeral. He had too, but I didn't pay him any attention, too wrapped up in myself at the time.

The last time I got a good look at him must have been a good five years before.

If his eyes and face weren't the same as what I saw in the mirror, I wouldn't have recognized him. He'd dropped a good fifty pounds he didn't need to lose, making him look sickly.

"Fuck don't tell me you're on rock or ice," I said, shaking my head as D let him in my office which wasn't an office at all but a ostentatious living room inside a housing project that was our headquarters. I could have afforded a nice place in a decent part of town, but when you ran the streets, you had to live in them too.

"Call off your boy," he said, jerking his head toward D.

"Take a walk," I agreed and D excused himself.

"I want in," he said, taking a couple steps into the room, not even bothering to look around at the TV that took up most of the wall or the sound system that cost the down payment on a mid-size car.

"In on what?"

"This. What you got. I want in. I'm fucking over slaving away to make pennies. I'm sick of swallowing the shit men feed to me just because they have a salaried position. I'm done. It's over."

"Annie wouldn't want..."

"Mom's dead. Mom has been dead a long time. I respected her wishes when she was around to care. She's in the ground and all I got is myself. And I want better."

"She ain't all you got. You got me too."

From that day on, he did.

He worked his way up.

He got his own reputation. If possible, somehow meaner, bloodier, and crueler than mine. He had, after all, ten years of feeling under-appreciated, overlooked, poor, and weak to draw anger from. Not to mention the loss of what looked like a promising career in basketball. He threw every bit of disappointment and rage into earning and keeping the respect of the men. He put in hours that made everyone else in the organization look like they were slacking; he made it possible to rise up in the ranks in under a year. He put on sixty solid pounds of muscle. He protected the girls. He watched over the new blood on the streets. He helped balance the books. He went with me to meetings.

Then one night, we got word of one of our girls getting roughed up and raped by one of our own. First, it was against the rules for any of the guys to get anything from any of the girls whether they gave it away for free or they paid for it. It wasn't done. Second, there was no fucking way you put your hands on them at all, let alone force yourself on them.

So me and Enzo, we grabbed knives and guns and we headed out.

See the thing is, we knew the important members of our crew. We knew the men who kept an eye on things, who handled our big clients, who enforced the rules. But we didn't know the names or reputations of every punk on the streets handing out bags of smack. So when we showed up at D'angelo's house, we had no idea he was just a kid. Meaning, no more than sixteen. He was big and heavy, having the body of a grown man, making it easy for him to overpower one of the girls, but in the face... just a boy.

Enzo pounced.

SAVIOR

Because age didn't matter. You were old enough to live through a beat-in and possibly offer up a nice chunk of your life to jail for the gang, then you were old enough to take your punishment when you earned it.

I froze.

I froze because I saw for the first time what I was doing. Not necessarily in that moment, because even free of the gang and older, I don't regret that shithead getting his face bashed in. Rape was rape, didn't matter if you were of legal age for a beat down or not. But, all the arrogance and power fell away as I stood there and watched the boy I had grown up with, the one with fucking potential, with the grades and skills to get out of our shit upbringing in a straight-up way, bash into the face of a street kid I had employed to sell drugs, a position that ultimately gave him access to our women.

And it wasn't just the two in front of me. It was the dozens of men, and the smattering of women, that I employed. Yes, I gave them a way out of poverty like Terrell and Darius offered me when I needed it. But in exchange for that, how many men died at my hands? Rival gang members, sure, but my own too. Ones I had ordered to be taken out, ones who had caught a spray of bullets during a drive by, ones that went away to jail and got shivved and left out the back door in a casket.

In that moment, slumped back against the wall in a house that obviously didn't belong to the kid getting his jaw busted, I was done.

It was over for me.

The problem being, it didn't work that way.

If you wanted out, you got out by death and death only.

Leaders especially didn't get the luxury of walking away.

Maybe they would have let me run. I could have rounded up my family and went to the West coast. But it wasn't just about my family at that point. I liked Navesink Bank. It was all I ever knew. I'd made friends outside of the gang that I didn't want to lose. I wanted out, but I wanted to stay in the area.

And, well, that meant my options were limited.

95

And the options I did have, yeah, they were bloody.

"Enough, Enzo," I snapped, dragging him backward by his shirt as the kid rolled to his side and spit out blood on his mother's carpet. Enzo shook me off and stormed outside, needing a minute to calm down. "You're out obviously," I told the kid. "We see you anywhere near our operation and especially our women again, your mom will be picking out funeral flowers. Got it?"

It took me three weeks to build up the nerve and steel my stomach to do what needed to be done.

Half of the men in Third Street ended up with knife wounds or bullets.

This included Enzo who spent two nights in a hospital bed recovering from a shot to his shoulder.

It was all bravado and it only worked for about a week before some of the men I attacked came at me in my new life in the industrial part of town. But I had been expecting them.

I spent two years fighting before they got tired of losing and left me alone.

Enzo never came after me, but I also lost my brother the second I put a bullet in him.

By the time I was thirty-four, I was fully free. No one messed with me and I got a following of ink lovers who kept me in business. I still had my nest egg that I earned illegally that allowed me to have the nice things I liked, the car I liked, the spending money I liked.

Enzo had a bloody fight to get to the top. A couple of the other guys who had been around longer kept him down and called shots until either he, or someone else, took them out. Things had been crazy since I left them, but had finally started to shape up once Enzo got in power. His men still needed some reining in, but he was doing better. Things were more controlled, less paranoid. People respected him, maybe partly because he reminded them of me in my younger days, but also because nothing about Enzo invited questioning or disrespect.

96

Things between us were fine for a while, both of us ignoring the other, pretending there wasn't history.

That all stopped when I found out Third Street sold H to my little sister, a girl who had once been like a sister to him as well. Granted, it wasn't him directly, but it happened under his watch. I handled my sister first, shipping her off to rehab even though she had only been high twice. Then I grabbed my gun and sneaked into Enzo's place, walking up behind him as he sat on the couch and put then cocked a gun against the back of his neck. "Sell my sister smack again and you won't live to regret it, Enzo."

The next time I saw him was when my friend Shooter had his girl kidnapped a year back by the Third Street gang's heroin supplier. It wasn't a warm reunion.

It was a sick thing, but I missed him.

I missed the boy I grew up with, the man I did business alongside, the face that used to sit across from me at Thanksgiving, Christmas, and Easter dinners.

But there was no going back from what we had done.

In general, as well as to each other.

NINE

Elsie

"You shot your brother?" I heard myself ask when he stopped telling me his story.

It wasn't an easy story to hear. Worse yet, I imagined, because I came from such a privileged background. That kind of dark and twisted didn't happen in my world. In my world, the worst that you'd suffered through was someone talking behind your back, destroying your image. Maybe a little drug addiction thrown in here or there- alcohol or cocaine mostly, high society drugs. But there were no beatings and backstabbing and shooting and killing.

But the way Paine told it, with a sort of detachment, was a testament to how normal it was in his life. Like that was just how life was where he grew up.

"Yeah, baby. I shot my own brother."

"Wow," I said, sitting down on my couch and looking down at my hands for a second.

"Wanna run screaming now?" he asked and, if I wasn't mistaken, there was some kind of vulnerability in his tone. He expected me to reject him because he had a past. Maybe a wiser person would, but nothing about Paine said he was a bad person. He had done bad things to get what he wanted and needed out of his life. The same could honestly be said about men like my father. He'd sunk smaller businesses to build his up, laying off thousands of families that needed paychecks, throwing them into financial uncertainty. He did this without a thought, without a flinch. He never stopped to think about what his actions did to others, what they did to himself.

Paine did.

So I wasn't going to fault him for having a sordid, ugly past.

"No."

"You should," he said, coming over toward me, sitting down on the coffee table in front of me, our legs touching. He reached behind him and put the jewelry box down.

"Probably," I agreed. "But I don't want to."

Paine's head cocked to the side as he watched me for a minute. "Pretty rich girl wants to go slumming?"

I felt my eyes lower as I stiffened. "Don't turn me into a trope. I'm not a God damn trope. I don't want you because you are a bad boy tattoo artist who used to run a street gang. I think you're a good man. You've been good to me as a whole. So don't you dare try to pull the 'oh the poor little rich girl can't get fucked right by the rich guys so she needs some back street guy' thing on me. I deserve better than that. And, quite frankly, so do you."

Somewhere along in my speech, Paine's lips tipped up and by the time I was done, he was full-on smiling. "You want me, huh?"

I felt my eyes rolling. "Of course that was all you heard."

"You want me," he repeated, his hands landing on my knees as he slowly moved to stand, raising one hand to rest on the couch behind my head to balance his weight as his body curled, forcing me to press my head against the couch to tip my head up and look at him. His other hand slid up my thigh, over my stomach, over my breast, then cradled my jaw. "Say it," he demanded, his voice low.

I wet my lips, swallowing hard.

"I want you," I admitted because, well, I did. I wasn't the kind of woman to play coy and evade when it came to sex. I knew what I wanted; he knew what I wanted. What was the use in denying it?

"Fuck babygirl," he said, fingers stroking up over my cheek slightly. "Any idea how good that is to hear?"

"How good?" I asked, head tilting, smile teasing.

His hand left my cheek, going down the side of my neck and sliding down my arm until he found my hand, grabbing it, pulling it up, and placing my palm against the crotch of his jeans over his hard cock. I heard a low, needy sound escape me as he curled my hand around him. "That good," he said, his voice getting deeper as I grasped him and did as much of a stroke as his thick jeans would allow.

I looked up into his light eyes, mine a challenge. "You know what I find with you?"

"No, what?" he asked, his hand digging into mine as I did another stroke.

"You're all talk."

"Is that a challenge, babygirl? Because, let me tell you, you open up for me, I can make you scream louder than any man or battery-powered device ever has before."

My free hand went up, snagging the back of his neck and pulling him down toward me, kissing up the side of his neck. "Maybe I'm quiet as a mouse when I come."

"Not for me," he promised, his hand moving off mine, tagging me at the waist as he simultaneously dropped down onto the couch beside me and hauled me up and over until I was straddling him. I adjusted my legs and sank my hips down, feeling his hardness press against my heat and throwing my head back on a silent moan. His hands sank into both my hips, using them to stroke me over his length and the silent moan became a not-so-silent one. "Barely touching you," he said as I leaned forward and rested my forehead to his.

"Yeah, what's up with that?" I asked and was rewarded with a small chuckle as his hands shifted around and down until he was cupping my ass, his fingers squeezing in hard.

"Did I tell you yet what a fucking phenomenal ass this is? Been thinking of it since that first night in those jeans. And in that purple dress... fuck me."

"Yes please," I invited, getting another chuckle before I pressed my lips to his and the sound disappeared on an erotic little growl.

A current passed through my entire system at the contact, making every inch of my skin feel electric and buzzing. I sank lower against him, my chest pressing hard into his. One of his hands snaked up my spine and curled into the hair at the nape of my neck. The other released my ass but only so he could pull back and smack it hard enough to make my body jump unexpectedly. My teeth sank into his lower lip in retribution, earning me another smack that had my thighs and lady bits contracting hard. His hand curled harder into my hair and tugged backward, making me release his lips and pulling me far enough back so he could look at my face.

When he could see me, he smacked again, harder. My body jumped, my mouth parted, and a small whimper escaped me as I stroked over him again, trying to get relief from the pressure low in my belly, begging for fulfillment. "Oh, babygirl, we're gonna have fun," he said with a sexy half-smirk. He released my hair. "Arms up," he instructed and up they went. The material of my sweater felt scratchy and uncomfortable on my heated and overly-sensitive skin. His hands went to the hem and snagged the material, pulling it up slowly, exposing me one inch at a time. I said a silent 'thank-you' to early morning hungover-me for choosing the pretty tan and black lace balconette bra and matching panties and not the plain white 'fuck this shit' bra and panties I almost put on. The material went over my head and Paine flung it across the room. "You wear this shit on the daily?" he asked, hands moving to my ribcage just under my bra line.

"Mostly," I said, grabbing his wrists and moving his hands up to cover my breasts. His hands squeezed hard before his thumbs stroked over my hardened nipples. My palms moved to brace on his thighs behind me as my hips ground against him.

"Fuck," he said, shaking his head as he watched me, my pace unhurried though the need was like a coil wound too tight inside. His hands followed the band of my bra to my back and made short work of the clasps. I pressed back straight so he could slide the straps down my arms. As soon as the material was gone, his hands moved up and covered my bare breasts, the roughness of his palms moving over my sensitive nipples and wrenching a groan from me.

They were good breasts, not huge, but not tiny either. His big hands completely covered them, squeezing them tightly before he took the hardened buds and rolled them between his fingers, almost to the point of pain. His hands went to my sides, squeezing in, and pulling my body forward. My hands braced on the back of the couch behind his shoulders as his head ducked, tilted, and his mouth closed over my nipple, sucking hard and deep as his other hand worked my other breast, overwhelming my already too-stimulated system.

"Paine, please," I pleaded as his mouth closed over my other nipple.

On a growl, his hands went to my ass again, digging in as he knifed up and to the side, making me land longways on the couch and bracing himself on his knees on the side and between my thighs. His hands left my ass and moved across my stomach, fingers slipping under the band of my pants and toying with the edge of my panties. They moved to the center and pushed the button. It took every ounce of self-control I possessed to keep from writhing shamelessly.

"Ready to scream?" he asked then, before I could even nod my agreement, his hand slid inside, not bothering to tease me first and going right under my panties. One finger slid up my cleft leisurely as if I wasn't just about ready to explode before hitting my clit and pressing in. I let out a moan that echoed off the walls in my quiet house. "Not quite there yet," he said, eyes heavy as he slid his middle finger down my cleft and slipped it inside me. He thrust a few times, making my hips rise up to meet his rhythm, before his finger curled up and started to work over the top wall, hitting my G-spot.

I was close. So freaking close. Every muscle in my body was tense and waiting for the rush of pleasure as my inner thighs started to shake in anticipation. His finger on my clit picked up its pace as his other moved to match inside me.

I felt myself tightening, Paine's eyes too hypnotic to look away from as my moans turned to whimpers, feeling too strangled for air to manage anything else.

"Come babygirl."

I was going to. I was...

My doorbell chimed, making my whole body jump, my eyes going huge. Paine's face spread into a slow smirk as he kept up the unrelenting pace on my clit and G-spot, pushing just to the edge.

"Else, open up! I left the key at my place," Roman's voice called through the door.

My eyes went even bigger and Paine's smirk got a little more sinister.

"Paine, I can't..."

But then his finger stopped working me in circles and pressed into my clit hard. He moved fast, arm whipping out and hand slapping down over my mouth just as my orgasm crested, just as strong as I had expected, my entire body jerking as the waves crashed over me and I screamed out against his palm, thankful for his foresight to muffle my cries. His finger thrust through, drawing it out, turning all my bones to liquid as I sucked in air greedily.

Spent, his finger pulled out of me and he sat back on his ankles as the bell chimed again. "Come on, Else. I have gelato and Kiss Kiss Bang Bang. Let's stuff our faces, watch the best witty, sarcasm-laden crime drama ever made and forget about the world."

Paine's hand left my mouth and I shot up on the couch, leaning over the arm of it to retrieve my shirt. "Hold on!" I yelled, giving Paine big-eyes as he just sat there watching me with an amused smile. "You have to go," I whispered at him as I found my bra and stuffed it under the couch as I wrestled myself into my sweater.

"Tell him you can't tonight," Paine said back in a normal voice and when I shushed him, he just chuckled.

"I can't. I mean... I'm sorry. I know I'm leaving you high and dry, but I've been a shitty friend to him and things have been awkward since..."

"Since you figured out he wants to fuck you," Paine said, sitting as I moved to stand in front of him.

"Else, it's fifteen degrees out here. What the hell are you doing?"

"Paine, I'm sor..."

"Stop apologizing," he said, shaking his head as his hands snaked out and reached for the front of my jeans, using them to drag me forward slightly so he could zip and fasten them. Finished, he stood, taking up all my space, making our bodies touch from the knees up. The coffee table behind me blocked any retreat. His head ducked near my ear and he said in a quiet, sexy as all hell voice, "Told you I'd make you scream." Then he kissed my cheek and took off toward the kitchen where, I figured he learned from his breaking and entering, he knew there was an exit through the back.

"Elsie are you okay?" Rome's voice asked, starting to sound worried.

I ruffled my hair and rushed toward the door, feeling both come-drunk and frazzled at the same time. I slipped the locks and pulled the door open. "Hey, Rome. Sorry, I was just trying to..."

The rest of my sentence fell away as the bag he was holding fell to the steps and his hand moved out toward me, catching the ends of my hair and pushing the mass of it behind my shoulder. "Else, what the fuck happened to your neck?"

Shit. Shit shit shit.

I'd ripped off my scarf in the kitchen.

And the bruises were in no way better after another full day. If anything, they almost looked worse.

"Rome, I..."

"Is this why you were wearing that scarf the other night?" he asked, his hand settling on the side of my neck as his brown eyes that I always found sweet looked almost... devastated. His other hand went around my back and pulled me against his chest, holding me there tight. I felt his lips press into the side of my head. "Why didn't you tell me? Anything, Else, you can tell me anything. If some asshole did... something..."

Oh, God. No. While that would certainly be an easier thing to explain, I couldn't let him think I was assaulted like that.

"No!" I yelped as his arm squeezed me tighter. "No, it wasn't that. Rome, I promise. I was... just... mugged. It was nothing. No big deal. Ease up, I can't breathe," I said, swatting his back and letting out a fake laugh.

He released me, brows drawn down slightly. "Since when do you keep shit like that from me, Else? This is not 'no big deal'. This is a big fucking deal. Did you report it? Does your father kno..."

"Rome, I'm a big girl. I handled it." Sort-of. Really some big, arrogant, jackass of a private investigator handled it for me, but regardless, it was handled.

"Okay," he said, looking hurt again as he leaned down to retrieve the bag he dropped.

"What kind did you get? I asked, trying for lighthearted and, despite my best efforts, it came off forced.

"Salted caramel for you and..."

"Brownie swirl for you," I finished, giving him a smile that I actually did feel. It was nice to realize that, despite my entire world being turned on its axis, some things never really changed.

He gave me a tight smile that he didn't feel and moved to step inside, making me take a step back, somewhat frantically looking around to make sure Paine had disappeared. I went to the kitchen and got us towels to wrap around the ice cream tubs and spoons and walked back to the living room where Rome had already loaded the DVD into the machine and got the movie going.

He pulled the top off my gelato and handed it to me, gesturing next to him on the couch. The couch where Paine had just given me a mind-numbing orgasm with just his fingers. I sat down awkwardly, putting my legs up over his as was our usual TV-watching position, and tried to focus on the movie, not the memory of Paine's hands and mouth on me.

Two hours later, we were watching the credits, ice cream long abandoned on the coffee table. Empty, of course. What monster got a pint of gelato and didn't eat it all in one sitting?

One of Rome's hands landed on my knee and squeezed, drawing my attention. "What's going on here?" he asked, face impassive, but I knew him well enough to know there was weight behind the question.

"What do you mean?"

"Else, honey, things have been weird here," he said, gesturing to the air between us, "for a while now."

"Rome, it's just been a hell week at..."

"No," he cut me off, shaking his head. "Not just this week. This has been almost a month. Ever since Elana took off on some harebrained vacation." I closed my eyes tight at that lie and I knew my guilt was all over my face. I knew it and Rome saw it. "Is Elana not on vacation? Is she at some kind of clinic somewhere?" he asked, knowing Elana took her rebellion a bit more seriously than he and I had ever dared. It wasn't crazy to think that she had ended up at some kind of rehab.

"She's not at a clinic, Rome," I said, feeling tears well up unbidden and trying to blink them away before they were seen.

But Rome was Rome and he saw them. "Else, honey, what's going on?"

"She's missing. Not legally, but... she's missing. They wouldn't let me file a report, telling me she probably just took her money and hit a beach somewhere. But she left Alfred in her house without food, Rome. She never would have just... left him to starve to death so she could go get a tan, sip margaritas, and have sex on the beach. No way."

"Jesus Christ, Else. Why wouldn't you tell me?"

That was a good question to which I didn't have an answer. I hadn't been the one who originally fed Roman the lie about her going on vacation. That was my father spreading the information far and wide. It got back to Roman's dad, Rhett, and then that got back to Rome. Way before I had even stopped freaking out enough to tell him the truth myself. Why I hadn't corrected him, set things straight, yeah that was completely beyond me.

I guess I got so busy chasing down leads, trying to understand what happened. I knew Rome would get my need for answers, but he also would have made me be careful, contact the cops again, let him get involved. He damn sure never would have let me go check out the warehouse on Kennedy all by myself.

I didn't want anyone slowing me down.

And that made me, well...

"I'm such a shitty friend," I whimpered, putting my hands up over my face to keep the ugly cry hidden.

I really, really needed a free hour to myself to get these emotions out of my system so I stopped crying at the drop of a dime. It was getting pathetic.

"Else, no," Rome said, voice soft again as his arms grabbed me around the back and under the knees, pulling me up onto his lap and letting me pull it together against his neck.

It took me an embarrassingly long two or three minutes before I remembered that I couldn't do that with Rome anymore. I couldn't cry on his chest. I couldn't sit in his lap. I couldn't keep confusing him. Feeling me stiffen, Rome's arms fell from around me as I scooted off his lap and dropped down on the seat beside him.

"Sorry. I'm a mess."

"Oh please. This is nothing. Remember when Alexi dumped you junior year? That was a mess," he teased, bringing up the memory of me ugly snot crying on the abandoned bleachers after school one afternoon, using Rome's school sweatshirt sleeve to wipe at my running mascara. When he had finally gotten me into his car a while later and I pulled down the mirror, yeah, let's just say it wasn't pretty. "This is just someone who works too hard and doesn't ever let anyone else help shoulder her burden so she gets over-tired and emotional thinking she's a shit friend, when she's really the best friend anyone could ask for."

"Oh yeah? Then how come I haven't asked you what led to gelato and a kickass Robert Downey Jr. and Val Kilmer movie on a Sunday night when you like to get extra sleep for work Monday morning?"

"Because you have more important things on your mind than my stupid work problems."

"I never have too much on my mind when you need to talk, Rome."

He gave me a smile, tucking my hair behind my ear. "I know that, Else. But not tonight. Tonight you need to get some sleep. We will catch up over the week, okay?"

"Rome really..." I pressed as he moved to stand.

"Shush. Go on. Go up to bed. Put a cold compress on those eyes and that throat. We'll get coffee after work whatever day works for you, okay?"

"Okay," I said, giving him a smile as I followed him to the door.

He pulled it open, turning, then turning back. "You need to talk about this, call me. Don't bottle it up. Okay?"

"Okay," I agreed and he kissed my forehead and took off down the steps.

I closed and locked the doors, turned off the DVD and the TV, cleaned up the ice cream, then made my way back upstairs, stopping in my bedroom doorway to untie my shoes and kick out of them before going inside.

"Don't scream," Paine's deep voice said from somewhere inside the dark room, repeating the first words he ever said to me and making me jump, my heart going into overdrive.

TEN

Elsie

"Jesus Christ," I said, hand slapping down over my heart as I heard his heels kick the platform of the bed as, I imagined, he rose from it. "You were supposed to leave."

"We had some unfinished business," he said, arms going to my hips and sinking in slightly.

"You were seriously just up in my bedroom in the dark while I was watching a movie with Rome?"

"Yep."

"That's kinda creepy," I said, fighting the urge to lean forward and press my face into his chest, breathe in his spicy scent, steal some of his strength.

"Flick that light on, Elsie," he demanded, pushing me back a step toward the door and the light switch.

"Why?"

"When I finally slide inside you, babygirl, I want to watch your face."

My sex clenched hard, making my thighs tense and my breasts get heavy again. I reached blindly behind me and hit the switch. The room got bright, making me squint for a second until my eyes adjusted. Then Paine was advancing toward me, each step predatory, animalistic. I found myself retreating until the wall prevented any more backing away. Once he got close, his hands went around my back to my ass and sank in hard, lifting me up and off my feet, coaxing my legs into going around his waist. My arms went around his shoulders as he slammed me back against the wall hard as he thrust his hips upward, making his hardness slam against my cleft, and having me moan out his name into his neck.

His hips pressed in hard, pinning mine to the wall as his hands left my ass. "Arms up," he barked and I hesitantly raised them, a little worried he would drop me. His hands grabbed the material and ripped it off. His hands closed over my heavy breasts, squeezing and kneading. I leaned back against the wall, using all the strength in my legs to move my hips against him while still holding on tight, feeling his cock part my folds and press against my clit. His head moved forward and lowered toward my neck, kissing up to my ear then licking a trail back down, sinking in his lips and sucking.

I was pretty sure I was going to come just from that.

Wanting to draw it out, I slipped my legs from around his waist, settling them down on the floor for a second to make sure they would hold me, then pressing Paine back a foot as I lowered down in front of him, hands going to his button and zip as my eyes stayed on his.

To be perfectly honest, I was hit or miss on whether I wanted to give a blow job or not. Sometimes, well, it was simply a lot less work to have sex. But right then, at the feet of one of the sexiest men I had ever known in person, I wanted nothing more than to take him in my mouth, to hear his hisses and gasps and groans as I worked him, to feel his hands go into my hair, curling in tight when things started to get intense. I wanted his pleasure at my mercy. I wanted that power.

I pulled down his zip, reaching up and grabbing his pants and boxer briefs and pulling them down at the same time.

I drew in a long breath as his cock came into view, long and thick and promising a fullness greater than I had known before. But that would come later. After I got to taste him first.

My hand reached out and closed around his shaft, my thumb stroking over the wet head, before stroking down to the hilt before I ducked my head and moved forward, sticking my tongue out and lavishing heat over the tip of his cock.

"Fuck," Paine groaned, his hand slamming down on the crown of my head and squeezing, curling into my hair like he was fighting the urge to push me forward.

On a thrill of accomplishment, I closed my mouth around his cock and sucked hard as I took him as deep as I could before my gag reflex engaged, which was, given his size, about halfway. I moved back up slightly, turning my head in a circular motion as I did so and continuing it as I moved back down, pressing my tongue flat and taking him a little deeper. His taste filled my mouth as he got more turned on, urging me to move faster, each time I got to the tip, running my tongue over and slightly under it, hitting that sensitive spot there before taking him deep again.

"Fuck Elsie," Paine's voice growled.

There was a tapping sound on the wall behind me and I thought it was Paine until his hand released my hair and he hissed out, "What the fuck?"

I flew backward, flinging my hair out of my face.

"Sounds like someone is having a good time in there," a familiar, cocksure, jackass voice called from the hall. "I hate to interrupt but me and Elsie have some matters to discuss."

"Fuck off, Sawyer," I growled, hands frantically covering my breasts as I tried to get to my feet. Paine had already snagged his pants and pulled them back up, reaching an arm out to help steady me as I reached for my sweater.

My life could not be so ridiculous.

No way had I been interrupted during sexy times twice in one night. By two different men. No way.

"Sawyer Anderson?" Paine asked me as I struggled into my shirt.

"The one and only," I snapped, lowering my eyes at the hall.

"I'll be downstairs while you put your fun bits away. Elsie, babe, I promise I won't be thinking about what your fun bits look like," he commented as he moved down the hall and toward the stairs.

"How do people keep breaking in here?" I asked, enraged, as I turned to look at Paine.

"He's a PI who is a bit loose with the law, babygirl. Breaking and entering is nothing to him."

"Do you have any idea how much that alarm system cost me?" I asked, stalking over toward my bathroom and flicking on the light, trying to get my hair back into some semblance of order as Paine zipped up. "Do you like the guy?" I asked, coming back out into my bedroom.

"Not particularly."

"Want to kick his ass for me?" I asked with a small smile at the idea.

"Say the word and he'll have a nice bed right beside his brother," he said casually and, well, I actually believed him. And that was mildly terrifying.

"Alright, let's go get this over with," I said on a sigh as I made my way into the hall.

Paine was behind me as we rounded into my living room to find Sawyer standing there twirling my bra on his finger. "You'd think if you got started down here, there'd be more of a trail leading upstairs," he paused, cocky smile slipping a bit as he watched Paine walk in and settle behind my shoulder. "Should have known that was your Challenger down the block," he commented before turning his attention back toward me, jiggling my bra again. "This mean you're commando under there, babe?" he asked.

I lunged forward, grabbing the bra out of his hand and balling it up best I could in my fist. "What are you, fifteen? Oooh, she wears a bra. Grow up."

The snippy-ness was all bluster because, deep down, all I was feeling was mildly mortified. The bra under the couch... that wasn't so bad. Hell, women whip those things off the minute they walk in the door sometimes. It could just be there by happenstance. But, well, he had totally heard me going down on Paine. And while I was a mature, sexually confident person, that kind of thing was personal. No one was supposed to know about it unless I chose to tell them. Certainly no one was supposed to hear or, heaven forbid, see that. Even if someone did accidentally hear or see, they weren't supposed to comment on it. That was a whole new level of rude and disrespectful.

Paine's arm landed hard across my shoulders, trapping my hair, and pulling me against his side. "What do you got to talk to her about?" Paine asked, badassery practically wafting out of his pores. I tilted my head to look up at him, giving him a small smile that I hoped said 'thank you'.

"Got coffee?" Sawyer asked, jerking his head toward the kitchen.

I sighed slightly and nodded. Paine let me go after a small squeeze and they both followed me into the kitchen where Paine set to work making the coffee and I jumped up on the counter, staring the occasional dagger at Sawyer who leaned against the island looking casually comfortable and amused.

"Alright, we're not waiting for it to drip for you to start talking," I told Sawyer as Paine moved over toward me and stood beside my hip. I wondered if he was aware it was both predatory, like he was staking a claim, and also that he was forming a united front against the guy I kind of wanted to watch Paine put in his place a little. But not really. "I told you we were done. Barrett, and by extension you, are fired."

"Nice try, babe. But now I'm on a mission to make some mother fuckers pay for putting my brother in a hospital bed with a concussion, stitches, and busted ribs."

"Cory Wad," Paine interrupted, drawing both our attention. Paine looked at me. "You told me about the scar on his lip, baby. Only one Third Street guy got a cleft lip scar."

"Still can't believe you got my fucking brother wrapped up with those shitheads," Sawyer said, shaking his head at the ceiling.

"Yo," Paine broke in, drawing Sawyer's attention. "Ain't her fault he didn't get more information or backup before he dove in."

Sawyer sighed, nodding a little, knowing he was right. "Babe, you might not be paying me or him anymore, but I'm not off the case. And I'm pretty sure once Barrett has access to a computer again, he won't be either. It'd be easier if you could tell us what we are in for this time. Save us some time."

"Why would I want to make your life easier?" I asked with a smile and Paine snorted. "You do realize you've been nothing but an ass since you first talked to me."

"Not here to make friends, Elsie. I'm here to get a job done. You want answers to something, I'm the man. I won't apologize for not being Mr. Congeniality while I put my life on the line for you."

Well then. There was really no good way to rebut that, was there?

I looked at Paine who gave me a small shrug.

"Alright fine," I conceded. "My sister is missing."

"Elana," Sawyer declared.

"Yeah, Elana. She was acting weird for a while and then she wasn't answering. I went over, she was gone. My father told me she cashed in her trust fund. He and the cops think she's off on a beach somewhere."

"But you think not."

"She found a jewelry box with a good fifteen dime bags of smack with a Third Street tag on them."

"So you think she's somehow involved with them? Trust had to be in the millions, babe. Know who your father is. No way could your trusts be under five mil each. She can't spend that kind of money on heroin."

"We went over that," Paine said, resting a hand on my knee and squeezing.

"So you're thinking she's dead or wishing she was and her money is circulating in some banger's pockets." I felt myself visibly flinch at his bluntness and, to his credit, Sawyer looked repentant. "Sorry, babe, but we have to consider the worst-case scenarios. Best case, she's on a beach. Slightly less good, but not awful, she got conned. Third, she's in love with some shithead and handed over the money because she was too high to care."

"But if it was any of those not-awful scenarios, why would she just up and leave her life? Her pet? Her family? The money was hers; it's not like she stole anything."

"Dunno how much you know about addicts, babe," Sawyer said, moving over toward the coffee pot and helping himself to one of the mugs Paine had put out, "but they're selfish and entitled. That's what the drugs do to you. Nothing and no one matters but the next hit, the next high or not feeling sick when you're on the down slide. She's not your sister if she's heavy into heroin. She likely doesn't care about her house, her family, her friends, her pets. She cares about the drugs. That's it. Case closed. So if she thought that you or her father or her friends might stand in a way of her next high, she's gonna want nothing to do with any of you."

As harsh as that was, as hard to swallow, it was somehow almost comforting. Maybe it was just that easy. Maybe she was just so wrapped up in her drug-packed lifestyle that nothing else mattered. I could live with that. Addicts could be reformed. She could get help. She could move on from this, even if her trust was gone for good. There was still a way to have my sister back.

"But if someone is controlling her, babe, I don't think I got to tell you... that makes things complicated. Third Street can be wild and unpredictable. Especially if money is a factor. No disrespect," he said, jerking his chin toward Paine. "Know you used to run shit. Know your brother calls shots now, but it's a gang and they've been scrambling for a year trying to hold down a new supplier since your buddy put a plug in their last one's head."

My eyes went wide and focused on Paine. "He kidnapped his girl. Shooter is a sniper. He did what he had to do to get her safe."

"How... how does all this stuff happen right under my nose in this town and I don't know about it?"

True, we knew there was crime. Especially in the slums. We had The Henchmen MC who were definitely involved in some kind of illegal activities. A couple years back, a bunch of buildings in town were bombed. Then some guy named Lex Keith was brutally murdered and it came to light that he was a serial rapist that the NBPD ignored because he paid them a pretty penny to do so. But it was a big town, we had a really diverse population. With a large number of people came an expected amount of crime. But Paine and Sawyer were discussing drugs, gangs, snipers, and murder like it was an every day occurrence.

"Baby, you know that Italian place you like?"

"Famiglia?" I asked, head tilting to the side.

"Mob," Paine said with a smile.

"What!" I exploded, slapping my hand down on the counter. "You can't be serious."

"Antony and his sons: Luca and Matteo."

"My father and I had drinks with Antony. I had a date once with Luca! He stood when I got to the table and opened car doors. And you're telling me he's a part of the Italian mob?"

"They run the docks."

"Oh my God," I groaned, covering my face with my hands.

"And, hey, you know that bar you and your friends go to..." Sawyer went on, sounding amused.

"No. Not Chaz's!"

"Charlie and his sons are loan sharks."

"Shane was my personal trainer when I first started going to his gym. Mark fixed my flat once!"

"Surrounded by bad guys who aren't so bad," Paine said with a small smile.

"Aw look at the moment you two are having. Good girl and former gang banger getting all big-eyed. How sweet."

"Do you get some kind of commission every time you're a complete asshole?" I snapped, rolling my eyes.

"Just saying," he said, putting his mug down and making his way toward the back door, "do you really see this going anywhere? You gonna bring home a former pimp and drug dealer to meet your daddy? Come on now. Have your fun, get your rocks off, but don't think there's anything more than that between you," he warned, the door slamming settling with a weird feeling in my chest.

I hadn't really stopped to analyze what had been going on with Paine. First, because it had been a really weird situation. And, second, because I just hadn't had the time.

I had been focusing on my sex drive and nothing else. And, well, there was nothing wrong with that. Every red-blooded adult needed to get laid occasionally, even if that turned out to be all it was- sex. It wasn't something I did often, but once in a while, I had affairs. Was that what I was doing with Paine? If that was the case, why did I involve him on the situation with my sister? Guys who were nothing more than sex to me before didn't even know I had a sister. Granted, the situation was weird. And Paine had kind of forced his way into my life, throwing it even further off its axis.

Was I just some notch to him? Bag the rich bitch and brag about it to your buddies? If so, was I offended by that or okay with it?

"You're thinking too much," Paine interrupted my train of thought.

"What?" I said, shaking my head and looking for him because he wasn't beside me anymore. Somehow without my

118

noticing, he had moved away toward the coffee pot and made us each a cup. He was walking back then, handing me the mug.

"Sawyer is a dick and he likes pushing buttons. That's what he does. You start thinking about the shit he says, you'll drive yourself crazy."

"Right," I agreed, sipping my coffee and silently telling myself that the only reason he could push a button was because it existed in the first place.

"You're tired. I'm beat. We've had a weird fucking night. Let's just call it a wash, yeah?"

"A wash?"

"We ain't fucking after that," he said with a smile, waving a hand out.

"Oh, okay." Yeah, that was kind of the last thing on my mind anyway.

"So let's sleep."

"Let's?" I questioned.

"Your bed is comfortable as fuck and I don't feel like driving home this late. You can try to relegate me to the guest room you stick poor Roman in, but I'll end up beside you regardless," he said, putting down his coffee mug and moving out toward the dining room.

I took a long sip of my coffee before putting it on the counter, hopping down, and following him upstairs.

I was going to sleep with Paine.

In the most literal way.

Somehow, that felt almost more intimate than sleeping with him in the figurative way.

When I got into my room, he had already kicked out of his shoes, his pants were gone, and so was his shirt. I felt my feet falter as I stepped into the doorway, taking in his broad back covered in dark tattoos. And while they were fascinating, the muscles were even more so. From the width of his shoulders, the strong plane of his back, to the muscular ass that filled out his dark boxer briefs way too well, he was a specimen of male perfection.

He turned slowly, as if sensing me looking at him, ducked his head to the side, and gave me a small smile. "Figured I'd leave the boxers on just this once."

I swallowed hard. "Yeah. Sure. Whatever is comfortable."

"Comfortable would be skin on skin with you, cock buried in that tight, wet pussy while you moan into my ear. But I'll settle for this."

So that whole... sex being the last thing on my mind thing? Yeah, that wasn't true anymore. My sex clenched hard and it was an effort to force myself to move forward toward my dresser, snagging whatever my hands reached for first and throwing myself into the bathroom. I stripped out of my clothes, washed my face, brushed my teeth, took out my contacts, and reached for my pajamas. It was right then that I realized I hadn't grabbed one of the chaste silky Victoria's Secret sleep shirts I thought I had, but a God damn white and pink nightie.

Great. That was just great.

I sighed at my blurry reflection and rolled up the nightie, slipping it over my head. It slithered over my sensitive skin in a far too erotic way and I knew that anytime I shifted in that bed, I was going to be washed over with that sensation again. Plus, the whole... Paine was going to see me in something overtly sexual while he was mostly naked thing. I said a silent 'thank you' to the universe that I had picked one that was solid silk and not one of the see-through lace ones.

On a shrug, I walked out of the bathroom, turning off the light and drawing Paine's attention from where he was sitting off the side of the bed.

"Fuck babygirl," he groaned, running a hand over his cheek. "You own stock in a lingerie company?" he teased, crooking a finger at me. And, well, when a man as sexy and mostly naked as Paine crooked a finger at you, you went to him. His hands moved up the sides of my thighs, whispering up my skin until they came in contact with the nightie then settled at my hips. "Alright," he said after a long minute, "climb in."

"Climb in?" I repeated dumbly, half-expecting him to grab me and finish what we started earlier.

"Yeah, baby, climb in. We're sleeping, remember?"

Yeah, I was pretty sure I wouldn't be sleeping. But I moved beside him and climbed in, settling against the pillows as Paine turned, snagged the blankets, and pulled them up over both our bodies. He settled back then slid an arm under my neck, curling it and pulling me toward him until I was nestled into his side. Uncomfortable, I pressed up and moved to rest my cheek on his chest. His arm curled tighter around me as I settled in. My hand went up to the other side of his chest, my finger tracing over the large, bold '3' tattooed onto his pectoral.

"You live through the first year, you have to get the gang ink," he explained.

"You haven't covered it."

Beneath me, he shrugged. "It's a part of me. Covering up the mark on my skin doesn't make those years I spent disappear. It was a huge chunk of my life. I'm not gonna lie about it or pretend it didn't happen. Now sleep, baby," he said, his voice going soft and my belly did a flip-flop I tried to ignore.

It had been a long while since I fell asleep with a man. I forgot how nice it was to feel a firm body beneath yours and a strong arm around you, anchoring you to him like he didn't want you to accidentally slip away, to hear a heartbeat under your ear.

It was soothing.

Within minutes, I was out.

ELVEN

Elsie

I woke up tucked in tight with blankets, slightly disoriented until the events of the night before came into focus. Confused, I shot up in bed. First, checking the clock to make sure I wasn't late for work. I had an hour and a half still. Second, looking around to see if Paine's clothes were still on the floor like he had gone down for coffee or something. Even his shoes were gone.

I squelched the unexpected twinge of disappointment, grabbed work clothes, and headed into the bathroom to shower. Forty minutes later, I was in steel gray slacks, black heels, and a black lightweight sweater. My hair was dry, my makeup done. I grabbed a black, gray, and white swirled scarf and tied it around my neck then went downstairs to head out early. There was no reason to sit around my house for a half an hour over-thinking what it meant that Paine sneaked out in the middle of the night or early morning.

I already had those thoughts on my mind all through my shower and prepping and, well, let's just say it wasn't helping my sour mood any.

My feet hit the bottom landing before I heard it, too consumed with my own depressive inner monologue to notice it before. There was clanging and the low, throbbing bass beat of hip hop music coming from my kitchen. I didn't realize I was smiling until my cheeks started to hurt. Cursing myself and making the smile fall, I moved through my dining room and into my kitchen to find Paine, changed, standing in front of my stove and pouring something into a pan, something I definitely did not have in my house the night before.

"Did you go shopping?" I asked, making Paine's head swivel toward me, doing a slow inspection as if there was anything sexy about my work attire, landing for a second on my neck.

"Come here, babygirl," he said, turning from the stove and going toward a small bag sitting on my island.

"Why?" I asked, already moving further into the room.

"Here," he said when I got close, reaching out for my scarf, untying it, and pulling it off. He reached into the bag and pulled out a small tube of something skin-colored, holding it up. "Sell this at the shop. It covers tattoos. It should work on your bruises," he said, twisting off the cap. "Pull your hair up for me," he said, squeezing some of the makeup onto his hands and reaching out toward me.

Yeah and then he totally rubbed makeup all over my neck. Incredibly gently, I might add. Finished, he inspected it for a second, squinting his eyes. "Did it cover?"

"I know it's there so I can make it out the tiniest bit, but I don't think anyone else will see. Especially if you throw a necklace on to distract them," he added as he went to the sink to wash his hands. "Baby, do me a favor and flip those pancakes."

I looked over at the stove dubiously. "You do know who you're talking to, right? I didn't even know I had to remove that plastic stuff."

"Spatula, scoop, flip, drop. I have faith in you."

Well, when he put it that way, it seemed like a seven year-old could do it. I flipped the pancakes, revealing the perfect golden side that made my belly growl. "You can cook," I commented, looking down at the circles.

Paine laughed, coming up behind me, his arm snaking around my belly as he reached for the box of pancake mix beside the bowl he used to mix it and held it up. "It's just add water and drop it into a pan. Not really a way to fuck that up. You smell good," he said, leaning down and nuzzling slightly into my neck in a way that engaged the lady bits that went to sleep unfulfilled the night before.

"Thanks," I mumbled as he reached for the spatula, scooped up the pancakes and piled them on a plate beside the stove. "What, are you feeding an army?" I asked, laughing at the massive pile of pancakes he had already made.

"Like the way your ass fills out jeans, babygirl. Want to make sure you keep it. Sit," he said, jerking his chin toward the stools at the island.

Feeling a little awkward, I followed instructions. I'd never had a man cook for me before. And, seeing as I didn't cook myself, I'd never really shared an intimate breakfast with someone before. Paine slid a plate with four pancakes in front of me then came back a minute later with utensils, syrup, and coffee.

"Eat," he said, shuffling around as he, I imagined, made himself food.

Maybe he liked the way my ass filled out my jeans, but if I kept eating junk, it was going to positively bust out of them sooner rather than later. I wasn't the kind of woman blessed with the metabolism of a fifteen year-old boy. If I didn't watch what I ate and workout, I put on weight easily, effortlessly. I made a mental note to hit the gym an extra night or two that week and dove into my pancakes. Because, well, he made them for me. No way was I rejecting them because of some ridiculous concerns about my waistline.

Paine sat down silently and started eating. Feeling uncomfortable with the silence, I reached for my coffee. "What time did you get up if you managed to get all of this done?"

"Five," he said with a shrug like that was totally normal.

"Five? Farmers aren't even up at five."

Paine gave me a sweet smile, reaching for his coffee. "I usually get up and hit the gym before I open the shop."

"Thank you for cooking," I said, reaching for another fork full. There was no way I was going to finish all of it, given how unaccustomed my stomach was to eating at all in the morning, let alone loading up on carbs and sugar.

"Why are you being weird?" he asked, making my head pop up.

"What?" Weird? I was being weird?

"Yeah, baby, weird. All awkward and shit. Not like you."

Shit. He was right. I was being awkward. That was because I felt awkward.

"Sorry. I dunno. I'm in a strange mood I guess," I said and it was mostly true.

Paine's stool scraped across the floor as he stood, coming around the end of the island toward me. I instinctively turned on my stool to face him just as both his hands moved, reaching out, and cradling my face as he lowered down toward me, his lips hitting mine hard and hungry and tasting like syrup and coffee. All of it was way too intimate and demanding for a good morning kiss. But damn if it wasn't nice. My hands went out and grabbed his hips, using them as leverage as I moved to stand, pressing my body against his. His head tilted and his tongue traced my lips until they parted, sneaking in and claiming mine as his hands left my face, pressing down my back and circling around my hips, pulling upward slightly until I was on my tiptoes. My arms went around his neck tight, holding on, as a small whimper escaped me.

At the sound, Paine slowed and stopped the kiss, pulling backward and waiting until my eyes opened. "Feel better?" he asked, eyes bright.

"Ah, I..." I stumbled, feeling all tingly and sated.

"You feel better," he said with a self-satisfied smile. "You better get going or you're gonna be late. I'll clean up and set the alarm before I leave."

"Oh, um, okay," I said, nodding as I released his neck and took a step back.

"Bring this in case you need a touch-up," he said, handing me the tube of tattoo cover-up.

"Right... thanks..."

"Go," he said with a grin.

With that, I turned to grab my purse and keys and did what he said, ignoring the voice that was telling me that interaction felt a lot like a goodbye.

I threw myself in my car and backed out, cranking up the stereo and hoping I could drown out the voice inside.

Because, even if it was goodbye, so what?

He wasn't my boyfriend. He didn't even seem like boyfriend material. Nothing about him suggested he was a relationship-type of guy. He probably got around as much as he could. I couldn't fault him for that exactly, but it said he was used to the hit-and-quit kind of situation. And while I might have had two or three affairs in my time, I was not a hit-and-quit kind of girl.

Though maybe just this one time...

No.

Okay. I needed to get my shit together and focus on the things that mattered: work, friends, finding my sister. I didn't need to waste brain space thinking about a non-relationship that had absolutely no potential to become a relationship.

So yeah.

That was the plan.

--

Nine and a half hours later, I felt marginally better. I threw myself into work. I hit the gym for a good, heart-pounding workout, spending most of the time running on the treadmill. First, because it was great cardio. Second, because it was a good way to focus because I hated it so much. Third, it worked off some of the stress and sexual tension.

"Running like you think you can actually outrun your problems," Shane Mallick, the gym owner, and also, apparently, the loan shark, commented as I made my way toward the doors afterward.

"Hell, maybe if I commit hard enough, I can."

"Wishful thinking, sweetheart," his voice followed as I walked outside.

And, well, I knew that was true. But still, I felt alright as I pulled into my drive and went into my house. I went up and took a shower, watching the tattoo cover-up run down my body after scrubbing with a loufa. It even lasted through a sweaty workout. That stuff was amazing. I imagined if my bruises didn't start fading, I was going to be using it for a while.

I had just slipped into a very unappealing outfit of oversize sweats and a roomy, ratty tee when my doorbell chimed. I ran down the stairs, blindly pushing on my glasses as I fiddled with the locks.

"Oh," I said, jumping back slightly at the image of Paine standing on my front steps. Not only was he standing there, but he was cleaned up. Meaning, that he had on black slacks, a tailored, tucked-in black button-up, a black belt with a nice solid silver buckle, and a watch on his wrist that years of watch buying for my father told me cost at least five grand. "Um... hi," I fumbled, realizing I had been staring.

"Hey babygirl," he said, doing an inspection with an amused smile.

"What are you doing here?" I blurted out.

"Taking you to dinner," he said, slipping his hands into his front pockets.

"You're taking me to dinner? Now?"

"No, next Thursday. I got dressed for the fuck of it."

"Why?" I asked, brows drawing together.

I had pretty successfully managed to convince myself Paine was a thing of the past over the past few hours. So him standing at my door, all cleaned up and asking me on a date, yeah... I was a little confused.

"Gotta eat. I can do it alone. I'd rather do it while looking at a gorgeous face. I left an hour for you to get yourself together. Don't know how long it takes you to slip into a dress and heels, but judging by how long it takes my sisters, we'll probably still be late for our reservation."

I shook my head, trying to clear it of the fog. "I, ah, I'll be done in half an hour."

"Miracle," Paine said, rocking back onto the heels of his black dress shoes. "You forgetting something, babygirl?"

Forgetting something? What could I be forgetting seeing as I hadn't expected him in the first place?

"You gonna kiss me or not?"

"Oh," I said, feeling a silly smile pull at my lips as I stepped into the doorway, leaned up, and pressed a quick kiss to his lips.

"I don't know what the fuck that was, but it wasn't a kiss," he complained as soon as I went down on my flat feet.

My lips twitched. "Maybe you need to show me what a kiss is then," I challenged.

Before I could even finish speaking, his hand was at the back of my neck and he was simultaneously moving into the entryway and slamming me back against the wall as his mouth crashed down on mine. There was nothing tentative or gentle about the kiss. His lips seared into mine, claiming them, branding them, guaranteeing I would feel him there for hours afterward.

Just when I felt like my body was going to melt into a puddle of need, he pulled away, released my head to push my glasses back up my nose a little. "For future reference, that was a kiss. Now go get into something that shows off those pins of yours; I'll occupy myself for a while."

I moved off the wall, nodding, a bit too dazed from the kiss to say anything. As he crossed toward the living room, he slapped my ass hard enough to make my step falter. When I looked over my shoulder at him, he was smirking.

Before I could run across the room and jump him, I hurried upstairs to get myself put together. He didn't tell me where we were going, but judging by the way he was dressed and the request for dress and heels, I imagined it was somewhere nice.

I grabbed a black lace underwear set, black garter belt, and sheer stockings, a simple little black dress that showed barely a hint of cleavage but a whole helluva lot of leg, and a pair of ultra-thin spike heels in a matte black color. I fixed my hair, applied more tattoo makeup, made my eyes a little smoky and slipped into my clothes. Contacts in, I spritzed a little perfume and added simple diamond studs to my ears. I slathered on some lip balm, because no way was I putting on lipstick that might discourage more kissing like we had just done, then made my way back downstairs with five extra minutes to spare.

At the sound of my heels on the floor, Paine turned his attention away from the TV and looked at me. Letting out a low whistle, he patted his knee.

A part of me knew I really shouldn't always go to him when called me like a dog, but... come on. A man like Paine told you to follow him into hell, you ignored the demons and fire and went with him. So I moved toward him, stepping between his legs, then lowered myself down on one of his thighs. One of his arms rested across my thighs, the other went around my waist and pulled me to the side against his chest, nestling my face under his chin.

When the silence stretched, his arm tightened around me slightly. "What's up with you?"

"What do you mean?"

"Don't know you that well, but I do know you're not the quiet type. So what's up?"

"Paine we have to get to dinner before we lose our reservation."

"Fuck our reservation. I want to know what's up. Was it that shit Sawyer dropped last night?"

"Paine..."

"Listen, I'm not the emotional touchy-feely kind of man, but I don't like a woman bullshitting me either. So tell me what's up; we'll talk it out. If you don't want to talk about it, then you need to fucking let it go."

Well then.

That was... refreshing.

I was used to men doing one of two things: demanding to know every detail of what I was thinking, or men not wanting to hear word one about my thoughts or feelings.

It was nice to be given an option.

And, well, I think I've established that I am not the kind of woman who could let things go. So I was going to swallow my pride and talk it out with him.

"Why are you taking me to dinner?" I asked, my focus on the TV. "You don't really seem like the kind of man to wine and dine."

"I'm not," he said bluntly, making me try to pull away to look at him, but he wouldn't let me. "You want the truth?"

"Always," I said honestly. Even if what I heard was something I didn't like, it was way better than what would go on in my head if I was left to come to my own conclusions.

"I obviously haven't been a boy scout. When I was younger, it was all about money and power. Now, money is still important. So is respect, not so much the power. But one constant since I was old enough to chase a skirt, I've liked women. Meaning, a wide variety of them. I've never been a man for exclusivity. That being said, I'm up front about that shit. I don't lie or feed lines or tell women I'm going to call when I'm not. You know exactly what you're getting from me."

"Then why do I not know what I'm getting from you?"

"'Cause, baby, I got no fucking idea what is going on here." He paused, letting that sink in. "I like being around you. You're interesting, different. You're hot as shit. And, babygirl, I don't remember the last time I wanted to fuck someone as much as I want to fuck you. That being said, this ain't no promise of anything. Maybe we'll fuck and I'll want to move on. Maybe I'll want to hang around and keep fucking you until it's out of our systems. Maybe something else. Fuck if I know at this point. If you can live with that uncertainty, great, let's go to dinner. You think you can't, maybe we should call it a day because I'm not gonna be that guy."

"What guy?"

"The one who pulls you around, promising one thing one minute, then when you get comfortable and feel safe, changes his mind. I've seen assholes do that to my sisters; I've had countless nights of them showing up at my place crying. I don't want to be that guy. I don't want you to get comfortable, feel safe and stable, then fuck you over. So I'm sharing this with you now so you know not to latch on because this shit is new to me and I don't know how it's going to go."

"You never know how it's going to go," I said, shrugging a little.

"So you can live with it."

Could I? Honestly, I didn't know for sure. But the only way for foggy things to get clearer was to progress into them. So I just had to wrap some barbed wire around my heart and hope that, along with some surprisingly good communication skills, he wasn't equipped with wire cutters too.

"I'm a big girl, Paine. And I'm also really hungry. So where are you taking me?"

"Sushi," he said, pushing me onto my feet then standing himself. "Figured you didn't want any more comfort food after that workout."

I turned back on my way to the door. "Are you following me?"

"No, babe. Doesn't take a genius to guess that after the pancakes, you were feeling guilty and would hit the gym after work," he explained, letting me slip into my coat then putting a hand at my lower back as he led me out the front door.

Just like the apparent mobster Luca Grassi, Paine was the opening doors type. It was a quality I really appreciated. While, sure, I could open the thing my damn self, it was nice that there were still men out there who employed good old-fashioned chivalry, provided it didn't come with chauvinism. Something told me that since Paine grew up with a strong mother, aunts, grandmother, and two little sisters, there was no way he was going to pull that sexism shit on me.

Twenty minutes later, we were out of Navesink Bank and walking up to the best sushi restaurant in the area. It was situated right on the beach, the back deck allowing an uninterrupted view of the crashing waves, even in the dead of winter. The inside was sleek, sticking to a classic theme of orange and black: black tables, chairs, sushi bar, and drink bar, black hardwood floors, black textured walls and orange hanging dome lights, orange upholstery on the booth backs, and water color black and orange understated artwork. The music, as always, was low and bluesy, inviting conversation. Paine walked me up to the hostess, his hand at my lower back, and I realized that it was a quality I really liked about him. Around other people, he liked to have a hand on me, claiming me. Maybe I was setting my sex back a couple of years to admit I liked it, but I did.

We sat and ordered drinks. Paine kept up light comments on the menu selection. I had my own menu up, but I hadn't so much as glanced at it, far more occupied watching him read his.

"What?" he asked, looking up with a smile, catching me.

"Nothing," I said, averting my eyes.

"Nuh-uh. You aren't getting off that easy."

"Nothing. You look nice," I admitted with a casual shrug. "And," I rushed to add, feeling almost a little shy at the admission which was completely unlike me, "I hadn't expected you to be a sushi kind of guy."

"You think I look nice, huh?"

"Shut up," I laughed, swatting him with my menu.

"I mean, can't blame you for thinking that, babygirl. I'm fine as fuck..."

"And so humble," I smiled.

"Know what?"

"No, what?"

"You look nice too. And by 'nice' I mean it's taking just about every ounce of self-control I got to not drag you off to the bathroom, hike up that skirt, and fuck you hard enough for this entire restaurant to know how much I like how you look in that dress."

He said this, mind you, as the waitress came back to drop our drinks. So, yeah, she overheard the entire thing and her cheeks went pink and she couldn't quite make eye-contact with either of us as she took our order.

"What?" he asked when I shook my head at him as she walked away. "Pretty sure everyone in here knows we want to fuck each other."

"Well they can assume things, but you didn't have to confirm it."

"You embarrassed?" he asked, picking up his craft beer with a smirk.

"No, I'm not embarrassed, but our waitress obviously is."

"She'll get over it. It'll give her a story to tell all the other servers later. So," he said, letting the word hang.

Oh, the small talk part of the evening. Usually it was something I excelled with, but mostly because I shared numerous friends or relations with the men I went on dates with. It was always easy to commiserate about sharing prep schools or ridiculous social engagements we had been forced into at young ages. I had nothing like that to play off with Paine. "So..." I repeated.

"Tell me about your sister," he offered, sitting back, making his legs push forward under the table and his knees pressed into mine.

So then I told him about my sister.

Elana was always a good topic for me. While Roman was my best friend, my confidant, my partner in crime, Elana was the one who first sneaked me a cigarette and a bottle of scotch. Our mother dying early put her in the strange position to, at once, feel the need to mother me, but also corrupt me like all good big sisters do. She was the one to sit me down and have the period talk. She was the one to explain to me what a penis looked like, what it felt like, what losing my virginity would be like. She was the one to pick me and Rome up when we got knock-down drunk at a friend's house and sneak us up into my room before our dad could see us. She was the one to push Dad's buttons to draw his attention away from me when he was being too hard.

In a lot of ways, we were alike. Physically, we were both blond, tall, and thin. Whereas I got the ass, she got the boobs. Where I got my mom's blue eyes, she got Dad's gray. And we both were raised up under a strict parent who was always very concerned about things like appearances so we both learned to rebel at young ages. But where I had my quiet rebellions I always tried to keep my father from finding out about, Elana practically waved hers in his face. She didn't even try to tame her sex hair when she came home from one of her lover's houses when we were teens or sneak in the back door when she came in drunk. She spent money on ridiculous things she didn't need or want just to piss off our father. She crashed her first three cars he bought her.

When I was young, I had always seen her as kind of badass and strong. It took me a long time to see that all the rebellion was her way of getting attention. That was what she wanted. She didn't want love, she wanted people to notice her. Especially men. Every guy in her life was a sad testament of her need of validation from them because she never got it from our father.

Elana had 'daddy issues' written all over her.

And, worse yet, she didn't even realize it.

Regardless, she was my big sister. Where Roman was my sun growing up: bright, warm, uplifting, Elana was my moon. She was the one I cried to at night in our beds after I got reamed for not doing the extra credit in a class I was already getting an A in. She was the keeper of my secrets, a place I could bury my hopes and fears and know no one else would ever find out about them. She was a dark, deep kind of comfort.

Maybe that was why my nights had felt especially lonely since she disappeared.

"What about your sisters?" I asked when I realized we were both halfway through our meals and I hadn't shut up except to chew.

"Kenzi is a real ball-buster. She's a lot like my mom in that way, always up in your business, never shy to share her very emphatic opinions. Reese is a lot more shy, quiet. Mom managed to keep them both off the streets. Kenz went to design school and has her own small line in one of the boutique shops in Milltown. Reese got her masters in library science and, obviously, works in the local library."

I paused to take a sip of my drink and finally got the nerve to ask something that I had wanted to since I met him. "Can I ask how the heck you got a name like Paine?"

He laughed a little, pushing his plates toward the end of the table for the passing busboy to grab easily. "I was a big ass baby. Ten pounds, four ounces. Mom was a skinny thing, hips like a twelve-year old boy. She couldn't get me out. So they gave her a massive dose of Ketamine and took me out. She was out of it for almost a full day after. Couldn't even hold or feed me. So my dad, the shit he was, filled out all the paperwork. He was probably high at the time and thought it would be funny because of how much pain I put my mother through before they finally decided to do a c-section."

"She didn't want to change it once she was back to functioning?"

Paine shrugged. "It's hard to say what went down between her and my dad. I know shit went bad as I got older, but I think when I first came around, she was head-over for him. She probably decided to humor him and leave it. It worked out in the end. There might have been a little ribbing when I was too small to know a fist to the face shut up a bully, but come on... a gang member with a government name like Paine?"

I smiled, imagining it was definitely better to be a gang banger by the name of Paine than to be, say, Billy or Brian.

We talked over green tea ice cream, skimming over the topic of my father, concentrating a bit more on silly, nothing things like hobbies and cars, both of us being fans of a nice ride.

When the check was dropped, as customary, on Paine's side of the table, I nodded my head toward it. "I don't suppose you're going to let me..."

"Nope," he cut me off, reaching for a wallet, pulling out a credit card and putting it inside the book without so much as looking at the bill, and held it out just in time to hand it off to our passing waitress. It was all so smooth you'd swear it had to be practiced. But, I guess, Paine was always just effortlessly smooth like that.

"Can I persuade you to let me leave the tip?" I pressed, growing up with a father that insisted it was a power move to pay. Whoever went out of pocket had the upper hand. I had to admit that in my dating life, it proved all too true.

"This matter to you?"

"Yes."

"Then knock yourself out, babygirl," he said with a shrug. When the waitress came back, I snagged cash from my purse and slipped it inside the book after he signed (an obnoxious amount of money because, first, I had no idea what the bill was and, second, to make up for the fucking in the bathroom comment.) Paine stood and waited for me to shrug into my jacket. "I tell my sisters to make that move too."

"What move?" I asked as his hand landed at my lower back again.

"To insist on contributing," he said, pushing open the door. The January air hit me hard, knocking my breath out of my lungs for a second.

"Why?"

"Hard for a guy to think you owe him shit when you put money in too. Not a lot of men around these days," he went on as he opened the car door for me. "Got a lot of bitch ass guys who think that fifty bucks for dinner means they got a right to demand pussy as payment."

I smiled as he slammed my door and made his way around the car, deciding that I was only ever going to date men who grew up with single mothers and little sisters from that point on.

"All that being said, we both came outta pocket tonight. So when I get you back to your place and finally get the fuck inside you, I don't have to worry you feel like it's some bullshit obligation."

"Oh, gee. I dunno," I said, trying not to smile. "I don't know what kind of girl you think I am, but I don't put out on the first date."

I think I caught him off-guard because he let out a strange snort sound before he threw his head back and laughed. It was so open and, at once, boyish and masculine that it warmed up my insides way better than the heat cranking in the car.

"Well, baby," he said, recovering, leaning across to my seat and grabbing me at the back of my neck, "maybe you're a good girl, but I'm pretty sure I can make you bad for the night," he promised.

My lady bits thrilled at the idea and I pressed my thighs together to calm the chaos there. "Well when you put it that way..."

He smirked, turning back to the windshield. He got a one-hand feel at the twelve o'clock position of the steering wheel. He did this because his other hand was occupied snaking up my thigh to rest just under the hem of my skirt which had slid almost indecently high when I scooted into my seat.

It took every bit of control I had to keep myself from squirming the whole drive home.

Judging by his small smile as he watched the road, he knew exactly what he was doing to me.

Oh yeah. I was definitely open to having Paine turn me bad for the night. Or week. Or the rest of our time on Earth.

TWELVE

Elsie

Never before had I been quite the combination of aroused and nervous as I was on the impossibly long drive back to my house. It wasn't like me to be shy about sex. And besides, he'd seen me mostly naked. And I'd seen him fully naked. Just not all at one time. That was always the most insecurity-inducing part. I had no doubts that the sex was going to be good. Maybe the nervousness was the fear that having sex would get me 'out of his system' and he would be ready to move on.

Because, fact of the matter was, I liked Paine.

True, I didn't know him that well. But I knew him well enough to know I enjoyed his company. I liked his strange mix of old school manners, modern respect for my ability to handle myself, street smarts, alpha manliness, and well... sexiness. Let's face it, that was a huge factor. The man was hot. And he had a mouth on him that was positively pantie-melting.

I liked him.

And I was pretty sure I wanted more than one night with him.

So yeah, by the time we pulled up to my drive and made it to the front door, I was a ball of nerves and definitely over-thinking everything.

This stopped, oh, say, five seconds after the front door closed. That was because as soon as my finger hit the last number on my alarm code, a strong arm was around my belly and I was being pulled back against his broad chest. His hard cock pressed against my ass and I felt myself wiggle against it slightly. His other hand went up to my neck for a second, brushing my hair to the other side before his lips landed there, kissing a slow trail up toward my ear. The hand then made no pretense at taking things slow because he was stroking his fingers up my thigh, moving inward, forcing them to part just enough for his palm to cup my sex, drawing a ragged moan for me.

My brain might have been a million places on the drive home, but my body had a one-track mind.

I was already hot, wet, and ready.

Paine's low, appreciative growl in my ear sent a shiver through my body.

His hand moved up then slid down into my panties, his finger circling my clit once before tracing a path downward and slipping inside me, thrusting slow and constant until my legs started to feel wobbly. Just when I was close, he pulled out, turned me, pressed me against the wall, and took my lips.

It wasn't the hard, hungry kiss he had given me before.

It was deep and thorough but slow, intimate, unhurried. I circled his neck with my arms and his hands slid down my back to cup my ass, lifting me up until I wrapped my legs around his waist. Then, like it was nothing, he wrapped his arms around me and carried me up the stairs.

While I was fit, I was tall and leggy; I wasn't the kind of woman who found herself carried around by a man. In fact, this was the first time it had happened since I was a teenager. I found that, like a lot of things Paine did, I really liked it.

My back hit the bed gently, but Paine's weight didn't follow me down. He pulled up, untangling from my arms and legs. He had placed me at the edge of the bed and he stood at the foot. His hands went to my knees, pressing them open, as he lowered himself down to his knees between my legs. He looked up at me for a minute, eyes hungry, before he dipped his head. His hand yanked my panties to the side, seemingly too impatient to bother taking them off, and his mouth was on me.

His lips closed around my clit, sucking in a pulse-like rhythm, his tongue moving out to stroke over me in unpredictable intervals. My legs shifted, one moving up beside his head, the other slipping over his shoulder. His hand landed on one of my knees, fingers digging in.

Every ounce of me was poised for the coming waves, my back arched up off the bed, hands grabbing the back of his head, fingers digging in as my hips thrust upward, begging for fulfillment.

He pulled hard against my hold, taking his finger out of me, reaching down, grabbing my panties and dragging them roughly down my legs. I suppressed the disappointment, reminding myself that the sooner I felt him inside me, the better, and pushed up on the bed, putting my feet on the floor. Paine reached behind his back, snagging his shirt the way I had fantasized that one time, and dragged it off, revealing his strong chest and abdomen, his perfect dark tattoos. My hands went to his belt, fumbling a little with clumsy fingers before I finally got the hook free and pulled it from its loops. My head tilted to look up at him as my fingers pushed his button through and pulled his zip down. His light green eyes were heavy lidded, sexier looking than ever before, needy, and I knew he found a similar look in mine. My hands grabbed his slacks and boxer briefs, pulling them down to his knees and letting them fall the rest of the way.

My gaze left his, but only because my focus went to his cock, hard, straining, heavy-looking. My hand moved to hold him at the base as my head moved outward and my lips opened around him, taking in just the head, lavishing my tongue over it. His hand went into the hair at the base of my neck, curling in, as his breath rushed out of him in a hiss.

"Fuck," he growled. "Elsie, baby... fuck. Okay," he said, his voice rough from arousal and still somehow amused. "Don't have the control for that right now," he told me, pulling me backward by my hair. I sucked hard as he slipped away from me and angled my head up with a smirk. "Christ, woman," he said with a smile of his own.

He reached downward, grabbing me at my ribs and pulling me up onto my feet. His hands sank into my ass before slowly drifting upward, tracing my spine until he found the zip for my dress and ever-so-slowly dragging it downward. He pulled the material at the shoulders and moved it down, exposing me inch my inch. My skin prickled at his touch, making a small shiver course through me. When the material got free of my hips, I shimmied until it fell to my feet, stepping out of it.

"Nope," Paine said as I moved to step out of my heels. "Heels stay on," he demanded as his hands traced back up my spine. "Garter and stockings too," he added, unclasping my bra and pulling it down my arms. My nipples were already straining and as soon as they were free, he pulled me tight against his chest, the contact sending a thrill down my belly and between my thighs. I would have let out a groan, but his lips stole mine, pressing in hard and hungry. His tongue moved right in, rough, demanding. His hand moved back up into my hair, grabbing, turning, and pulling slightly. The stinging in my scalp only intensified my need for more, for everything.

His teeth sank into my lower lip hard, hard enough to bruise if he didn't release it as quickly as he snagged it. "Paine, please," I groaned, too overwhelmed to not beg.

His head pulled back slightly. A slow, sexy smirk spread that screamed he was up to something. Before I could wonder what, he grabbed me at my waist and threw me backward on the bed. I landed with a slight bounce and before my body had even settled, he was over me, kissing a line from my navel upward.

Everything about him was unexpected. One moment he was soft and gentle, the next he was rough. I had no idea what was coming and the fluttering in my belly told me I liked that.

His fingers traced up the silky material of my stockings, stopping at the garters, snagging the bands, pulling backward, and snapping them against my skin. My body jolted and he smiled as he pressed upward and pushed back so he was standing again. "Legs up," he commanded as he looked down at me for a moment. I put my legs up, crossing my ankles. "Great fucking view," he commented before he leaned down, snagged his pants, grabbed his wallet, pulled out a condom, and made short work of protecting us.

The bed depressed as he climbed in, kneeling right behind my legs, pulling my ankles onto one of his shoulders where he turned to bite the outside of one. A surprised yelp escaped me, followed by a gasp as he grabbed each ankle spreading them, and pushing them toward my body. My knees pressed into my chest as I felt him thrust hard and deep.

"Fuck," I cried out, hands slapping down on top of the ones he had on my knees, holding them against my chest. It was part surprise, part pleasure, and just the tiniest twinge of pain. I was right when I said he would fill me like no one had before. I felt a pressure in my lower belly he was so deep, my walls stretching to accommodate him, holding him tight.

"You good?" he asked, voice deep and rough as he stilled inside me. I felt my head shake. "No?" he asked, stiffening a little.

"Not good. Great," I said wiggling my hips a little, moaning at the friction.

"Thank fucking Christ," he said with a smirk as he released my knees.

He kept them in place with his torso as he leaned slightly over me, his arms going under my back and grabbing my shoulders from behind, fingers digging into my clavicles.

And then all there was was wild, hard, fast fucking.

He slammed into me, using my shoulders to drag my body down as he thrust up, making me take him to the hilt, hitting me so deep there was a slight pinch that was the most erotic kind of pain I had ever experienced.

Paine had a dirty mouth when talking about what he wanted to do to me, but as he fucked me, there was only the sound of my moans getting louder by the second, his ragged breathing, and the sounds of our bodies slamming together. I'd take that over any words he could give me. It was raw, primal, animalistic.

I clamped down tight around him, feeling myself get closer as he fucked me up the bed he was so rough. Until my head slammed up against the headboard and there was nowhere else to go.

"Paine... I..." I groaned, fingers digging into his arms hard enough to cut as his pace didn't so much as falter.

"Come babygirl. Come," he demanded again.

And then I did.

And I swear it shot through every inch of my body, a wave of pleasure so intense I couldn't even cry out for a long minute. Then when I did, it was his name. And like he had promised, it was a scream louder than I had ever made before, louder than I thought was possible.

He thrust until every last wave washed over me. Then he buried deep and jerked slightly upward, coming on a curse, his fingers crushing my clavicles so hard I worried he could have actually broken them for a second before the pressure let up.

"Fuck baby," he growled into my neck, his breathing ragged and warm on my skin.

My legs fought against his body weight and he lifted up just enough for me to slide them out and wrap them around him.

My arms went around his shoulders and I held him to me as he rested over my hammering heartbeat.

My fingers drifted slowly down his back, snagging slightly on the occasional scar that I knew must have come from knives with their perfect, straight lines. He'd been stabbed. It shouldn't have come as a shock, but it did. Everything about Paine seemed fierce and capable. It was hard to imagine someone besting him, hurting him. But, then again, even the most skilled of fighters lost sometimes. I found my mind wandering, wondering if they had been bad enough to land him in the hospital, what his mother and sisters must have thought, if he sought retribution.

"Like my scars," he mumbled against me.

"What?"

"You like my scars," he said, pressing up, balancing his weight on his forearms. "You're tracing them," he told me and I realized he was right. My mind had drifted and I hadn't noticed that both of my hands had found different scars and were stroking over them almost lovingly.

"I guess," I said, self-consciously moving my hands away.

"You don't have any."

"Huh?"

"Scars. Not one. Every inch of your skin is fucking perfect. If it wasn't so fucking gorgeous, it would be obnoxious. No one should be completely fucking flawless."

"I'm not," I objected.

"Tell me one flaw."

"My eyes suck," I supplied.

"Best shade of blue I've ever seen."

"Maybe," I allowed, "but they don't work right. Contacts and glasses every day."

"Glasses are cute as fuck. Doesn't count."

"I have a birth mark..." I started, then stopped when I realized what I was about to say.

"Just inside the crease where your thigh meets your pussy," he supplied with a smirk.

"God, you're observant."

"It's shaped like a fucking heart. Doesn't count."

I thought for a second, then let out a short laugh, waving a hand out a little. "Then what can I say... I'm flawless," I said with a smile.

"Damn straight," he agreed, leaning down and pressing a hard, but quick kiss to my lips. "As much as I'd like to stay inside you all night, I gotta get up and deal with this condom. Unwrap me," he demanded and my legs and arms fell begrudgingly. He slid out of me and I let out a small, objecting noise that made him chuckle quietly. "Don't worry, I'm getting all up in there again as soon as I can," he promised as he disappeared into the bathroom and closed the door.

Alone, unseen, a huge, satisfied smile spread across my face. My hand slapped over my mouth to cover it, knowing it was a bad idea to let myself feel that way. True, the sex was freaking phenomenal. And, yes, he said he wanted a repeat. But we were on shaky ground and I needed to tamp down the 'I feel happy when I'm around him' thing before it got out of hand.

I heard the water run and quickly relaxed my face and shifted up on the bed, crawling under the covers. Paine came out and climbed under, moving over me slightly and I was sure he was going to kiss me. But at the last second, his head moved quickly downward and he bit into one of my still-hardened nipples, making me squeal in surprise and pain and amusement all at once.

He settled onto his side, facing me so I moved onto my side as well, hands in prayer position under my cheek. "You're very unpredictable."

"Gotta keep you on your toes. Can't have you getting sick of me."

"If anyone gets sick of sex like that, they're not human."

"Oh, babygirl, that was nothing," he said with a smile.

"All talk," I said, suppressing a small yawn. What can I say? It was a long day that included work, the gym, a nice dinner, and a solid fucking. I was beat.

He smiled sweetly, his eyes softening. "I'll prove it to you once you've gotten some sleep. Deal?"

"Deal," I agreed, wanting to snuggle in toward him, but unsure of the protocol. Usually snuggling followed lovemaking, not screwing like animals.

But then the uncertainty was taken from me as he slid one arm under my pillow and the other around my waist, pulling me into his body. My head rested on his arm, my face pressed slightly against his chest as he tucked my head under his chin. One of his thighs moved slightly over mine, making it slide between his.

And just like that, cuddled against his chest, I drifted off to sleep.

--

I woke up tucked in again and took a long minute to smile up at my ceiling, snuggling up in the warmth and enjoying the soreness in my thighs from the activities of the night before. Figuring he was downstairs making coffee or whipping up another food-coma inducing breakfast, I climbed out of bed. As soon as my feet were off the side, I saw them.

I kept a small square memo pad on my nightstand, always worried I was going to remember a chore I needed to do or an idea for a work project when I was in bed at night. I wanted something close just in case. Two pages had been ripped off and used, laid out on the surface. I reached for them with a smile. They were sketches. It was easy to forget that Paine was a tattoo artist. I'd never actually seen him at work and

147

it wasn't something he talked about much. But he was. And to be a tattoo artist, you first had to be an artist.

One was a drawing of animated sushi: a block of rice with blushing cheeks, a sushi roll with a smirk, and chopsticks kissing. The other was a simple picture of a barbell. I took that to mean that he got up and went to the gym as was his usual early morning activity.

I'm embarrassed to admit how long I sat there and looked down at those sketches with a goofy grin on my face. Snapping out of it, I took them over to my jewelry box, slipping them in and storing them for safekeeping. I was always that kind of girl; I saved things. I had the movie stub from my first date when I was a teen and the label off the first bottle of liquor I ever tasted in a scrapbook. I had seashells from every beach I had ever visited in a vase in my dining room. I liked having little reminders of things that once made me smile around me.

And, well, Paine's artwork made me smile. Huge.

I showered as I thought of him sitting off the side of the bed in the very early morning light, scribbling those pictures for me before he left. It was infinitely better than waking up to a note.

I decided then to only date men who grew up with single mothers, little sisters, and could draw from that point on.

I had half-expected him to show back up before I left for work and had to suppress a surge of disappointment when he didn't. I left early and stopped to get coffee, buying an extra one for him and cursing myself for doing so. As I drove across town (my path to work making me pass his shop), I tried to convince myself to not stop, to not be that girl. Needy, borderline desperate to be around the guy she was crushing on.

But I found myself pulling up behind his Challenger when I noticed the shop was open for the morning already. The shades were half-closed on the windows to block the brutally bright morning sun and, as such, I hadn't spotted the small group of people inside until I pulled the door and it was too late.

"Oh," I said, taken aback when three sets of eyes fell on me. One set was Paine's light green ones. Another were very dark green ones on the face of a man with an old school kind of handsome mixed with a post-punk look: tattoos all up his arms and across his neck, gauges in his ears, plain white v-neck tee, tight black jeans, and black and white checkered creepers. To say the charming smile he was giving me was enough to melt any red-blooded woman's panties was an understatement. The final set of eyes were blue and belonged to a man Paine's size build-wise with blond hair in an undercut, pulled into a small bun at the crown of his head. He also had a blond beard and a knowing little smirk on his face. "Um, sorry to interrupt," I said, my words almost tripping over one another I was so flustered. I turned to Paine, thrusting my arm with his coffee out a little awkwardly. "I just wanted to say thanks for dinner. I, ah, need to get to work."

He took the coffee from my hand, brows drawn together slightly as I yanked my arm back and turned to move back toward the door. Or, at least, I tried to make my way back toward the door. I failed because suddenly my wrist was snagged in Paine's giant palm and I was turned and pulled back the distance I had just created. "Fuck was that?" Paine asked when my gaze found his.

"I'm sorry... what?" I asked, painfully aware that the other guys in the shop were staring at us. And while I couldn't see, I was pretty sure they were still smiling.

"'Thanks for dinner, I need to get to work'?"

"And coffee," I reminded him, trying to lighten the mood.

But then what little space was between us was gone and Paine's face ducked down toward my neck, his breath in my ear where he said just loudly enough for me to hear, "Babygirl, I was inside you less than twelve hours ago. Can't even give me a good morning kiss?"

"You have company," I reminded him.

"Oh, honey, sugar, darling," one of the other guys said, making me jerk back to place him. It was the green-eyed, post-punk one. "Please tell me someone as gorgeous as you isn't wasting your time with this ugly fuck," he said, jerking his head toward Paine.

Paine rolled his eyes. "Elsie, this is Shooter," he said, indicating the green-eyed one.

He reached for the hand I offered, but turned it knuckles-up and leaned down to kiss it. To say I let out a girlish giggle would be a giant understatement.

"And Breaker," Paine went on, ignoring both Shooter's hand-kiss and my subsequent reaction.

I held out my hand to Breaker who took it as offered, shaking it hard before letting it drop.

"Hey doll," he greeted me.

"What?" Paine asked as I pressed my lips together to try to keep a smile in.

"Paine... Shooter... Breaker..." I explained, shaking my head.

"Johnnie and Bryan if that helps," Paine explained, waving at Shooter when he said "Johnnie" and Breaker when he said "Bryan".

"And by Johnnie," Shooter explained, "he means Johnnie Walker Allen."

"Like the scotch?"

To that, he smiled. "Yeah, darlin', like the scotch. I had a dick of an old man too."

Unsure how to respond to that, I gave him a small smile before turning back to Paine. "I really do need to get..."

"You got another twenty minutes before you even needed to leave your place," he cut me off.

"Well I, ah, left my coffee in my car," I tried. I wasn't sure why I wanted to get out of there so badly, but I did. There was something about being around a man you were sort-of seeing when his friends were around that made a woman feel a lot like she was at some kind of audition. And well, with names

150

like Shooter and Breaker and the aura of badassery that was coming off of the men, I was pretty sure lame ole' me wasn't going to impress them.

"Coffee in the kitchen. You know where that blueberry shit is," he said, waving a hand toward his open apartment door.

"She knows where the blueberry shit is?" I heard Breaker's amused voice ask as I scurried quickly, but not quickly enough to look like I was running away, into Paine's apartment.

I had just gotten the blueberry bottle out of the cabinet when a voice behind me said casually, "Alright, peaches, spill," Shooter's voice called.

I jumped, spinning with the blueberry bottle held up like I might strike out with it. "Sorry," I apologized when his brows drew together at the action. "I've had some, ah, close calls lately. I'm on edge."

"Paine filled us in," he explained with such a casual shrug that I was left to wonder if what was going on for me and was extremely strange was just usual and commonplace to them.

"What did you want me to spill about?" I asked, turning to finish fixing my coffee before I focused my attention back on him.

"How you're still here."

"I'm sorry?"

"Pretty girl, I'm sure it hasn't exactly escaped your notice the kind of man Paine is. Meaning the non-monogamous kind. You're a smart woman. You can spot a guy like him a mile away."

"You mean a guy like you?" I countered.

"Formerly," he said. "Found my girl. Been settled for a year now. But we aren't talking about me. I want to know how you got Paine taking you out to eat and making a big deal about you trying to rush out of here."

"Honestly, I don't know. I'm not that special. I mean, compared to you guys, I'm painfully normal. I don't know what is, ah, making Paine act differently."

"If you think you're not special, you're seriously fucked in the head, sweetheart."

"I didn't mean it like that. It's just... I don't know. I don't get it eit..."

"Oh perfect!" a female voice called from the store and I felt myself start.

"Don't go for the blueberry bottle," Shoot grinned. "I can protect you from Paine's mother."

"Paine's mother?" I asked, true horror evident in my tone.

"This is gonna be fun," Shooter said, rubbing his hands together as he moved to stand in the doorway. "Hey Mama Gina," he called to the woman I couldn't see.

"Shoot! Wow. One stop today. I wanted to invite you and Amelia and Breaker and Alex and Paine and, well, whatever flavor of the week he's got, to dinner Sunday night."

Alright.

I was mortified.

Mortified.

I wanted one of those sinkholes to open up right underneath Paine's shop and swallow me up into it.

Whatever flavor of the week he's got.

Flavor of the week.

I was a flavor of the week?

Was that possible?

It seemed like it seeing as there had obviously been women he had brought to his mother's house in the past. So if he brought them to meet his mom, it really wasn't a big deal that he took me to dinner and drew me cute little pictures that made me smile like a lovesick teenager.

God.

I was so freaking gullible.

There was the loudest silence following her statement that I had ever heard before. I could tell all three men were shocked silent, given that they knew I was present and what I must have been thinking at that comment.

"Ma," Paine's voice finally broke in, "hold up a minute," he said and I could hear his footsteps moving toward the apartment. My head was shaking no even before he crossed in. I'm a little ashamed to admit this, but I actually backed myself into a corner. "Come on," he said, holding a hand out toward me.

"No." Nope. No freaking way.

He closed the gap between us, his hips pressing into mine which pressed my ass into the counter hard. "I've never brought someone home to meet my mother. She was being a smartass. That's how she is. Now stop giving me a look like I kicked your puppy while declaring to the world at large that you've got the sweetest fucking pussy I've ever tasted."

"Shut up!" I squealed, horrified, looking past him to the spot where Shooter was standing. But he was gone.

"Hey," he said, his voice getting a little firm as his hands cupped my face. "Whatever the fuck is going on in that pretty head of yours, shut it down. You ain't some bullshit flavor of the week. I'm gonna prove that by dragging your sweet ass out there to meet my mother so she can personally invite you to dinner at her place on Sunday night."

With that, he dropped my face, grabbed my hand, and turned away. With his strong hand claiming mine and outweighing me by a good hundred some-odd pounds, well, there was no choice but to follow him.

Paine's mother looked, well, absolutely nothing like him. First, she was small. As in both short and thin. Paine was right when he said she certainly didn't have the hips to birth a baby as big as he was. Hell, I found it hard to believe her small body could carry a baby as big as Paine. She was just past middle age with pale skin and dark hair that she had cut in a way that didn't scream "mom!" but was actually pretty stylish. Her eyes were

153

similar to Paine's, but not quite. Hers were such a light green that they were almost see-through. Paine's had a bit more depth and I wondered if maybe the father had green eyes as well somehow. She had on dark wash jeans that she had tucked inside her tan heeled boots that matched her sweater I could see underneath her winter jacket.

She had been smiling huge at Shooter because of something he said and I got the overall impression that he was a real charmer. But her eyes moved over toward us when she saw motion and the smile faltered, fell, then reappeared but with drawn-in brows like she was confused.

"Ma, this is Elsie. Elsie, this is Gina. Now you gotta explain to her that fucking flavor of the week comment."

Oh, good Lord.

Seriously, where was a good sinkhole when you needed one?

"Oh, Elsie honey. I didn't mean anything by that," she rushed to correct her transgression. "He's never brought a woman to my table before because he's well..."

"A bit of a ladies man?" I supplied, my voice a strange strangled imitation of itself.

"I was going to say slut," she said bluntly with a smile, "but lets go with your term. I've been waiting close to twenty years for him to introduce me to a girl."

"Well now you're introduced," Paine supplied, dropping my hand but only because he slid an arm around my hips, pulling me to his side slightly.

"Do you have any plans Sunday night?"

Normally, I would. I'd had the standing Sunday night dinner with my father since I first moved out to go to college. But since I kinda... killed that tradition a couple days before, I was free. "No plans," I said with a smile. If I thought the audition with his buddies was bad, an audition with his buddies and his mother was all kinds of torture.

"Wonderful. Paine will pick you up and bring you to dinner. I don't need you to bring anything at all. Me and the

154

girls have it all covered. Shoot and Breaker will be bringing their girls too so you won't feel like I'm interviewing you all night," she said with a knowing smile.

"Sounds great. Thanks for inviting me."

She gave me a smile then turned to her son, the smile falling. "Don't fuck it up before then," she told him firmly before turning to Shooter and Breaker. "See you guys Sunday. Elsie," she said, reaching for my hand and squeezing it the way only mothers do, "it was so nice to meet you."

"Nice to meet you too," I said, then watched as she turned and left.

"We good?" Paine asked when his mother got into her car and pulled away.

"Um, yeah, we're good. I really do need to get to work now though," I said, glancing at the clock.

"I'll walk you out," he offered. Well, 'offered' wasn't the right word because it wasn't an offer. It was him narrating events as he pulled me toward the door.

"See you guys Sunday," I managed to call before the door slammed behind me.

Paine pulled me toward my car, pushed me back against the driver's door, and slammed his lips down on mine. It was by no means a 'good morning' kiss. It was hot and hungry and promising all kinds of fun carnal things that he couldn't give me because I was almost late for work and, you know, we were in public.

"I'm not even close to fucking done with you," he said in a deep, smooth voice before turning away and going back toward his shop.

With a strange fluttering feeling in my belly and wobbly legs, I got into my car and went to work.

And couldn't concentrate enough to get a damn thing done all day.

THIRTEEN

Paine

Drawing helps me focus. It lets my mind find what's important through all the bullshit that was always rolling around. Elsie had shifted away from me in her sleep and I had managed to get up without bothering her. A part of me had wanted to stay, to climb back, sleep in, wake up with plenty of time, and fuck her senseless before we both had to get off to work. But that was exactly the reason I needed to get my ass up, hit the gym, and get myself some perspective.

The sketch of the barbell was first. It was a simple explanation to where I went so she didn't wake up and freak out. It was also supposed to be the only one I left, but as soon as I put it down, the animated cutesy sushi came to me and I just started to draw it out. Obviously, it was something that was on my mind.

First, because it was a relatively new experience for me. I'd shared coffee with women, or drinks at a bar. I'd even taken a few out to an early morning breakfast after an all night fucking. But I never just... took a woman to dinner. For the fuck of it.

Second, because in doing so, I got to see Elsie. See past the pretty and the smart and the rich, all the things that assaulted you when you saw her. I got under that. I saw the funny and awkward and silly. I saw the way her eyes lit up when she talked about her sister. By all accounts, Elana seemed like her shit was whacked, she was all over the place. But it was clear that Elsie loved her fiercely and loyally. And, well, Elsie was a pretty level-headed chick. If she thought you were worthy of fierce and loyal love, then you must be, despite all the outward appearances of crazy.

As I plowed through a rough workout, I couldn't shake the question why. Why Elsie was different. Sure, she was drop dead gorgeous. But I'd bagged beautiful women before. She was smart. That was also something I'd known before. The rich thing, that meant nothing to me. It wasn't like I was the kind of man who would ever let a woman take care of him.

There was just a 'something', a thing I couldn't put my finger on, but she had it and I wanted a piece of it.

Maybe it was her contradictions. Sure she was pretty, but she vegged out in ugly sweats and wore giant glasses when her contacts were out. She was rich, but she worked her ass off to take care of herself despite the trust. She seemed to have her shit together, strong, independent... but there was also a hint of vulnerability about her that made any good man want to protect it at all costs. She cared about her body, but not in a way that made her deny good food when it was in front of her.

And, well, shit, that woman wore a sexually confident vibe that a man could sense a mile off. And it wasn't the sad, desperate vibe you found on lonely women in a bar. It was something else, something infinitely more attractive. It was something that said she owned her sexuality, she liked to have sex if and when she wanted it with whomever she chose and that she didn't let it define her or in any way lower her.

The sex? Off the fucking charts.

Sure, there had been women in the past that I hit it off with in bed and spent more than one night with. Some that I called whenever the mood struck, alone and horny and in need of some headboard breaking, no strings attached sex. But that was clearly all it was.

With Elsie, once I was inside her, I got this strange as fuck feeling like that was where I was supposed to be.

Factor in that she could take it as hard and fast as I gave it to her, the fact that she gave good head (though it got interrupted), that her pussy tasted like fucking candy... yeah, no way was I going to pass up the opportunity to explore that with her.

I showered and left the gym, texting Shoot and Breaker to meet me at the shop to talk about the Elana situation, see if either of them knew anything.

Breaker got his name because he was good at breaking things. Mainly, people. That was how he made his living, through intimidation, through beatings. Shooter, well, obviously he was good with a gun. Meaning, he was the best sniper and contract killer on the East coast. I came across Breaker when he was squatting in abandoned storefronts as a teen. There was a certain connection street-kids felt for one another. Me and Break, we got along straight off. A couple years later, Breaker took in a younger Shooter like a little lost puppy. Breaker was, outside the gang, the best friend I had. So, by extension, me and Shoot got tight as well. It helped that we all lived outside the law; we understood one another.

Through the years and me getting outta the gang, they were by my side. Both still worked their illegal jobs and, therefore, both had an ear to the streets at all times whereas sometimes my information was weeks or months too old to matter.

"Fuck man," Breaker said, shaking his head with a smile after we had discussed the situation for a while.

"What?"

Shoot laughed. "You watched the two of us go through it and you don't know what?" he asked.

See, Breaker and Shooter used to really enjoy the company of women too, many different women. Then Breaker met Alex. Because he was paid to kidnap her. Long story short, they ended up together. Then Shooter had to go back to Alabama to handle some family shit. He met Amelia. Amelia got herself wrapped up into some trouble that Shoot tried to get her out of. Lots of action and shit with both of them that ended up leading to serious relationships.

"That's not what's happening here."

"Sure it ain't," Breaker agreed, lips twitching.

"What do you give it?" Shoot asked Breaker. "Week? Two?"

"For what?" I asked, knowing I would regret doing so.

"Until you're completely pussy-whipped," Shoot supplied.

And that was exactly when Elsie decided to come in and bring me morning coffee. Which, well, was sweet as fuck. I'd never had a woman go out of her way to bring me anything before.

Then my ma showed up and dropped that flavor of the week line with Elsie within earshot. I mean I love my ma, but I seriously wanted to throttle her for that, especially when I walked into my kitchen and Elsie backed herself into a corner, eyes wide, looking both terrified and horrified at once. And I didn't fucking like that one bit.

I could see in that moment that she wasn't that girl. She wasn't the girl guys used and threw aside. She was class. The men who courted her, courted her. And the men she maybe fucked just for a fuck, guaran-fucking-tee they wanted more when she was done with them. That was what she was used to and the thought that anyone saw her as a disposable fuck toy really bothered her.

I didn't like the idea either.

So yeah... things were a bit more fucking complicated than I was used to.

On top of that shit, Shoot and Break hadn't heard anything. Nothing about Elana or anything about some extortion or kidnapping ring in the area.

So short story... things were fucked.

I was hoping Sawyer dug something else up. He might have been an ass, but he was an ass that got shit done. If there was someone I was comfortable with being on the job, it was him.

If all else failed, I was willing to cross over to my old streets and start causing some chaos until I got the answers I wanted. Enzo would flip shit, but that was too fucking bad.

I focused on work, never finding anything that I could concentrate on quite like I could drawing or tattooing. But as soon as I shut the shop, she came rushing back.

She was in.

Under my skin.

And I didn't know what the fuck to do with that realization.

So I went to the grocery store, like I had planned.

Then I went over to Elsie's.

FOURTEEN

Elsie

"Hey Elsie, wait up," Shane Mallick called as I skirted the front desk. I paused, turning, brows raised. Sure, he'd been my personal trainer once upon a time, but we barely shared more than hellos and goodbyes anymore.

"Yeah?"

"Got something for you," he said, reaching for something under the desk and coming back with an envelope.

Alright. Truth be told, now that I knew he was some kind of knee-breaking loan shark... I kinda felt a little weird taking anything from him. But he was holding out the envelope like he expected me to take it. So I did. The front had my name on it but that was it. I slid a finger under the seal, opened it, and pulled out the sheet of paper inside.

Curious, I unfolded it.

It was from Paine.

I knew this because it was another drawing.

This time, a perfect replica of my kitchen. Except there were grocery bags on the island which absolutely did not belong there seeing as I did not keep much in the way of food in my house.

"Uh oh. I know that look," Shane's voice broke in and my eyes sought his guiltily. It was then that I realized I was doing the goofy grin again. I had to make sure I didn't do that in front of Paine. Seriously.

"What look?" I asked, feigning ignorance.

"Oh fuck off babe," he laughed, giving me an amused smile. "You know exactly what look. You're so fucked. Paine, babe? Shit."

"It's not like that."

"Sure it's not."

"It's not," I insisted.

"What'd he give you?"

Seeing no reason not to share, I showed him the picture. "It's my kitchen."

"This supposed to mean something?"

"I think it means he's cooking me dinner? I don't keep food in my house and there's food on the counter in the drawing."

"Paine is gonna cook for you?" he asked like I implied Paine was going to paint my toenails while watching a Sex and the City marathon.

"He already made me pancakes."

"Shit," he said, shaking his head as he handed me my drawing back.

I carefully refolded it, knowing it was going right in my jewelry box once I got home. "What?"

"You're both fucked," he said with a shrug.

"Gee thanks for that," I said, shaking my head. "See you next time," I added, going toward the door.

I drove home with both a knot of uncertainty and a thrill of excitement spreading through my system. And, sure enough, Paine's Challenger was out front. I grabbed my purse and gym bag and hustled into my place, expecting to smell dinner cooking, but all I was met with was the sound of my TV playing some kind of game. Paine was reclined back on my couch, legs up but feet (and shoes) hanging off.

"Hey babygirl," he called, not looking up from the TV.

"I got your, ah, note."

"And you got a kitchen counter full of groceries."

I felt my brows draw together. "About that..."

"You're gonna cook me dinner."

"I'm sorry, I'm what?" I asked, completely thrown off.

"Cook me, well, both of us, dinner. After you get that fine ass over here and give me a kiss."

"Paine... I can't cook. At all."

"Sure you can. And you're going to. I'll help."

"Paine..."

"Baby, you take care of yourself in every other fucking way. Wouldn't it be nice to know you can throw some food together too?"

Well, he did sort of have a point.

"Okay."

"Good. Now what part of getting your fine ass over here to give me a kiss didn't make sense to you?" he asked, but there was humor in his voice.

"You have legs too, you know," I said, standing my ground. "And if you want me to cook dinner, I think getting near a couch and kissing might delay that for, say, the rest of the night."

At that, he knifed up, turning over his shoulder to give me a wicked smile. "Might have a point there," he agreed, standing and making his way toward me.

I threw my gym bag and purse, knowing that whatever kind of kiss he had in store for me was going to require my hands as well as my lips.

He stopped when his toes touched mine, slid one foot between my feet, slipped one arm around my lower back, then sank one hand into my hair at the base of my neck, curling and yanking it backward. The second my mouth opened on a gasp, his was on mine, tongue moving inside to claim mine. Claim. That was the only way to describe it. Every time Paine kissed me, it felt like he was marking me, branding me, making me his.

What's more, I wanted to be his.

My hips pressed into his as he bent me slightly backward, throwing me off balance, and if his hand wasn't around my hips, I'd have fallen over. Against me, he was hard and straining. Which wasn't helping the fact that I was already hopelessly wet and almost painfully aroused.

"Alright," he said against my lips, getting me back on my feet and releasing my mouth. "Gotta stop or I'm gonna fuck you right here."

I fought the urge to tell him I had no problem with that and nodded.

Then he led me into the kitchen, my body still humming with arousal, and pulled items out of the bags.

"Starting easy. It's hard to fuck up spaghetti," he said with a boyish smile. "Boil water, put in spaghetti, stir. Put a pan of sauce on, stir. Ten minutes later, dinner is done."

"Sounds pretty idiot-proof," I agreed, going toward my cabinet to get a pot.

"You cooking for a football team, baby?" he asked, making me turn.

"What?"

"Swear to fuck, you're so clueless about this that it's cute. That pot is too big. Something half that size for the pasta. Then something half the size of the pasta pot for the sauce."

"Right," I said, finding the right pots, filling one with water, filling one with sauce and putting them on the stove as instructed.

"Want wine with dinner?" he asked, moving toward the rack.

"Sure," I said, watching the pot.

While I waited for the pot to boil, he asked me about my day, handed me wine, found excuses to casually touch me. It was all so... normal. Casual. And I realized I could really get used to it.

But I told him I wouldn't do that.

The night before, I agreed to let things play out how they were going to play out, to not expect things.

So yeah, I watched the bubbles pop up in the water and tried to tamp down the warm and gushy feelings inside.

"Salt the water first," Paine said as he handed me the box of pasta. I followed instructions. I mixed the pasta a time or two.

Then I couldn't mix it anymore.

This was because Paine had snagged me around the belly, pulled me across the floor, turned me, and pushed me up against the island.

"Got ten minutes. Twelve if you can deal with your pasta being on the soft side."

"Twelve minutes for what?"

"To fuck you," he growled, grabbing the waistbands of my pants and panties and dragging them down to my knees. He pulled me backward by my hair, sinking his teeth into my neck. "First let's have a quick birth control talk. Pill?"

"IUD," I corrected, groaning as his hand moved down my belly and started working my clit. "Had a screen at my last gyno visit six months ago. Haven't had sex since then."

"Checked last month. Always use a condom. You wanna wait for the paperwork..."

"I trust you," I said as his teeth bit into my neck hard.

"Thank fuck," he groaned, grabbing my hair again, twisting in it, and using it to push me downward hard and fast, pressing my upper body and the side of my face against the island, holding me there. "Tip your ass up," he demanded and I quickly moved to comply, the need for him inside me a throbbing, insistent thing. His palm swung out and swatted my ass hard enough for me to go up on my toes at the sting, my pussy clenching hard in excitement.

His other hand pressed hard into my neck, holding me against the counter, then he slammed inside me to the hilt. "Fuck," he growled, stilling inside me for a second.

And then he was fucking me.

Not fast, but hard.

With each stroke, he almost fully left me before slamming all the way forward with so much force that it made my hips slam into the counter.

All I could think past the clenching tightness of my growing orgasm was... never. No one had ever taken me so hard before. The men I had been with before had always been tentative at first, just shy of gentle. When they got more comfortable, there was some headboard knocking, but nothing even in the same hemisphere as the way Paine took me.

On a strange growl, he released my neck. Before I could try to push up, his hands closed around my hips, his fingers sinking into my hipbones hard as he lifted me up and off my feet. I repeat: he lifted me off of my feet, thereby taking away any ability I had to thrust backward, or do anything at all but take him. My arms went out in front of me, grabbing the edge of the counter as he held me up and continued thrusting hard, getting faster, and I knew I was going to be done way before the pasta.

I clenched down hard as I teetered on the edge, letting out low, quiet whimpers.

"Come Elsie," he demanded, his tone tense.

Then he slammed forward, tilting up slightly once fully inside, and I did.

My entire body shook as my muscles contracted hard around him, a throbbing, seemingly endless wave of pleasure that had me crying out his name. At the sound, he buried deep, dropping me back onto my feet, and came.

I was still trying to even out my breathing as he slowly slid out of me. I pushed myself up on my elbows, but didn't

trust my legs to fully hold me yet. Paine leaned down, grabbing
my panties and moving them up my legs and into place. He
went back for my pants, struggling with them slightly. Then he
slid an arm around me, just under my breasts, and pulled me
backward against his chest.

"You alright?" he asked, nuzzling his face into my neck.
I felt my head nod tightly and his other arm snaked around my
lower belly, both of them tightening hard enough to almost cut
off my air. "Sure? I got a little carried away."

I drew in a breath that was still a bit shaky. "I like carried
away."

He was in the middle of kissing my neck and I could feel
his smile against my skin at my words. "Good. Now go get
cleaned up. I'll strain the spaghetti."

"Okay," I agreed, sliding out of his arms and making my
way out of the room. I went up the stairs, grabbing some more
comfortable clothes, meaning gray yoga pants and a black long-
sleeved tee, cleaned up, then made my way back downstairs.

"Knew you had to have at least one pair of those things,"
Paine said as I walked in, carrying the plates over to the island.

"Why?" I asked, brows drawing together.

"To have an ass like that and not have a pair of yoga
pants would be a crime against fucking humanity, that's why."

Then we sat and ate the first real meal I had ever made.
Paine led most of the conversation, talking about Shooter and
Breaker, how they met, the crazy things they had been involved
in. He explained how Breaker met Alex and how Shooter met
Amelia, doing so with a fondness that made it clear he wasn't
just friends with the women because they came along with his
friends, but because he genuinely liked them. Alex, he said, was
some kind of computer hacker who could be a bit standoffish at
first, but once she warmed up to you, was pretty funny.
Apparently watching her and Breaker fight was the highlight of
almost every gathering. Breaker liked to pick at her and she
always rose to the bait. It sounded downright popcorn-worthy.
Amelia, Shooter's girl, was a drug and alcohol counselor. She

could occasionally come off as prickly, but was soft underneath it all.

When he was done and we were just sipping wine, he asked about Rome, him being the only truly close friend I had.

I felt almost guilty talking about him with Paine, like it was a betrayal to both of them somehow. Which was ridiculous. But, after a while, I was smiling and laughing as I told him about all the stunts we had pulled together, the vacations we had gone on, the things we had helped each other through: my mother's death, his mother's stints in rehab before she finally got sober five years before, my father's relentless, demanding presence, our breakups, our failures and successes.

"Babygirl..." he said when I finally ran out of things to say. The word hung heavy with meaning.

"I know," I said, looking down at my empty plate.

He nodded, letting it drop, and moved to stand. "You the type who can't go to sleep with dirty dishes?" he asked, bringing both of ours over to the sink.

"I have no idea. I doubt it."

"Good. Then let's go to bed."

Then we went to bed.

Tired and, quite frankly, a little sore from our earlier carnal activities, we just went to sleep.

--

Again, I woke up in my blanket cocoon. And, again, I realized this with a smile. I immediately rolled to my side, looking over at the nightstand. I found another two pictures. I sat up against the headboard and reached for them. The first was a picture of a tattoo gun, which I took to mean he had to get to work. The second, well, the second one was of a man with a red woolen tunic under an armored chest and shoulder plate, a helmet, a sword, and a giant red shield. It didn't take a history major to recognize a Roman soldier. Also, the man had a startling resemblance to Roman. Underneath was a scribbled "set this straight".

So I guess that was what he expected me to do with my day. I wondered if that meant I wouldn't be seeing Paine after work because he wanted me to finally have that supremely awkward conversation with Roman.

And then I internally yelled at myself for thinking that thought because it was a bit too needy early on in our, er, relationship. Hell, as far as I knew, it wasn't even a relationship at all. So I definitely shouldn't have been thinking thoughts like that.

So I totally didn't think about the way his eyes got bright when he talked about his friends, soft when he talked about his friends' girlfriends. I also did not wonder if it meant something that we were at the point of something serious because we were having sex without condoms. If what he said was true and he always used them and I had only ever not used them with one serious long-term boyfriend in my early twenties, that kind-of implied we both felt like there was something different between us, right?

"Augh!" I growled at my reflection, pissed at my internal monologue and annoyed because my hair was doing that 'I'm not going to lay right no matter what tricks you try to tame me' thing. A little rougher than necessary, I tied my hair back. I applied more of the tattoo cover-up, threw on the barest hint of mascara, and headed out the door. The bruises were getting better. I figured by Sunday dinner, there would be next to nothing left there anymore. Which was good because half of the tube of that tattoo stuff was gone.

I got into my office a full hour before anyone, except the early morning cleaning crew, showed up. I pulled out my phone and texted Roman asking him to come over so we could chat after work. It took him almost an hour to answer me, which wasn't like him, saying yeah.

So then I worked.

Seven-thirty rolled around and I wrapped things up, checking my phone on my way out the door and realizing I didn't even have Paine's number. I mean I knew the number to his shop, but not his cell. And, as far as I knew, he didn't have my number either. I was pretty sure that was a pretty huge sign that we weren't in, or heading into, something serious.

I kept up these swirling, infuriating, frustrating thoughts the entire drive home, pulling up beside Roman's car in my drive. He was climbing the steps and looked back at me over his shoulder and, just like that, my thoughts finally quieted. Because I had never seen Rome look as beat-down as he did right in that second. I threw my car into park, grabbing my stuff in a rush, slammed my door, and almost ran up the steps to meet him inside my front door.

"Rome, what's up?" I asked, watching him hit the code before turning back to me, giving me a second to stash my bag, phone and keys.

"Guess you haven't seen the news," he said, his voice almost hollow.

"No," I said, shaking my head as I followed him into the kitchen. I couldn't remember the last time I actually watched TV. I caught that movie with Rome and then about two minutes of the game Paine was watching, but that was it. "What's on the news?"

"We got robbed, Else."

"Robbed?" I repeated, moving toward the coffee machine to make a fresh pot.

"An entire truckload of cold medicine meant for all the pharmacies in the state."

"Cold medicine?" I repeated, brows drawing together.

"It's a fucking PR nightmare. You have any idea how tightly that shit is regulated now? We tried to keep it quiet when

170

we first investigated, but we had to report it and now it's all over the news."

"Aw, Rome... I'm so sorry. I wish I had known... I could have..."

"Nothing you could do, Else. Besides, you have your own stuff going on."

"Stuff?" I repeated, not liking the tone he used.

"I was going to drop in last night. I had pizza and another movie..." he paused, looking down for a second before meeting my eyes. "You had a car out front."

Shit.

Well, I guess it wasn't going to be as awkward a subject to bring up as I thought. "Rome..."

"It's the tattoo guy, isn't it?" he asked bluntly.

"How did you..."

"Else, I've known you your entire life. You get dragged out of a bar by that man then come back in lips all swollen and bent on drowning something in alcohol. It wasn't too hard to come to the conclusion something was going on there."

"I was planning on telling you tonight. I just... it's new and I wasn't..."

"I've loved you all my life," he cut me off, the sensation of a stab wound searing through my stomach. "Around sixteen, seventeen, it became more than that."

"Why didn't you ever tell me?"

He let out a humorless laugh. "And fuck up the chance to spend my time with you because you didn't reciprocate? I'm not stupid, Elsie. I knew you always saw me as a brother. And I would always rather have a best friend who was clueless to the fact that I was in love with her, than to never get to see the woman I loved again because she felt guilty for not loving me back."

"I love you Rome," I said sadly.

His hand covered mine and squeezed. "But not like that."

"No," I admitted reluctantly.

"So I need to let go already," he said, dropping my hand.

171

"Rome," I said, my voice a plea.

"I'll always be here for you. Always. But I need to move on." He moved toward me, arms going around my shoulders, pulling me against his chest. I always liked that about Roman, his hugs. All other guys put their arms around my waist to hug me, leaving me to put my arms around their shoulders. Rome was always different. My arms went around his waist tight, tight enough that I knew I was making it hard for him to breathe, but not caring. He pulled against my hold, dropping a kiss on my forehead. "I'm glad you found someone. I want you to be happy."

"I want you to be happy too," I agreed, feeling the familiar sting in my eyes and I knew I was going to start crying.

"Don't," he said, knowing me too well. "It's not goodbye. No crying," he said, pulling away and putting yards of space between us.

See, the thing was, in a way, it was a goodbye. It was a goodbye to the intimacy of our friendship that I had always viewed as chaste and due to knowing each other so long, but was really the result of his feelings for me. It was the end to me feeling comfortable talking about sex and boyfriends with him.

I heard the door open and the bleeping of the alarm started. My eyes shot to Rome who had a look of resigned understanding. The bleeping stopped and Paine's footsteps came toward us. As soon as he was in the kitchen, he made a beeline for me, putting an arm around my waist and kissing the side of my head. And it was such a clear message that he was claiming me that the knife thing started in my stomach again.

A shutter moved down over Rome's eyes and he shook his head slightly, turning his attention to Paine. "I hope you end up deserving her."

"If I don't, you'll be there for her. That's big of you."

Rome visibly shrank away from the praise of a man he knew was having sex with the woman he loved, but nodded tightly. "She's worth it," he said, turning to move out toward the dining room.

I moved to follow him, but Paine's arm tightened and held me in place. "Rome," I called, but the front door clicked closed and I knew he wasn't coming back. Not anytime soon anyway. Alone, I wrenched away from Paine, shoving him hard in the chest as I turned. "That was not necessary!" I screeched, my voice shrill, as close to a yell as it had ever gotten during an argument.

"Babygirl, it was," Paine said, voice calm, moving toward me.

"No, it wasn't. He had just admitted he loved me since we were sixteen and that he knew it was time to let go and you came in here acting all alpha-dog claiming his fucking beta. That was really shitty of you," I seethed, backing up as he kept advancing.

"Baby..."

"Don't 'baby' me. Pet names don't erase that you just..." my voice hitched and I shut my mouth to keep it from becoming a full-on sob.

"Hey," he said, his voice suddenly soft as I backed up into the counter and he came up in front of me. His hand raised and his fingers brushed the first tear off my cheek. I ducked my head only to find myself crushed up against his chest, his arms wrapping me up tight. And, well, something about being held opened up the floodgates. "It's gonna be okay," he said softly, the arm around my upper back loosening slightly so he could reach up, pull my hair tie out and run his fingers through my hair.

"He's... not going to... want to be around me," I sobbed into his shirt.

"Stop. You know that's not true. He loves you. He might need a little more distance than you're used to, but he won't go anywhere."

"You don't know that."

"I know you."

"What's that supposed to mean?" I asked, doing an oh-so-attractive sniffle.

"I don't know you one-tenth the way he does and I know a man would be out of his mind to stop hanging around you just 'cause you don't want to fuck him."

"Don't be crass."

"Just honest."

I pulled against his hold slightly and he loosened enough so I could swipe at my cheeks. "I still think it was shitty of you to do that," I reminded him, not willing to let it go.

"You gotta remember something, babygirl. Men and women, we communicate differently. You guys like to choose your words and pussyfoot around the issue so as to not cause any conflict. Men don't do that shit. In fact, if we can get our point across with a look or gesture instead of words, we will. You don't get it, but Roman did."

"He got what?"

"That you're mine. And what's mine is mine and he better the fuck not cross any lines with you from here on out."

I'm pretty sure my entire body froze at that, including my heart. It just stopped dead in my chest for a second. "Yours?" I choked out after several awkwardly silent seconds.

"Yeah, mine," he said with a squeeze of the arm around my hips.

"I'm... yours?"

"You been paying attention, baby? It was you I fucked in your bed, right? And it was you who met my friends and my mother. And I'm pretty fucking sure it was you who I've been leaving notes to every morning. And I'm almost damn positive it was you I fucked raw in your kitchen last night. Know you don't know me that way, Elsie, but that's a big fucking deal for me. I don't do that. I don't lead women on if I plan on getting shot of them. And I never, as in ever, fuck a woman without protection. So you and me, we have something going on here."

"Okay," I said, ignoring the way my stomach was swarming with happy little butterflies, because I knew that for my peace of mind, I needed actual clarification. "But... what does that mean? What does 'something going on here' mean exactly?"

"I'm sure it's pretty clear by now that I've never been a relationship guy."

"It's come up," I agreed, lips tipping up slightly.

"So this is all new to me. I don't know what you're looking for here. You need assurances? I have none of those. You want labels? You're mine. Call it what you want: girlfriend, partner, main squeeze. I don't give a fuck. It all means the same thing: mine."

"So, as it stands, this," I said, waving a hand between our bodies, "is a relationship? It's exclusive and..."

"Babygirl, when I say you're mine, I mean everything. Mouth, tits, ass, pussy. It's all mine. And in case your mind is going there, let me shut this shit down right now. That means everything I got is yours too."

The fluttering thing intensified. "You don't think maybe this is a little... fast?"

To that, he put his head back to look at the ceiling and let out a sigh before looking back down at me. "What? You want six weeks of sitting across from each other in restaurants and talking about our favorite colors and all that bullshit that means nothing? We got something here. Only way to fuck that up this early on is to over-analyze it to death. So quit it. Let it happen."

Let it happen.

"Okay," I said, though a part of me knew there would always be that niggling little voice in the back of my head begging me to over-think every little thing. I was convinced it was a voice all women were born with.

"So we're good."

"Yeah, we're good."

"Thank Christ because I'm starving."

"Listen," I said, smiling, "I think me cooking one meal a week is plenty fair."

"Chinese?" he asked, already releasing me to go fetch a menu from on top of the microwave.

"Sure. Lo mein," I said, walking out toward the dining room. "I'm gonna go get changed."

I hemmed and hawed over my pajama selection for a truly embarrassing length of time. Agreeing we were in a relationship certainly seemed like the occasion to slip into a slinky nightie. But we would be eating dinner and a delivery guy was going to show up...

Eventually, I settled on a baby pink silk nightie, no bra or panties because the length was decent enough. Then I found a white and pink floral silk robe and slipped it on, knotting it. It would be a fun little surprise for later.

Or, at least, I thought it would be.

That was until I got into the living room to find Paine sitting on the couch, some rerun of a sitcom on the TV. He wasn't actually watching it, but it was on and the volume was almost to the point of being loud. "Not a fan of silence, huh?" I asked, leaning against the doorway.

He looked up, eyes running over my robe, brows drawing together slightly. "Grew up in a two bedroom apartment with two sisters, a mom, and a grandma in a building that was constructed with the thinnest walls imaginable. Then, with the gang, there was always men and women around. It was never quiet. Silence feels unnatural to me," he explained, tossing his phone onto the coffee table. "Come here," he said, patting his knee.

I rolled my eyes, but crossed toward him, moving to sit on his thigh like he had requested, but he grabbed me instead and pulled me to straddle him. His hands went immediately to the knot I tied and worked it out. He parted the material and a slow, sexy smile spread across his face. His hands drifted inward, sliding to cup my breasts. At the warmth of his skin on the cool material, my nipples hardened against his palms and his eyes went hooded.

"Twenty," he said oddly, looking up at me.

"Twenty what?"

"Minutes to delivery," he explained, rolling my nipples between his thumbs and forefingers.

"That's a long time. I wonder what we could do to make it pass faster," I said with a smile.

His hands slid from my breasts and down my belly, landing high on my bare thighs so that his fingers slipped under the material. "No panties?" he asked, cocking his head to the side.

"It was supposed to be an after dinner surprise."

"Yeah well now it's a before dinner treat. Slide back," he said, pushing my hips slightly backward. He reached down, unfastening his pants, reaching inside, and pulling out his hard cock.

"Is that my treat?" I asked with a devilish little smirk, ready to slide down to my knees.

"Gonna have that mouth on me again, baby. But right now, I need to be in that tight pussy. Ride me," he demanded, still holding his cock at the base so I could position myself. Not needing any further encouragement, I moved back over him, lifted my hips, then slowly slid down on him as my fingers sank into his shoulders. One of his hands moved to squeeze my ass, the other up toward my neck, holding on at the side.

I took him slow for a few glorious strokes, reveling in the feeling of fullness, in the perfect friction. But it wasn't long before the need became an urgent, clawing thing and my hips started working him faster and faster, quiet moans accompanying almost every downward stroke. My thigh muscles tensed and shook, my core tightened, and I knew I was getting close.

But then I lost it. My rhythm got sloppy and I felt it slowly drifting away. I was never good at being on top. I always got too into the sensations and couldn't keep whatever constant pace I needed to have an orgasm.

I collapsed on Paine's shoulder with growl/whimper hybrid.

"Lift up," Paine said, his voice sex-rough. I lifted up a bit and he started thrusting upward into me, his pace quick, but not overly rough, the position limiting him. I pulled off his chest on a moan and his hand curled further into my neck. "You need me to take over, tell me baby," he told me gently as he kept his perfect, relentless pace, drawing my orgasm back out of hiding. His free hand left my ass and slid between us, finding my clit and starting to work it in slow, hard circles that made my walls tighten hard around him. "You gonna come for me?" he asked, eyes holding mine and I wanted to take that moment: him inside me, his hands on me, his eyes pinning mine, I wanted to take it and freeze it, have it forever.

"Yes," I whimpered, rocking my hips back and forth as he kept thrusting up into me, making his cock rub over my G-spot at every turn.

"Squeeze my cock. Let me feel you come," he demanded then his finger did another circle, his cock did another thrust and my hips did another rock and I did. Hard. My body jerked almost violently as I fell forward against him, my legs shaking too hard to hold my weight.

Paine grabbed my hips, pulling up, then slamming down, burying deep and I could feel his cock jerk inside me, his hot come filling me.

I turned my face into his neck, kissing him just below the ear.

"You don't like being on top, Elsie, tell me."

"I like it," I said into his skin, taking deep breaths to take in his unique spicy scent. "I just suck at it. I get too wrapped up to remember to... move," I said with a silent laugh.

"Got it," he said in a way that made me pretty sure he was cataloging that fact to remember for a later date. I liked that about him too; when I talked, he seemed to genuinely listen. Again maybe a trait he got from growing up around so many women. I actually found myself really excited to meet them all, silently thank them all for the man they helped create. I was really enjoying him after all.

"Alright, off," he said gently, squeezing my ass with both hands.

"I'm comfortable," I objected, snuggling in further for good measure.

"Like that you feel that way baby, but I'm gonna be leaking out of you."

I cringed slightly and nodded. "Right," I said, carefully climbing off of him and hastily closing my robe as I tried to rush out of the room to clean up without said leaking happening too badly.

By the time I came back out, the food was on the kitchen island. "Are we ever going to use the dining table?" I asked, realizing for the first time that I had literally never used it before.

"So I can sit three feet away from you? No thanks."

And, well, that was a good point.

At dinner, he asked me questions and I talked. He occasionally weighed in, especially when we got onto the topic of my father. In bed, both of us realizing we apparently weren't going to be using the bed for sex often, we snuggled. This time, I asked questions and he talked.

He was surprisingly open about his past, never sparing any gory details, never trying to hide the kind of man he was once, the things he had done. I liked that. It was refreshing. Most 'normal' men hid, evaded, hinted at things but didn't explain, or outright lied even though what they had to hide or evade or lie about was nothing big. Paine's history was big, but he shared. It was like it never even occurred to him to be anything other than forthright.

I fell asleep on the tail-end of a story about him and Enzo playing pranks on Enzo's mom, lulled by the smooth, quiet tone of his voice, his warm chest, his strong arm around me, his steady heartbeat beneath my ear, excited to figure out what picture notes I would wake up to in the morning.

FIFTEEN

Elsie

Three things happened the next day.

First, I woke up to more picture notes.

Second, I had a relatively normal Wednesday at work. Meaning I worked hard for about four-point-five hours then kinda fell off and lost my steam and spent time around the metaphorical water cooler.

Third, I was kidnapped.

But back to the first thing.

I woke up like I expected to, in my blanket cocoon, smiling like a fool, feeling a warmth spreading across my chest that I knew, if things went south, was going to hurt like nothing before. On my nightstand wasn't a drawing of where he was or what he was doing; it seemed we had established that he spent his mornings at the gym then went to work. Instead, it was a drawing of... me. I wasn't sure exactly what moment he used for inspiration because the picture cut off at the neck, not showing any clothing, but it truly was an exact, perfect sketch of my face. He drew me with a smile, but not a full one, no teeth, just a turning up of lips that made the corners of my eyes crinkle the tiniest bit. My hair was a little mussed like I had just run a hand through it and it settled in slight disarray.

I smiled, placing it with the others, then went about getting myself ready for my day.

As I said, work was work. Wednesdays suck. I never found it comforting that half the week was over because it still meant you had half to go. Which was especially annoying when you had things you wanted to do with your weekend. Like spend it with your new... boyfriend.

Boyfriend.

That's what he was.

The term sounded absurd given that I was twenty-eight years old and Paine was in his mid-thirties, but that's what he was. He was mine.

So yeah, while when I was single, I often clocked sixty to eighty hour weeks happily and easily, I was struggling to pull off forty to fifty hour weeks with one.

I blamed the hormones.

And the mind-bending sex.

With a super hot, alpha, but in a sweet way, guy.

I left work and headed to the gym, planning on just putting in a good twenty minutes, just to keep things tight. Chinese food always made me feel greasy and bloated the next morning and, well, it wasn't easy to feel sexy when you were greasy and bloated.

I took a quick shower, dressed in plain jeans and my old college sweatshirt and headed out the door.

I did this while not looking up because I was searching for my keys.

As such, I ran into a solid wall of man.

"Oomph," I grunted on impact, my keys falling out of my hand as I took a hasty step back. "Hey sorry, I wasn't paying..." I looked up and froze.

He looked down and sneered.

Because we both recognized each other.

It was actually kind of hard to realize that it was only nine days before. It felt like a lifetime. But it was just the Monday before last that I found myself running through the streets of Navesink Bank being chased by a not-so-fit man named Trick who had at least half of a brain and a muscle-bound, brutish, single-celled organism named D.

Now, granted, I hadn't gotten the best look at either of them being that I was scared out of my skin and running for my life, but I'd caught a good enough look at D to recognize him as the man standing in front of me in black basketball shorts, black sneakers, and a too-tight gray wifebeater. Yeah, shorts and a wifebeater... in the middle of winter. I wondered if steroids somehow made your body temperature rise.

"Barbie," he smiled evilly.

In about point-three seconds, I took in the empty parking lot and knew the front doors were only about twenty feet behind me. There was a tree blocking it from view, but if I ran and screamed, there was a gym full of big, muscle-y guys who could run to my rescue.

I turned and had one leg out to start my sprint. But one hand clamped down around my mouth while the other arm curled around my belly so hard it felt like it was rearranging my insides, and lifted me up off my feet against his chest.

The panic started in a second, making my heart hammer in my chest, a sweat spread across my body, my throat start to feel constricted. I flailed as much as the position would allow as I was dragged backward. I needed to get my feet on the ground. I remembered a self-defense video I watched once where they grabbed a guy from behind and he said the only way to overpower a much stronger attacker from behind was to get your feet on the ground and jump as hard and fast as possible, thereby breaking his hold on you. Then you were supposed to run like hell. But my feet never hit the ground again as I was pulled across the lot.

We stopped beside an old tan sedan, as in old, like it had been alive almost as long as me. The next move happened so fast that I couldn't react. One second, a hand was still over my mouth and an arm around my middle, my entire body dangling. The next, my mouth was uncovered and my middle was released as my feet slammed down hard, the pain ricocheting up my thighs. But before I could even scream, a strong forearm was around my throat from behind, cutting off my air supply. My hands went up automatically, trying to claw his arm away to no avail as I felt my brain start to get fuzzy. I didn't know much about things like self-defense, but I did know it only took seconds to pass out while being choked. I was vaguely aware of D moving around behind me, of a trunk being opened.

But then, only a matter of five or six seconds later, I wasn't aware of anything as unconsciousness claimed me.

I woke up fully alert.

That hit me as strange. I figured I would wake up groggy, unfocused, a little unaware of what happened. But that wasn't what happened. One second, I was trying to claw a hand from my neck. Seemingly the next, I was rolling around in a trunk, acutely aware of what just happened to me. I was choked out and thrown in a trunk by a member of the Third Street gang.

I threw out my arms and legs automatically, hitting all four corners of the trunk and holding myself in place as the car took a hard turn that made my stomach do an uncomfortable flip-flop.

Okay. I needed to focus. I needed to ignore the painful thrumming of my heart in my chest, the throbbing points of my pulse in my throat, wrists, and temples. I had to swallow the nausea.

I needed to not panic.

Everyone knew the story about car trunks. Hell, we all learned that in assemblies at school. Newer cars had an emergency escape latch. Older cars didn't. This was an older car. In older cars, your best bet was to kick out the brake lights. I scrunched up in the small space, finding the corners where the

183

lights were situated and slamming my heel into it three times before, on the fourth strike, my foot went straight through. I turned again, thrusting my hand out of the space and waving it around frantically, wondering if anyone was even around to see it, let alone try to intervene.

The car took another sharp turn and something slammed into my side. I reached for it with my free hand, feeling the familiar slippery material of my gym bag. I always locked my purse in my trunk when I was leaving work for the gym, not trusting leaving it in a locker room even though I had a lock. Two things came to me right at that minute. One, I had a lock. As in a padlock. As in a solid piece of metal that could really cause some pain. Two, while I locked up my purse in my trunk, I always threw two essentials into my gym bag along with my clothes and water bottle: my Ipod... and my cell.

I pulled my hand out of the hole, knowing that was probably not going to help me anyway, and fumbled through my bag, cursing the sweaty gym clothes and tossing them into the dark of the trunk. My hand found the metal of my gym lock first and I pulled it out, clicking it closed, then slipping two fingers into the loop so I wouldn't lose it. I found my cell with a sharp exhale. I got it in my hands and tapped in my passcode when I felt the car stop. Not more than a second later, the driver's door slammed.

He was coming.

He was coming and I had no time to call the police.

And I didn't even have Paine's number.

Christ.

Okay.

My hands shook as my screen came up and I clicked my Facebook app, thankful for good service even in a freaking trunk parked God-knew where. I hit my status and dropped a pin.

It was a long, long, long shot.

But it was all I had time to do.

I prayed as I heard the key slip into the trunk lock, turning off my phone and slipping it into my back pocket, that Sawyer and Barrett were still on my case. If Barrett was, he would see the pin. And, if maybe he was suspicious enough, he would know something was wrong. And then I hoped to hell he would call his pain in the ass, cocksure, annoying, baddass mother effing brother who would call Paine and they would come save me.

But like I said, I knew that was a long shot. As in, it was probably never going to happen. So I had to try to save myself. I curled the lock into my hand, knowing it was too awkward a position for me to hit him as soon as he opened the trunk. I didn't have enough of a range of motion to get a good hit in. So I had to wait.

"Gotta take you to the boss," he said as he reached in and curled his hand around my bicep, squeezing in hard enough for me to wince and hiss out a breath as he started dragging me out of the trunk. I scrambled out, trying to keep my feet. He slammed the trunk and then he slammed me against it, locking me there with his body. His pelvis was against mine and I could feel his erection through his jeans. "But maybe I can have a little fun with you first," he said with that ugly-freaking sneer again, his hand moving out and closing over my breast through my lightweight sweater.

And, well, that was apparently my breaking point.

I leaned slightly backward as I planted my feet. My arm went back and, without even pausing to think, I swung out with the lock. It made a sickening crunching sound as it collided with his cheekbone, making him rear back on a howl.

I didn't consider the chance of staying and fighting, hitting him until he couldn't see so he couldn't chase me. I just turned and ran.

I realized too late that I should have went with the blinding him idea because I was shoved so hard in my lower back that I fell forward, flailing, stomach dropping. I had the foresight at the last possible moment to throw my hands out to break my fall. But my momentum was high and the impact was hard, scraping across my palms which didn't hold my weight and I went down on my forearms, crying out in agony as it felt like something snapped inside as the pavement burned and ripped the skin. The side of my face collided too, but much more gently because I instinctively locked my neck. The road scratched my cheekbone, but not bad enough to cause any real damage.

I couldn't even blink away the tears before a hand reached down and grabbed my hair at the ends and pulled so viciously that I pushed up onto my busted palms just to try to ease the searing pain in my scalp. But it was no use, because he just kept yanking as I went onto my knees, as I moved to try to stand.

"You stupid fucking cunt!" he screamed, finally releasing my hair, but only because he needed his dominant hand to swing out and collide solidly with my jaw. The impact did two things at once. One, the pain spread out from the point of impact until the throbbing ache overtook the entire left side of my face. Two, it was enough to drop me to my knees.

And, well, my knees was somewhere I didn't want to be.

I knew this when his leg cocked back then kicked forward, hitting right above my navel and knocking out my air. I doubled over, gasping uselessly, taking in nothing but the taste of my own blood from the punch from before.

My hair was grabbed again, but closer to my scalp, pulling me back onto my feet.

At this point, I was done. My face was throbbing; my stomach was aching; my forearms and palms were burning and bleeding and I was just... done. He pulled and I went with him.

"I ought to slit your fucking throat for that you stupid cow," he roared as he pulled me across a lot. It was then I realized where he was taking me. Before me, a long, wide, windowless metal structure loomed at me, a perfect kind of irony. I wanted to know what was inside. I guess I would be figuring that out after all. "Maybe once the boss finds out what you got to say, I'll get the privilege of killing your ass. But not before making you wish you were dead first," he said, giving me a once over as we stopped outside the warehouse door.

I felt my stomach clench hard, knowing what he meant, knowing that he would take a sick amount of pleasure in beating and raping me before putting me out of my misery.

I swallowed hard, proud that my eyes were dry, knowing that while I was absolutely weaker than he was, that at least I wasn't looking that way.

"Is your chosen form of torture talking 'cause, let me tell you, I'd certainly take death over this."

D's fist banged on the metal door three times, the sound loud enough for me to shrink away from it. "You're going to regret this," he promised as the door pulled open, revealing the other guy from that night nine days ago. Trick. Paine had called him Trick and he was the one with more of a brain. I wondered if that worked for, or against, my favor.

"The fuck'd you do to her face?" he asked, looking down. "And her arms?"

"Bitch hit me with a fucking padlock. The fuck was I supposed to do, let her get away with it?"

Trick sighed heavily, like he'd hit his limit at having to put up with D's shenanigans. "I'll call the boss," Trick said, moving out of the way of the doorway so we could, presumably, enter. I was given very little choice because I was shoved forward with two hands to my back, making me trip over my own feet. I managed to stay upright somehow and Trick's hand reached out to steady me. "Ease up," he said over my shoulder toward D.

The smell hit me first. It wasn't something I could place, but it was chemical, unnatural. It made my nose burn to breathe it in. The air inside the warehouse was hot, stiflingly so. I felt sweat already start to bead up on my scalp as I heard the door slam behind me. My eyes quickly found the sources of the heat and humidity, locating long, low work tables in four rows down the center of the room. People stood almost shoulder-to-shoulder. Some were doing some sort of grinding, others stirring, but also some... cooking things. As in over fires. Small ones. With beakers over them. Like in science class.

No one even bothered to look our way despite the initial commotion. I guessed they were either too focused, too scared, or too used to such things to bother. Or maybe a combination of all three.

"Stick her over there," D said, waving a dismissive hand toward a small closed off space in the corner, like an office, except the walls didn't go all the way to the impossibly high ceiling.

"Come on," Trick said, his voice going low. "Better not to piss him off. The boss won't do the talking with fists and boots. You're better off laying low until the check in."

"Check in?" I found myself asking, immediately cursing myself for being nosy and cringing at the pain even the slightest bit of talking did to my, I imagined, hideously bruised jaw.

"Check in," he agreed, not dumb enough to elaborate as he opened the office door and ushered me inside. "You got about... two hours," he said, looking over the room quickly before moving back toward the door. "Sit tight." With that, he closed and locked the door.

For a long second, the panic swelled up to epic proportions. I felt like I was choking on it. It made my skin feel like it was crawling, like bugs were going to burst from the hair follicles covering my body. It made my mind race and my breath hitch.

There was some kind of slamming outside the door that made me jump and somehow managed to fight back the swirling thoughts so I could think clearly.

Panic wasn't going to help me.

I needed to think.

I needed to...

"Idiot," I hissed at myself, reaching into my back pocket and grabbing my cell. I was so nervous that my hands fumbled and screwed up my password twice before I took a deep breath and tried again. My screen unlocked and flashed bright and beautiful, like a lighthouse beacon to a lost ship. That was until I looked at my service bar and saw a big, ugly X over it.

My brows drew together, confused. I'd never seen an X over my service. I had service every-freaking-where. I was once in a field full of wind fans in the middle of bumbfuck Montana and had all my bars. It was never simply... gone. Not willing to accept the X, I clicked off of the now-blank Facebook page, and hit my number pad, typing in 9-1-1, hitting send, and bringing the phone up to my ear. I waited. I pulled the phone down when I heard no ringing, saw that it was doing the dot-dot-dot thing, trying to connect, brought it back up to my ear and waited some more. I hung up. I dialed again. I waited again.

But it was no use. There was nothing.

Maybe the Third Street guys had one of those signal-blocking things.

On a sigh, I slipped it back into my pocket and crept across the room, taking it in fully for the first time.

No windows, obviously, and just the one door. There was nothing on the bare Sheetrock walls. In the center of the room was a cheap Ikea-looking black desk and ergonomic desk chair. On the surface was a blank memo pad and two pens. I grabbed the pens and stuck them in my pockets, knowing it wasn't much, but it was something. As much as my stomach turned over at the idea of stabbing something like that into someone's eye, well, if it would save me from rape and death... I was willing to steel my stomach and do what needed to be done.

I took deep, slow breaths as I moved methodically over every inch of the small space, looking for any point of escape (there were none) or anything I could use to defend myself (aside from the pens, all I found was a heavy rock that I guessed someone used to prop the door open).

It wasn't much.

It certainly wasn't a metal, bone crushing padlock.

But it was something.

It was all that I had.

With nothing else to do, I sat down on the office chair, tried my best to ignore the pain that was overtaking my entire body, and tried to ready myself for anything.

SIXTEEN

Paine

I'd like to say I knew something was wrong, that I had a gut feeling, that I had some kind of fucking sixth sense that told me my girl wasn't okay. Sure, I'd love to claim that. But it wasn't true. I wasn't some superhero and I wasn't psychic.

So at eight when Elsie still hadn't showed up, I expected she had stayed a little longer at the gym, doing a guilt workout to work off the whole container of Chinese food she had devoured in one sitting. When eight-thirty rolled around and I was sitting in her kitchen next to the dinner spread of a giant salad, baked rosemary chicken, and side of green beans I had made, mindful of the fact that we both liked to keep our bodies in shape and to do that, you had to feed them right at least sixty-percent of the time, and she still hadn't showed up, I started to worry.

When another twenty minutes ticked and she still hadn't pulled up, I grabbed my keys and I headed over to Willow to check the gym. At first, I spotted her blue Porsche and felt my stomach muscles unclench, my hands relax their death grip on the steering wheel. She was just staying extra late at the gym. Hell, maybe she ran into a girlfriend and got to gabbing. But as I did a quick K-turn, ready to go and wait at her place so I didn't show up and look like some possessive prick, I spotted something that made me put the brake to the floor while pushing my car into park and running out of it. There were keys on the sidewalk.

This is where the gut feeling finally did kick in.

Sure, they could have been anyone's keys.

There were dozens of cars in the lot, any one of the owners could have carelessly dropped their keys on their way into the gym, shuffling to get their shit into their gym bags or whatever.

But that wasn't the feeling I was getting.

The feeling I was getting was that they were Elsie's and that something was wrong.

When I got to them, snatched them up, and saw the dozen or so keys she kept on a chain along with the Porsche key fob and the red Stanford "S" Roman had given her as a key chain, the stomach clenching came back, intensifying to the point of a sharp pain.

I turned and ran toward the gym, barely in the door before I started barking at the girl at the front desk. "I need your camera feed for the parking lot. Now," I growled when all she did was look at me with drawn-together brows. "Fucking now, babe. I don't have time to..."

"Paine, what the fuck?" Shane Mallick's voice called, walking up, shirt wet with sweat like he had overheard the yelling while doing a workout.

"I think Elsie was taken from your parking lot. I need your camera feed. Now."

"Taken?" he repeated, needing clarification.

"Third Street," I said through clenched teeth and his face fell as he turned toward the computers behind the desk, shouldering the girl gently out of the way and clicking through a few screens before finding the feed. I moved behind the desk uninvited and stood to his side, watching as he used a little ball to rewind the footage. People came and went. A couple made out against their car. A guy picked a wedgie. A girl wobbled on her heels, looking around frantically to make sure no one saw her.

Then there it was.

I wasn't sure it was her at first, just a blur of motion as a person disappeared inside a trunk, but as Shane slowed the feed and it kept moving backward, Elsie's limp body came back out of the trunk, came to life, then she wasn't being held in a successful rear naked choke, she was being pulled across the lot, flailing, gagged.

By. Fucking. D.

"Lost her," Shane said when they went out of camera range. "Hold up," he said, switching to a different camera and rewinding. Then there they were again. She hadn't been paying attention and she ran right into him.

Fuck.

"Shit," Shane cursed, standing, reaching for a phone.

"Cops?"

"They can put out a call to look for her. But they won't find her," I said, clenching my hands up. "Call Sawyer."

"Sawyer Anderson?"

"Yeah. He was working a case for her. Call him, tell him what happened. Get him on it," I said as I moved out from behind the desk and went toward the door.

"Where you going?" Shane called.

"Family fucking reunion," I growled, swinging open the door and running across the lot toward my still-open and still-running car. I threw myself inside and put it into drive, simultaneously peeling out of the lot and reaching into the glove for my gun.

Seemed like the only time I ever saw my brother anymore was when I had a gun on him.

Enzo generally occupied the old apartment I used to when I ran things. But he also had an apartment on the very outskirts of the slums, still technically on the streets he ran, but safer and more expensive. It was like a part of Enzo was constantly at conflict between his old life before and the one he chose to live in after, like he couldn't give up the money and power of running the streets, but also didn't really want to be associated with that 'low life' behavior his mother raised him to detest.

As I parked on the street, slipping the gun into my waistband and pulling down my shirt to cover it, I wondered if that was something he struggled with- what Annie would think of the man he'd become.

Knowing Enzo, it fucking haunted him.

I pushed those thoughts and the tug of connection away as I moved in the front doors of the red brick building that had a super that actually cared enough to keep things relatively up-kept though there was no automatic lock on the front door. I went inside and took the elevator up to the top floor and moved toward the far end of the hall near the exit staircase.

Enzo wasn't the door locking kind of guy so I reached for the knob while taking my gun back out.

The inside of his place was neat, orderly, almost obsessively so. Maybe like a part of him rebelled against the filthiness of his lifestyle and overcompensated with chronic housekeeping. All his furniture was sleek and modern, a style that made my lip curl. I liked a home to look like a home, like a place you could sink into and feel comfortable. I figured it was just another way to make his place look all the more orderly.

The living and kitchen space was empty and I moved down the hall toward the master bedroom. The bed was made, tucked down in full-on military fashion. Just when I was turning in the direction of the bathroom door, it opened.

Enzo froze, back illuminated by the harsh fluorescent light in the small tile room. But as he took a step out and his face wasn't in shadow, I felt my raised gun fall a few inches.

This was because Enzo, just as big and built and unbreakable-looking as me, had been worked over. Meaning his face was busted: lip swollen and broken open, one eye swollen almost shut, the other bruised with small steri-strips holding a large gash closed. And if the way he was leaning toward his side and bulkiness under his shirt was any indication, he'd bruised or busted a rib or two as well.

"The fuck?" I heard myself ask, not sure I'd ever seen anyone get the drop on him, let alone keep him down long enough to do that kind of damage. It looked like he'd been jumped. It looked like...

"Yeah," Enzo said, nodding slightly like he knew what I had been thinking.

"You got a beat-out?" I asked, brows drawing together. First, because as long as I had been affiliated with the gang, the only way out was death or disappearance. Second, because shot-callers simply didn't get beat-out. That wasn't how it worked.

"What the fuck are you doing here with a gun on me again?" he asked, moving into the room and lowering himself down onto the foot of the bed, wincing hard as the movement, I imagined, sent a stabbing through his ribcage.

"Elsie," I growled, lowering the gun, but keeping it at my side. Looking like he looked, moving like he moved, I seriously doubted he could get across the room toward me before I could get the gun raised again if need be.

"Elsie?" he repeated, shaking his head like the name didn't ring a bell.

"My. Fucking. Woman," I seethed, not having the time or patience for the runaround.

To that, Enzo's battered face twisted up into what would be considered a smirk. "Woman? You got a woman? As in... one you do more than just fuck? You?"

"Don't have time for this, Enz," I said, shaking my head. "About a week and a half ago, she was being chased down the street by D and Trick. About an hour ago, she was leaving the gym and ran into D again. He choked her out and threw her in his trunk. Now I need to know what the fuck is going on. You got beat-out, that sucks for you. But that shit is fresh so you were still in control of things nine days ago when they pulled the chasing stunt. So I want to know what the fuck is going on."

Enzo held a hand out, shaking his head. "Didn't know shit about that. You can come in here, testosterone stinking up the joint, but that don't change the fact that my men have been working with someone else under my nose for a long while now, slowly stealing their loyalty and my power."

"Then why the fuck are you beat-out and not lying in an alley somewhere?"

"Whoever this new guy is, Paine, he ain't Third Street. He doesn't know how we work. Seems like he don't care to either. He have their own agenda. Fuck if I know what that is seeing as I seemed to be the only one out of the loop over there."

"You have no idea why he'd want Elsie? I know she was sniffing around your warehouse but..."

"We don't have a warehouse," Enzo cut me off.

"The one on Kennedy," I elaborated.

"The fuck could we use a warehouse for, bro? We deal smack and sell women. Ain't like we needed manufacturing or to hold stock."

"She was chased from that warehouse to my shop by Trick and D. So whoever this new guy is, he's got a warehouse on Kennedy for something. And if..." I trailed off as my phone vibrated in my pocket. I reached for it with my free hand, seeing an unknown number and swiping to answer. "Paine," I barked, too impatient to deal with some bullshit wrong number, but knowing I needed to answer because if there was even a slight chance that it was Elsie, I'd never forgive myself for missing it.

"It's Sawyer," he said in my ear, sounding calm, dangerously so.

"Shane call you?"

"Yeah, but I got a call from Barrett first."

"Barrett?"

"Try as I might, couldn't keep his ass off the case once he got released. He's crashing on my couch with his laptop. Anyway, he must be keeping tabs on Elsie because he said she dropped a pin."

"She dropped a pin?" I asked, that meaning absolutely nothing to me.

"On Facebook. He said she used to do it all the time anytime she went out with friends. To check in or whatever. Until he told her to stop because that was just asking for a stalker. Anyway, she dropped a pin and he called because she dropped it in Third Street territory. Somewhere on Hoover. She pinned it at Barky's, but there's no way she's at a vape shop, let alone advertising that she's at a vape shop. But Barkey's is about a block over from..."

"The warehouse on Kennedy," I finished for him.

"You seen the place?" Sawyer asked and I could hear a little tension there. "It's massive. No fucking telling how many men could be in there. I got me and two of my men..."

"I can get Breaker and Shooter but that's about it..."

"Better than nothing. Call them. Meet me by Barky's in twenty."

He disconnected and I called Breaker to fill him in. He would call Shoot. They would meet me at Barky's. Then the six of us would go in and pray like fuck the warehouse wasn't full of the entire God damn Third Street gang.

"Yo," Enzo called as I made my way out his bedroom door. I turned back with a raised brow. "Under the sink in the kitchen. Both are loaded."

I nodded tightly. "Thanks."

With that, I went into the kitchen, grabbed the guns, and tore out of the apartment building, trying not to consider what it meant that Enzo was helping me, that he was out of the gang, that he was not my enemy anymore. That was shit I would think about when I got my eyes and hands on Elsie again, when I knew she was alright.

D was a wild card.

When I ran things, I was constantly having to keep an eye on him, make sure he wasn't getting some asinine idea into his head and running with it. He was violent and dumb which, as anyone with half a brain would know, was a really bad combination. He hadn't really hurt her in the video at the gym. True, he'd dragged her. And, yeah, he'd choked her out. But he hadn't beat her. He looked like he was focused on just bringing the mouse home to his master. Which was good. If she didn't piss him off, she would be alright.

She'd been smart. She'd used the phone to drop a pin, hoping or knowing that Barrett was keeping an eye on her. She was hoping for a rescue. I hoped that meant she knew not to try to fight her way out. There was no way to fight out. Especially not for someone untrained and nowhere near as strong as the men who she would be around.

I pulled up, parking behind Sawyer's massive SUV, walking up to the three men standing there: Sawyer, his giant wall of muscle named Tig, and Sawyer's other guy, a tall, thin, but strong guy around my age with buzz-cut blond hair, sharp features, and brown eyes. Judging by the wide-legged stance with his hands clasped behind his back, he screamed ex-military.

"Brock found the car," Sawyer said as soon as I joined them. "Over about half a block in a lot. She'd kicked out the taillight. He found her gym bag in there, but her phone was gone so she lost it, got it taken from her, or, hopefully, still has it on her."

"Anything else?"

Tig and Brock shared a look that immediately made me straighten. Whatever 'else' there was, it wasn't good.

Luckily for me, Sawyer wasn't the kind of man to sugarcoat anything. He turned to me and gave it to me straight, no chaser, no garnish. "Brock found her gym lock. She must have used it to hit D," he said and I felt my stomach start to churn. So much for hoping she wouldn't piss him off. D had a short trigger. You looked at him wrong, he was zero-to-a hundred in a second flat. You came at him with a fucking padlock? Fuck.

"Say it," I demanded through gritted teeth.

"Blood and a fair amount of it on the pavement. He said it looks like some of it was from falling and skidding and that some looks spit out."

"Drag marks?"

"No. When he took her, he either carried her or she decided to just go with him to save herself any more abuse."

Shoot's ridiculously expensive car rolled up behind mine and he was out of it before any of us could draw breath. "Break will be here in two, three if he decides to stop at any of the red lights. So... two," he said, nodding at the guys.

"Warehouse on Kennedy. She went at D with a padlock. She paid for it," I supplied, barely able to get that short retelling of events out with the fire churning in my stomach.

"And you'll make him pay for whatever he did to her," Shoot said with a look that said he understood. When someone fucked with Amelia, he'd made the entire fucking side of the man's head explode with a bullet. You didn't fuck with what was ours. At least not without expecting to pay for it with your life.

Breaker's SUV pulled up and he rambled up toward us, all long-legs and coiled muscles, ready for a fight. If it weren't for my rage making me hum like a God-damn psychopath, he would be the most formidable one in our group. Shooter was a bit on the thin side, wiry, great with a gun, but with a gallows type of humor in every situation, making you underestimate his skills. Sawyer and Brock had a calmness about them that spoke of inhuman self-control. Tig was huge, but he had a bit of a gut, making anyone who didn't know him think he would get winded in a fight. But Breaker, Breaker spent a lot of fucking time keeping himself in shape, never knowing who he would be paid to lay the hurt on and what shape they might be in. He was big, bulky, and lethal with a mix of control and rage that made anyone shrink away from him when he was on a job.

He was on a job.

And this was personal to him because it was personal to me.

And that made him all the more dangerous.

Shoot filled him in and we compared notes.

"I don't know how fucking long you plan on watching this place when who-knows what is happening to her in there," I growled as we stood beside a building to the left of the warehouse, watching the door.

We'd been there fifteen or twenty minutes already just fucking waiting and watching.

All we'd seen was D walk out for a smoke then go back in.

I took a bit of comfort in the nasty fucking bruise he had on his cheek.

If she hit him, at least she managed to do some damage.

"Quiet," Sawyer barked, pointing toward the building.

When I looked again, there was a new car parked out front. It was late model and expensive. The driver and passenger doors opened and two people stepped out. One, I recognized as one of Enzo's former higher-ups, the guy who he would bring with him to go pick up the shipments of H when it came in.

And the other person...

"No fucking way," I hissed.

SEVENTEEN

Elsie

The door opened and closed four times when I was in the office, the sound reverberating around all the metal walls. I flinched every time, my shoulders going up toward my ears, my heart starting to hammer in my chest. The first two times, nothing happened. Someone must have just went outside and then came back in. The second and third times, there was an automatic hush to all babble outside the office and I figured that meant that the boss was there.

A few minutes later, the door opened and I froze. But it was only Trick. "Come on," he said, sounding suddenly tired.

Pretty sure I had no choice, I slowly got up and moved toward him, stepping into the doorway and following where he was taking me which seemed to be toward the group of three people standing in a circle. One was D. Another was some guy I didn't recognize. The third was...

"No," I hissed, stopping mid stride and drawing the full attention from the trio.

I wasn't absolutely positive at first.

But then the second that they all fully turned toward me, oh yeah, I was sure.

Freaking positive actually.

"Elana?" I asked, my voice a strange, raspy sound.

Her hair was different. It had been long and blond when I had last seen her and now it was cut in a long bob, brushing her shoulders, and dyed a deep, rich brown which only made the gray eyes she'd inherited from our father pop all the more. She had on plain black slacks, spiky heels, and a tight gray sweater that stretched over her, admittedly much larger than mine, boobs. I hated to admit it because, Lord knew, if she was in the Third Street gang's warehouse on Kennedy then she was not in a good place mentally, but she looked good. She was standing straighter, her eyes looked clear, her hair cut and color really suited her. She looked like the best version of herself.

"Elsie?" she gasped and I figured she had no idea I was there. She turned back toward D so fast that she actually blurred to my eyes. "What the fuck happened to her?" she demanded with so much viciousness that D actually went back a step. Hell, I even felt myself straightening and she wasn't talking to, or looking at, me.

It was right then though, watching D flinch away in fear, that I understood.

Elsie wasn't there because she was looking for some heroin.

She wasn't even there because she was being extorted.

She hadn't fallen in love with one of the men in Third Street.

No.

Elana was their boss.

Elana had somehow replaced Enzo.

She was in charge.

She was in charge of a street gang.

My sister.

"Elana, what are you doing here?" I whispered as she took another step toward D, shoving her hand into his chest hard.

"That's my goddamn sister you brainless piece of shit!" she yelled and all eyes in the warehouse moved between us, I guess comparing us. Normally, before she changed her hair, there was an unmistakable resemblance. But now she had dark hair and gray eyes and I had blond hair and blue eyes. If you weren't looking for a similarity in our bone structure, it was easy to miss.

"I didn't know, E. I didn't fucking know!" D yelled back, but it was in actual fear, not anger. And I was left wondering what the hell she could have possibly done to make brainless, violent brutes actually fear her. A woman. A woman who grew up privileged who didn't raise a hand to someone because it would ruin her very expensive manicure. "She was snooping around the warehouse last week. I chased her, but I lost her and then I came across her tonight. I figured you'd want to know why she was snooping around."

"Oh, gee, I imagine she was looking for me. And in what universe does bringing her here for questioning involve fucking up her face and knocking her on the ground?"

"She hit me in the face with a gym lock!" he defended.

"Wow. Wonder why? Maybe because you kidnapped her? Maybe that's why she would hit you. Idiot. I'll deal with you later. Go help unload the truck," she demanded, waving a dismissive hand at him. It was the first thing she had done since she walked in that seemed like my sister. She was always doing the dismissive hand wave whenever she was done talking to someone she deemed too idiotic to entertain or when she trailed off while telling a story.

She turned back toward me, the anger draining from her face as she gave me what I would consider an apologetic smile. "Else..." she said in the old, familiar way she used to. But it was coming from the lips of a stranger.

True, I was glad she was alive.

203

But she was alive and she wasn't in a too-drugged-out state to pick up a phone and tell me she was alive. She was walking, talking, and ordering around gang members while still in town, while easily able to reach out and let me know she was okay.

So I was glad she was alive, I was also almost unreasonably pissed.

"Do you have any idea how worried I've been about you? You just up and disappear with no note, no call, no nothing, leaving your bird to starve in his cage and having me hire private investigators and get chased down the road by thugs!" I shrieked, only stopping when I realized one of said thugs was still standing beside me.

"Okay," Elana said, holding out her arms wide in a welcoming gesture. "Come on, let's go talk in the office..." she suggested.

But then the door opened, the sound making me cringe and my head snap over to see who was coming in. I relaxed slightly when I saw it was just D and two other guys carrying big cardboard boxes. They piled them on a table behind Elana as she slowly moved toward me, head tilted, like something about me was confusing her.

My attention went back to D as he reached inside the box and pulled out a plastic wrapped pile of smaller white and green boxes. I felt my stomach muscles clench. SinuEase was written clearly across the front. And I knew that name. I knew that name. And I knew that it was produced by Matthewson Pharmaceuticals. Matthewson. As in Rhett and Roman Matthewson. As in my best friend and his father.

My entire body went rigid, fire flooding my veins.

"You bitch!" I screamed as she got close enough, slamming my cut open wrists into her shoulders.

She stumbled back a step as I hissed in pain. Elana seemed more intrigued than angry. "Did you just call me a bitch?" she asked, almost sounding amused.

Alright, so we were sisters. And, well, we'd thrown the b-word around a few times when we got into fights over the years, but mainly in our adolescence when we were too immature to remember to filter ourselves.

"You stole from Roman!"

"Calm down, Else. It's not like I'm hurting his bottom line. They're insured to the hilt. They won't even miss this stuff."

"They're missing it. They're missing it and suffering a PR nightmare because of it. That stuff is heavily regulated because people use it to make..." I trailed off, my head snapping to our sides where all the people were pretending to not listen while they worked.

And what they were working on?

Yeah, they were cooking meth.

Meth.

That was why cold medicine was regulated and watched so closely, because it was the main ingredient in making meth.

"Are you fucking serious?" I asked, my voice low, as I looked back at my sister.

"Else..." she tried in her big-sister soothing voice.

"Don't Else me. You're working with a street gang and stealing from a mutual friend so you can cook meth? You have a trust fund! You don't need to..."

"Office," she barked at Trick who reached for my arm, holding it tight, and pulling me back toward the office. I struggled at first, but there was no use. By the time he pushed me inside and Elana followed in, I had stopped trying to get away. Trick left, closing the door behind him and Elana leaned against it, crossing her arms.

She watched me for a long minute. "I needed to get out."

"Out?" I repeated.

"Yeah, out. I was so over all of it."

"All of what, El?"

"Everything. Dad, the money, the cocky rich guys, the job I hated, the house that came with strings, all of it. That entire life."

"You could have just... walked away at any time, Elana. No one was forcing you to live in that house or drive that car or work that job or date those pricks. Those were choices you made."

"Choices," she laughed, shaking her head. "God, are you still that naive?"

"I'm not naive," I bristled. Sometimes, not often, but sometimes, I saw a bit of our father in her. It was in the condescension in her tone, in the way she made little, expertly placed jabs, knowing just where to poke to cause the most damage. In spending her life rebelling against him, she couldn't see that she had inherited some of his worst traits.

"Do you really think you have any independence? Why aren't you living in that small, unpretentious townhouse you really wanted? Why are you working in energy? Why do you still go to that ridiculous family dinner every Sunday?"

She had good points, she really did.

"I don't go to dinner anymore. Dad and I had a blowup. About you actually."

"About me?" she asked, and I could hear the neediness in her voice and wondered if she heard it herself. She wanted, she needed to know what our father thought or said about her.

"Yeah because I was mad that he wasn't looking for you and he called it a non-issue," I said and my voice was a little bitter as I dropped the last part, knowing it would hurt her.

Her lips tipped up but there was a deadness in her eyes at my words. "What did he have to say about the trust?"

"That you probably just emptied it and took off with some guy."

"He always had such a high opinion of me."

"Yeah and way to lower yourself to his expectations."

"Ouch, sis," she said, shaking her head. "You've never been so nasty before."

"Well I never had a drug dealing selfish brat for a sister before either. What is this? You want to stick it to Dad by what? Creating a criminal empire?"

"Could you imagine the look on his face when he found out?" she asked, smiling at the idea. "He would blow a gasket."

"Seriously? This is all because you want to piss off your father?"

"This is all because I'd never get free of him if I didn't make my own life! All the dinner parties and the charity events and the way he kept trying to make me get together with his business partners and..."

"Oh, please," I groaned, rolling my eyes. "He had no plans on trying to force you to marry anyone."

"Seriously?" she asked, laughing a little cruelly. "You really think he sees us as anything other than chess pieces he can manipulate across a board until he gets a checkmate. Grow up, Elsie."

"He never tried to set me up with anyone."

"He never had to!"

"What are you talking about?"

"Come on, there's naive and then there's plain dumb," she snapped and before I could open my mouth to object, she went on. "He didn't need to set you up with anyone because you already did that for yourself."

"I never seriously dated anyone he approved of."

"No, you didn't," she said with a smile. "But you were awfully cozy with Roman Matthewson weren't you?"

"Dad never wanted me hanging around with Rome!"

To that, I got another eye roll. "Reverse psychology, much? Dad's a pro at that stuff, Else. He knew that the more he objected, the more you would rebel and get close to him. He's been waiting about a decade for Rome to get his head out of his ass and make a move already."

I felt my stomach twist at that as well as the likely truth behind it.

"Too late now," I heard myself mumble.

"Too late?" she prompted and for a second, she was only my sister.

"I'm seeing someone. Roman knows and he wasn't happy. He's giving up on me. At least in that way," I admitted, taking a deep breath, the pain of hurting the person I cared about probably the most causing a sympathetic agony inside me.

"Stock broker? Lawyer?" she was teasing me, but there was a hint of malice there too. I had dated mostly professionals in the past. It was what I knew. It was what was familiar. I never thought there was anything wrong or close-minded or ridiculous about it.

"Tattoo artist," I corrected with a chin lift.

"Look at you, still doing your little rebellions," she mocked.

"Oh for God's sake. Not everything is about Dad. I met a man. We hit it off. Dad was never a factor."

"He's always a factor. Every time I went on vacation, he had something to say. Every time I went to a charity event with a man he didn't like, he made his feelings known. Every time I went to buy a new car, he had to bitch about the one I chose..."

And that was about all I could take of her woe-is-me-ing.

"Oh, poor little rich girl," I hissed. "I feel so bad for you that you got some flack when you bought a car worth six figures and you got some lip about it. And it must really suck to travel the world and go to swanky charity balls and date handsome, successful men. I feel so bad for you."

"Don't you dare go..."

"No. Don't you dare go trying to convince me that this little stunt of yours is anything other than the actions of a privileged, entitled, spoiled little girl. You wanted to stick it to Dad and be free... you'd have left every cent of that trust, let the bank have your house, the dealer have your car, and you'd take off to some new city and bust your ass building a new career and a new life free of him. That is how you stick it to him. This," I said, waving out one of my damaged hands, the blood crusty and filled with dirt, "this is just a little girl begging for Daddy's attention."

"I never wanted his..."

"You always wanted his attention. You wanted his attention and approval and it ate at you that you never got it. So what did you do? You looked for that attention and approval in the revolving door of men in and out of your life."

"Shut up!" she yelled, advancing toward me. It should have been scary and maybe, in a small part of my brain, it was. But while she might have been some criminal and drug dealer and God-knew what else, she was also my sister. It was hard to be truly terrified of someone you once watched throw up two bushels-worth of cotton candy when she got off a roller coaster and sing into her hairbrush while belting out Beyonce. There was just no way I was going to shrink away from the person I had shared my entire childhood and adolescence with.

"What are you going to do if I don't?" I challenged. "Hit me? Send D in here to rape and kill me like he was hoping you would let him do?"

She froze mid-stride, jerking backward like my words landed with impact. Her pretty features twisted up in a mix of shock and disgust. "Jesus... no," she said, her voice small. "God. Do you really think I'd let him do that to you?"

"Well I never thought you'd become a thief or drug dealer either," I said with a shrug.

"There's a big difference between what I choose to do with my professional life and what I do with my personal life."

I fought a snort I felt building when she said 'professional life'. "What personal life, El? You left me. You left all of us, let us worry sick about you, create God-awful worst-case scenarios in our heads."

"I was going to call and explain..."

"When? When we could legally declare you dead and bury an empty casket? When El? Because it's been weeks."

"I've been a little busy, Else!" she yelled, swinging away from me. "Do you have any idea what it took to do what I did?"

Still seeing no real way of getting out of my situation, I figured gathering more information was at least productive. "No, what?" I asked, sounding only mildly interested.

She took the bait. Of course she did.

"Do you have any idea how un-trusting a street gang is? How violent? And not to mention, unwilling to take orders from a woman. Luckily for me, they've been having some issues locking down a reliable heroin supplier. It was making the dealers antsy, worried about their income. It was easy to get some of the small timers with the promise of a truckload of cold medicine to make meth and create a new, steady source of money. Once I got them, got them working, got them some cash in their pockets... fake at first, just money from my trust because I didn't have any product on the streets yet like I told them I did, they started talking to the more important guys. They got on board. Then pretty soon, I had everyone but Enzo on my side."

"Enzo?" I repeated, my voice a little breathless. Because I found I was worried about him. Because no matter how Paine tried to play down the bond between them, I knew it would crush him if anything happened to his half-brother.

She rolled her eyes and waved a hand. "Former Third Street leader."

"Former?" I asked, feeling every muscle in my body tense.

God.

Could she have had him killed?

Was she really capable of that kind of awfulness?

"Yeah. I mean what kind of shot-caller lets someone sneak up under him and steal his business like that?"

"Shot caller?" I repeated.

Her lips tipped up a little. "I always knew my obsession with Gangland would come in handy one day," she mused and I almost smiled, almost. Because I remembered her talking my ear off about all the biker gangs and street gangs and stuff she used to watch on that show. I guess she wasn't watching it for the dark, gritty entertainment way it was intended, but as an educational device. "Anyway. He's out of the way now and I have this whole operation under my control."

"You like the power," I said, shaking my head a little.

"Everyone likes power. Everyone."

"That's not true," I objected. I liked control over my life, but I didn't want power. I didn't strive to claw my way up the corporate ladder and get a corner office position. I was happy being in the middle. I worked hard; I made a good living. I didn't need more than that.

"Oh please. You wouldn't have busted your ass as hard as you did in school and college if you didn't want a position of power in your future."

"I busted my ass in school because it was Mom's dying wish that I never be dependent on a man. I did it to have a comfortable, independent life. I didn't do it so I could harp on endlessly about how many people I have power over."

"So you think you're somehow... better than me?" she asked, eyes going a little dark.

"I think I didn't build my life around my father's approval when I claim to hate him so much. Christ, El, do you not see it? You're just like him now..."

The sound of the smack echoed up and into the metal room above and around us, the quick sting of pain smarting across my un-bruised cheek. Now, again, we were sisters. As such, I'd felt her smack more than once in my life, no matter how well we generally got along. One time it was over something as stupid as me borrowing her hairbrush and not cleaning my hair out of it afterward. Her anger had a quick trigger. But it burned hot and fast and was gone.

"The truth hurts, El," I said with a shrug as she dropped her hand to her side and balled it into a fist.

"I'm not like him."

"You know, you're right. No matter how pissed Dad has gotten with me, and he's gotten pretty pissed..." Like when I refused to go to his alma mater after he made a call to the dean to square away a donation and ensure my place. Or when I once took my spring break senior year in high school to 'rough it' by staying in a hostel in Amsterdam instead of taking him up on his offer for a lavish French Riviera vacation. "He never put a hand on me."

"It's different," she snapped and I could see the tiniest trace of guilt.

"You're right. Because the only people who can manage power right, El, are the ones who can control themselves. This," I said, waving a hand out, "is going to blow up on you one day. You think you can just haul off and hit one of these... these... gang members and they won't do anything? They obviously have no problem hitting women," I said, gesturing toward my face.

Was she really that dumb? I mean, my sister was smart. She had always done well in school, at work. She was knowledgeable. But, at the same time, she was always rash and impulsive, never stopping to truly analyze things. It was one thing when what she was rushing into was an ill-advised affair with a married English aristocrat who was only in town for two weeks. It was a whole other to decide all willy-nilly to become a drug kingpin. I mean... what could have been going through her head?

A slow, almost evil smile spread across her face. "Oh, they'd never put a hand on me, Else."

She sounded so sure that I felt a cold creeping across my skin, making goosebumps form on every inch, making a sliver of ice slide into my heart. "How can you be so sure of that? It's not like you have some reputation of being..."

"There's a lot you don't know about me, Else. I haven't been the sister you've thought in a really, really long time. You were just too clueless to see it."

The door to the warehouse opened, making me flinch.

But then there was commotion.

And not the good kind.

Elana tensed as the door flew open and Trick came in wide-eyed. "Trouble," he barked at her, reaching in his pocket and pulling out a gun. A gun. I mean I knew they were gang members, but still, it was one thing to know it, it was a complete other to see evidence of it.

"How many?"

"Six," Trick said as he moved back out.

Then something happened that, even if I had a lifetime to consider the possibility of, I never would have been able to come up with. My sister swung around and in a blur, she was no longer in front of me, but behind me. Her arm locked around my center. Now, we were both about the same height, but she had the slight advantage of heels, making her head several inches higher than mine. The arm that wasn't around my stomach, pressing into the spot where D had kicked me and sending a wave of pain through me that made me seriously worry I was going to throw up, went behind her for a second. When it came back, I saw the flash of silver. Then I felt something cold, round, and metal press into my temple.

I didn't have to see it to know what it was.

A gun.

My sister was holding a gun to my temple.

"El..." I heard my voice gasp and plead at the same time.

"Shut the fuck up," she hissed, pushing me forward. "Walk," she growled when I tried to plant my feet. And, well, I was too freaked, too shocked, and too scared to do anything but what I was told. I had been able to stand my ground and argue with her because, in my mind, she was just my sister. She was my sister who was playing a really stupid real life game of cops and robbers. That was all it was. She was still the girl who used to get my hair into wicked knots when she tried to braid it when we were in elementary school. She was the one who cried her eyes out with me when we went to see Les Mis on Broadway when we were teens. She was the woman who got so tequila-drunk at my housewarming party that she started taking all her clothes off. She'd been reaching for the strap of her bra when

213

Rome rushed up, cocooned her in my throw blanket off my couch as she bitched that she was too hot for clothes.

She was my sister.

I could argue with her.

Because she would never hurt me.

But all ideas of sisterhood and family loyalty went right the hell out the door when you suddenly found yourself at gunpoint by someone you thought you knew every nook and cranny of.

There were yells from the main room and I felt my body go ramrod straight as I was pushed out into the commotion. Because I realized another thing: I was being held at gunpoint, but I was also being used as a human shield.

All the action that had been going on at the tables had stopped. The people who had been working there were all cowering under the tables and I realized that, maybe, they hadn't all been gang members. Maybe they had just been like... workers.

In front of the tables were D, Trick, and three other men I didn't recognize all yelling, all with guns raised.

My eyes snapped toward the other side of the room and I felt two things at once: relief and bone-deep fear.

Because there was Paine, eyes locked on D and I saw the intention there, the desire to cause some serious damage and I knew, I knew that he somehow knew what happened to me. Fanned out around him was Shooter, who had a weird little amused smirk, Breaker, who had a coldness in his eyes that made me shiver involuntarily, Sawyer who looked almost... calm, Tig, the big guy who told me to ice my neck the night I was strangled, who seemed tense but unconcerned about the gang members yelling at them and aiming guns. There was one last man, someone who had the buzzcut look and stiff stance of someone in the military. He seemed calm like Sawyer. Suddenly I wondered if maybe they had both been military, if they had seen things much worse than a warehouse with a handful of gang members and that was why they were acting like what was happening was no big deal.

"Move," El hissed in my ear again, slamming her knee into the back of mine and making an involuntary cry escape me. At the sound, Paine's eyes flew in our direction. It wasn't easy to read him then. A muscle was ticking in his jaw which was a pretty universal sign of anger. There was a tension around his mouth that I took for anxiety. But his eyes, those light green eyes I wanted to get lost in, they looked downright horrified.

El kept pushing me along the side wall and I knew she was trying to make it around the group of my saviors and get toward the door. To hell with her men, I guess.

Paine pivoted with our motion, eyes following every step we took. I tried to convey a message with mine: I know this looks really bad, but I'm pretty sure she's not going to kill me.

As we closed in on the door, Elana jerked me hard, her arm crushing into my center and almost making me double over. If she wasn't holding me so tight, I would have. Her back was to the open space and she was walking both of us backward into it.

Until she collided into something that made me collide into her.

Unable to see anything, I looked to Paine's face for some kind of explanation. What I found there was uncertainty and surprise. Which, well, weren't exactly good things to see given the circumstances.

"I fucking dare you to move, bitch," a deep, smooth, threatening voice said. Whoever it was made my sister stiffen hard. Her hand holding the gun to my temple was shaking and I felt my stomach start to churn. If there was one thing you definitely didn't want, it was someone with a twitchy hand holding a gun to a part of you that would never survive a bullet wound.

"You won't shoot," Elana said in my ear, but she didn't sound as sure as I bet she wanted to. "You and your buddies aren't smart, but you aren't that stupid either. It'd be a suicide mission to open fire in a meth lab."

My eyes went again to the scene in front of me, everyone with guns raised, but no one who seemed all that willing to pull a trigger.

God.

I was an idiot.

Of course no one would shoot.

The reason there were task forces meant just for finding meth labs was because they were unstable. As in, they were known to blow up. All the time. Something as small as static electricity could send the already unstable materials a-blazing. Hell, meth lab explosions could decimate entire apartment complexes.

So, yeah, no one was going to shoot a gun, which was a small explosion itself, in a meth lab.

Everyone was at a standoff.

Except, apparently, whoever was behind my sister.

"Hey honey," he said, his voice still deep, but softer so I figured he was talking to me and not my sister. "Funny thing... know what is really hard to hold onto?" He asked, and I knew that whatever was to follow would be really important. "A completely limp body," he finished.

The second the words were out of his mouth and they registered, I let my legs buckle and the entire force of my weight pulled downward, making Elana's arm lose my middle and allowing me to slide completely to the floor.

I hit with an impact that shot into my stomach and I curled onto my side, sucking in a breath. I was vaguely aware of my sister yelping and I twisted my head over my shoulder to see her lifted off her feet and disappear out into the dark outside. But not before I got a look at the man who had saved me, who had threatened my sister, who had made Paine look both uncertain and surprised.

There was no mistaking it. It was in the matching caramel-colored skin tone. It was in the insane, chiseled bone

216

structure. It was in the height and width of their strong bodies. And, lastly, it was in the identical shade to their eyes.

Enzo.

Paine's half brother.

The only real difference between them, other than their voices, was the fact that Enzo's face was swollen and bruised like he had taken a very recent, very brutal beating.

It didn't really take much for me to realize that my sister was the one who had, in some way, made that happen to him.

I turned back and Paine's eyes were on mine for a second and I saw the split feelings there: the need to come to me, and the need to handle his business.

I waved a hand at him, hoping he took it to mean 'do what you need to do, I'm fine'.

The next second, his gun was tucked away, and he was flying, positively flying across the room toward D. Full force, his body slammed into D's, sending them both spiraling into the table behind D. Their impact landed with a slam and grunt from D as Paine pushed up, swung an arm back, and started hitting.

I watched for all of ten seconds, seeing his fist collide with D's face at least three times in that span, making a spray of blood fly up and spatter across his shirt and face.

That was about all I could take.

The rest of the men seemed to reach an understanding at that point, all of them tucking their guns away and realizing that this was not their fight. Shooter and Sawyer turned back to me and both started to move in my direction.

"I can't bend down, but I can pull you up," the deep, smooth voice of Enzo said behind me, making me visibly flinch as I rolled onto my back. He stood towering over me, one arm reaching downward, offering to help me up. Where was my sister? Had he actually taken her outside and... shot her? No. I hadn't heard a gunshot. So what... "She's gone. Told her ass to get the fuck out of Jersey 'cause if she don't, I'll find her. Come on, let's get you up, honey," he said, shaking his hand a little, encouraging me to take it. There was something about the way that he said honey that made me feel like maybe he wasn't quite so scary after all. I reached upward, forgetting about my raw hands and arms until he shrank away. "Fuck," he hissed, shaking his head.

"We got her," Shooter said as he and Sawyer moved down at my sides. "Always loved a good damsel in distress, darlin'," he said, reaching out and booping my nose before he slid a hand under my left shoulder. Sawyer did the same with my right (minus the booping, obviously) and then I was on my feet.

"Someone needs to stop him," I said, not bothering to look behind me, but hearing the unmistakable sounds of fighting still going on.

"Break will stop him when D's had enough," Shoot assured me.

"I think he's had enough."

"Babe," Sawyer said, shaking his head. "Look at you. Your face, arms, hands, and the way you're arching to your side, I'm guessing you got bruised or busted ribs too. He hasn't had enough yet."

I sighed, figuring I really had no say in the matter. "I'm fine. Really. A little soap and water, some triple antibiotic, and a couple ibuprofen and I'll be all better."

Okay. I felt like crap. I felt worse than crap. My stomach and side was screaming. Shock and anger wearing away, taking with it the adrenaline that kept me from feeling the searing sensation of road burn on my arms and the sting of the cuts that were caked in dirt and who-knew what else, it was really taking all that I had in me to not just fall into a puddle of tears on the floor. But I couldn't do that. Call it pride, but I had seven big, strong, fearless, badass men around me and I didn't want to fall into waterworks over a few boo-boos.

"Babe," Sawyer said, shaking his head like I was an idiot.

"She needs the hospital," Tig said, walking up. He reached out slowly, touching me under the chin to angle my head up. "I'd like to see you not-bruised sometime."

"That'd be nice," I agreed with a wry smile.

"I said enough!" Breaker's voice roared and all eyes turned to see Breaker wrangling a furious, rabid Paine off of a bloodied, mangled version of D. For a second, I was worried he'd beaten him to death, until I saw the telltale rise and fall of the unconscious man's chest and felt like I could finally take a breath of my own.

"Paine," I heard myself say. It wasn't loud, barely more than a whisper, but Paine's head snapped up toward me and all the tension drained from his body. Breaker, seeing he was no longer needed, released Paine who looked down at his hands almost... helplessly, like he couldn't believe what he had just done. There was a lot of blood. On his hands, his arms, his shirt, his face. I was fairly certain that not a drop of it was his.

"Get him cleaned up," Enzo called to, I assumed, Breaker. "We'll get her to the car." Trick and the remaining Third Street guys looked at Enzo who shook his head at them. "You're all fucking dead to me, traitors. Handle your own shit; see how long you last." With that, he turned out the door and disappeared.

When I turned back to Sawyer and Shoot, they both opened their arms. At my drawn-together brows, Shoot smiled disarmingly. "Pick one."

"Pick one for what?"

"To carry you, peaches, of course," he said and I felt myself smiling a little.

I looked between them, both having matching masks of masculine certainty that I was, for sure, going to pick them. It was almost as if they might have had some kind of bet on the outcome. I turned to Tig instead. "If you have an arm, I still have two legs," I said and he gave me a soft smile, putting an arm around my hips, low to avoid contact with any sore spots. I leaned into his side slightly and started walking, each step a tiny stab to my side and center and by the time we got into sight of the cars, I could feel the tears stinging at my eyes, begging to be released.

"Come on, honey," Enzo said, holding one of the car doors open. If I wasn't mistaken, I would put money on it being Shooter's car.

"No. I'm waiting for Paine," I objected, moving out of Tig's hold and wobbling over to lean against Paine's Challenger.

"The sooner we get you..." Sawyer started, but I cut him off.

"No. I can wait five more minutes."

"Babe..."

"Alright darlin'," Shoot said, moving to lean on the car beside me, looking off in the direction of the warehouse. "If there's anything I know about women, and I know a lot," he said with a devilish little smirk followed by what would normally be an absurd wink, but on Shoot it was charming and sexy. Oh, yeah, I bet he was quite the dog before Amelia leashed him in. "It's that there's no use arguing with you."

"Just 'yes' us to death and then do whatever the hell you wanted in the first place?" I mused.

"Eh, I think you've had enough kidnapping for the night. Though my trunk is rather spacious, you know."

I smiled, shaking my head, and turning back toward the warehouse. Out of a street on the side, I could see the outline of two giant men coming out of the shadows.

"Did he change?" I mused, meaning to only think it, but I had said it out loud.

Paine's eyes were on mine as they crossed the street, his white shirt replaced with a black one, his hands, arms, and face wiped clean of blood.

"Babygirl," he said as he got up close to me.

And, well, that was all it took.

I leaned forward, face-planting into his chest and letting out a really ugly, really pathetic-sounding sob. His arms closed around me slowly, gently, like I might break or crumble beneath his strength.

"Shh, baby," he murmured into the hair at the side of my head. "It's alright. I got you."

And, well, him being all sweet just made me cry harder.

After what was what I could only imagine an embarrassing amount of time later, I finally pulled it together, sniffling hard. I pulled back and Paine wiped my cheeks for me. "Got that out for now so we can go get you looked at?" he asked, the words at once sweet and a tiny bit teasing. Which I needed to stop the seemingly endless pool of tears inside me.

I nodded, pulling back. "Yeah."

I turned self-consciously back toward the group, giving them a small smile. "Thanks guys for ah... getting me out of there. You especially," I said, turning to Enzo who was looking the slightest bit uncomfortable.

"Darlin' anytime you need a knight in..." Shoot started, but was stopped when Breaker slapped him hard on the back of the neck with an eye roll.

"Go get all stitched up, doll. We'll all see you on Sunday," Breaker said, slapping Paine on the shoulder as he and Shoot moved to take off in their respective cars.

"Smart move with the pin, babe," Sawyer said as his men moved to their cars as well.

"I knew he was still looking into me."

"Good thing too," Sawyer agreed. "I'll check in with you after you're all pretty again," he said with a teasing smirk before swinging into his SUV and taking off.

"Enz," Paine said, his focus still on me, like he was afraid to look away. "You and me, we're having a talk. Soon."

"Yeah, man. I'm around."

"Come on, babygirl, get in the car," Paine urged, leading me to the passenger and helping me inside.

We drove to the hospital in absolute, ear-splitting silence.

And, of course, that gave my mind plenty of time to race and wonder and worry.

Why wasn't he talking to me?

Why wasn't he even looking at me when we stopped at the red lights?

Was this too much too soon for us?

Was it over?

Yeah, the little voice who narrated my worst fears, she was a pessimist by nature.

So by the time we parked outside the emergency room and Paine got out of the car, walking around the hood to open the door for me, yeah, that voice had pretty much convinced me that he was going to drop me, say he was going for coffee or something like that, and never come back.

"Elsie, come on."

I sighed hard, steeling myself for what I thought was the inevitable outcome, and got out of the car.

EIGHTEEN

Paine

"You need to fuckin' pull it together," Breaker
demanded as we watched the rest of the group move out, Tig's
giant tree-limb of an arm around Elsie as she hobbled out. She
was hurting. She was hurting and that fact made me want to
turn back around and rip mother fucking D's head clear off his
shoulders.

"Did you see her?" I demanded, fists clenching down at
my sides.

"Saw her. Saw my own woman with her face busted too
so I know how you're feeling. But she doesn't need you raging
out. She needs you to get your shit together, clean up, and take
care of her. She ain't from this life. She's gonna be a mess when
the adrenaline wears off and everything settles in, becomes
real."

You looked at Break and you saw muscle, you saw the
beard, you saw the ice blue eyes. No one immediately thought
upon seeing him that he was wise, but he was. He'd led a rough

life, living on the streets, eking out a living with his fists, dealing with all kinds of scumbags. The streets aged men and women beyond their years.

"Alright," I said, un-clenching my fists and releasing a breath that I had been holding so long that the fresh air I pulled in burned my lungs.

"There's a gas station with an outside entrance to the bathroom down the block. Go and clean up. I'll grab you a shirt and meet you there."

So that was what we did.

Then we made our way back to my girl.

The walk wasn't long, but it was long enough to give a man time to think.

Like think about the fact that Elsie was just held at gunpoint by her sister who had somehow managed to overthrow Enzo and get hold of the Third Street loyalty. And, well, the bitch was cooking meth. Meth. Christ. On top of that, she had a busted face, raw arms and hands, and damage to her torso: busted ribs or maybe just some nasty bruising. It also didn't escape me that Enzo had been the one to diffuse things, saving Elsie, trying to get her off the ground. That meant something. Then him telling the Third Street guys that they were dead to him, yeah, that meant something too. And that 'something' needed some clarification as soon as fucking possible.

But first, Elsie.

I had barely come to a stop in front of her before her forehead landed in my chest and a wrecked-sounding sob tore from her, making a stabbing feeling sear through my gut. I let all the other shit fall away and held her until she worked through the first round of grief. First. I had watched my mom, sisters, and aunts enough in my life to know that, with women, their sadness came on them in waves. Days, weeks, months, years. Another wave could always come crashing. I had no doubt that Elsie was going to have more to go through in her near future.

When I finally got her into the car and turned it over, the other thoughts came flooding back. I knew I needed to stay in the moment and give Elsie whatever she needed, but I couldn't fight the other things from crowding out everything else.

I got her shuffled into a room and sat in the chair beside the bed, waiting for the doctor. She went for an x-ray of her ribs which weren't broken, just a little bruised. Her face would heal in its own time and I made a mental note to pick up more of the tattoo cover-up cream. Her hands and arms took the longest, a nurse painstakingly pulling clumps of dirt and gravel out of the dozens of blood-crusted cuts. Then she had medicine smeared on and her hands and arms wrapped up in gauze up to her elbows. She got a script for pain meds and instructions on treating her wounds at home. All said and done, she had gotten off relatively easy. But if you tried to tell that to the seemingly bottomless pit of rage inside me, nah. All I could see was her gorgeous face with a nasty bruise, a cut on her perfect lips, gauze all up and down her arms. All I could see was that some mother fucker put his hands on what was mine.

It didn't matter that D would likely be eating through a tube for the next year. It didn't matter that his face would never look the same again.

It wasn't enough.

But then again, even if he had paid with his life, it never would have felt like enough.

Because who I was really pissed at was myself. That shouldn't have been able to happen on my watch. My people did not get busted up. It didn't matter that I was out of the gang and had been for a long time, you didn't fuck with what was mine and that was how it was. But I had been too fucking wrapped up in spending time with her, getting to know her mind and her body that I hadn't done the most basic things to keep her safe. Like give her my God damn cell phone number. Instead of calling or texting me, she'd needed to drop a fucking pin and hope to hell that Barrett was paying attention. I hadn't given her mace or a self-defense key chain or taser like I had given my mom and sisters. I hadn't done shit.

She was sitting on a hospital bed all bruised and battered with tear-stained cheeks and sad eyes because I dropped the ball. I had to live with that. And when she got some sleep, some food, some time to think things through, she would start to see that I didn't protect her. Then she would look at me differently. And I would have to learn to live with that too.

The door opened and a middle-aged, graying, detective with a hangover of a waistline walked in, pen and pad already in his hands. I didn't have to ask for identification to know who he was.

"Collings," I said, giving him a jerk of my head as his younger partner walked in behind him.

"Paine," he said back, giving me a nod. "We have a couple questions for you, Miss Bay," he said, addressing Elsie, his face softening.

"Sure," she said, giving him a small smile and avoiding looking at me.

"Can you describe the man who attacked you today?" he asked.

I felt myself tense. If she described him too well and he showed up in the hospital later and Collings clocked the cuts on my knuckles, yeah, things wouldn't go too well for me. But that was a problem for later. I sure as fuck wasn't going to ask her to lie to the police.

Elsie shrugged a little. "Tall, but not super tall. A couple inches taller than me. I'm five-nine," she clarified as Collings nodded and wrote in his notepad. "Really built. Like... he had to have been using steroids to get muscles like that. He had on basketball shorts and a wifebeater. Nothing really distinctive about his features. Sorry..."

She was being evasive. She wasn't outright lying, but she wasn't giving the full truth either.

"Ethnicity?" Collings asked.

"African American," she supplied.

"Can you give us a plate number or partial plate number? Make or model of the car?"

"I didn't get a plate number. My back was to the car and then I was... unconscious. And I'm great with new cars, but I don't know anything about older cars. It was older. Very squared, tan or gold... old enough that there was no release hatch in the trunk."

"Okay," Collings said and I could see him mentally writing off the case. There wasn't enough to go on and we all knew it. True, Shane's security footage might eventually surface and then maybe D would be caught and sent away. But it was a long shot. It was something I needed to discuss with Elsie when she had a chance to process things; what did she want to do with the information? Did she want D in jail? Did she just want to let things stand? He wasn't a threat to her anymore, but if she needed him behind bars to feel safe, I would make that happen for her.

"Put your hand on me one more time!" I heard a loud, booming, commanding voice outside the door demand.

Don't tell me how I knew for sure who it was. Maybe it was the way Elsie stiffened, looking at once relieved, worried, and angry. Maybe it was the authoritative way he spoke, as if he wasn't used to anyone telling him what to do. Maybe it was just the most obvious explanation.

Edward Bay had somehow gotten wind of his daughter being in the hospital.

Not more than a couple seconds later, the door burst open, making the rookie cop stiffen and put his hand over his weapon. Collings simply slowly put away his notebook and pen and nodded at Elsie. "We'll be in contact, Miss Bay, if we hear anything." He nodded his head at Edward Bay as he passed. As he turned out the door, he caught my eye and gave me a look that I swear to fuck said he understood the situation and was leaving it up to me. Such was the way Collings, a twenty-something year member of the NBPD, handled business: let the streets handle their own shit until he absolutely needed to step in. He was clean. He didn't take bribes, but he understood the power balance in our town and he had no intentions of fucking with it.

"How the fuck did this happen?" Edward Bay asked as he closed the door. There wasn't an ounce of softness in his form, not literally or figuratively. Meaning he kept himself in shape underneath his five-thousand dollar gray suit and had a personality that would make a fucking ice cube shiver.

"Nice to see you too, Dad," Elsie said, her voice sounding suddenly exhausted, like the night's events had drained every last drop of energy from her. "This is Paine," she said, waving a bandaged hand in my direction. My head tilted at the guardedness of her tone, wondering where it came from, if she was reconsidering us as a couple because of all the shit that went down. Even if that was the case, it wasn't something we could talk about in front of her father so I let it drop, but it stayed as a clawing feeling in my stomach.

"Paine?" he repeated, turning to look at me.

"Mr. Bay," I greeted him, tucking my hands behind my back, making it clear I had no intention of shaking his hand. I knew it was a slight and if the fire in his eyes was anything to go by, he took it as such.

"Seriously, Elsie? Is this what this is all about? Why you've been so irrational lately? Blowing up at Sunday's dinner? Because of some itch you're getting scratched by some..." he trailed off, waving a hand dismissively.

I expected her to shrink away, to let it drop. From all I could tell about their relationship, she always backed down, always cowered. That was what he raised her to do. But she didn't. She sat up straight which I knew sent a stab of pain through her body, but she was trying to stand her ground. "Some what, Dad? Where were you going with that?"

"Drop it, Elsie," he commanded, voice frigid.

"Were you going to say something about him having tattoos? About him not wearing a suit at all hours of the day? Or

228

were you going to go deeper than that? Comment on the fact that he's not the right shade for me? Is that it?"

I felt my brows go up. She was on a tear. Her entire body looked like it was vibrating with rage. And while a part of me was pleased that she wanted to stand up for me, the other part was wondering why she would be so livid over a little nothing comment.

"I'm not a fucking racist, Elsie Ann," he barked and I honestly believed him.

"Then what, Dad?"

"You can do better," he answered simply.

Maybe I should have bristled at that, but a part of me might have agreed with him a little. She did deserve someone who didn't keep company with people who could shoot people from a distance an eagle couldn't see from, who didn't have a brother who just got beat out of a street gang, who didn't lose his shit and nearly beat a man to death.

"You don't even know him. You can't say that."

"Fine," Edward conceded, turning slightly to me. "I will get to know you over Sunday dinner at my house then."

"We can't. We have plans at Paine's mother's house this Sunday."

"Sundays are mine."

"Until you refused to talk about Elana being missing."

"For the last God-damn time, Elsie, Elana is not missing."

Elsie's head jerked back at the same time I felt myself stiffen. There was something in his tone, something off. Elsie's head tilted a little, her air rushing out on what was almost a sigh. "You knew, didn't you? You knew she was still in town."

"Of course I knew," Edward said in a tone that suggested he was offended she might think he was in the dark about anything.

"Did you know what she was up to? Did you know she stole from Rhett and Roman? Did you know she was taking over a street gang and cooking meth?"

"This is family business," Edward said, giving Elsie a look that was meant to make her drop it.

"You knew. You knew all of that. Oh my God," Elsie groaned, looking down to her lap and shaking her head. "And you just let me worry myself sick over it."

"I told you to drop it."

"And I thought you were being an unfeeling asshole!" she shrieked, making my brows raise and her father actually falter back a step in surprise. "God what a shitty family it turns out I have, huh?" she asked, looking over at me, but all I saw was pain there.

"Baby, I don't think this is the time or place for this. You've had a rough night. You're tired. Let's just let this go for right now."

"Tuesday night," Edward said to her, but also to me as well, then turned and left the room. No hug for his daughter. No hoping she felt better soon. No offer to be a call away should she need anything.

I wondered how Elsie came out of his house as she did. She was warm and sweet and affectionate. Even when she was riled, she didn't pull that holier-than-thou attitude her father wore like a shield. Was it her sister that pulled her through? Those two had definitely seemed like they'd had a strong bond if the way she had spoken about her was anything to go by. If that was the case, she must be especially hurting to have had that bond ripped from her a couple hours ago.

She still had Roman though.

As much as I wasn't exactly thrilled about her best friend being a guy who was admittedly in love with her, I understood the situation. I trusted her. I didn't need to trust him. And he was good for her. They had history. He was like family to her. Now, with her sister gone and her and her dad on the outs, she needed that more than ever.

Granted, I planned on sharing my crazy family with her: my mom, sisters, aunts, grandmother, as well as Breaker, Alex,

Shooter, and Amelia. But I knew that wasn't the same, at least not at first. Maybe down the road she could see them that way.

Christ.

Was I really thinking things like 'down the road'? With regard to a woman?

Seemed like I was.

A couple minutes later, the door slowly opened and into the doorway stepped Roman, as if my musings about him had somehow summoned him. He had on slate gray slacks and a deep blue dress shirt, his hair mussed like he had been raking his hands through it. And, judging by the tightness of concern around his eyes, I imagined that was exactly what had happened.

"Else..." he exhaled her name as he looked at her.

Elsie looked up, a strange, humorless smile on her lips. "Let me guess... Dad called you."

"Else, why didn't you call me?" he asked, looking like he wanted to cross to her, but either my presence or her uncharacteristic coolness was keeping him just inside the door.

"It's late," she went with, though we all knew what a bullshit excuse that was.

"Hey, babygirl," I called and she looked over at me and, if I wasn't mistaken, it was almost reluctantly. What the fuck was that about? "I'm gonna go to the hospital pharmacy and fill your scripts. You guys talk. I'll be back in twenty."

Walking past, I clamped a hand down on Roman's shoulder. His head turned to me and I could see he understood the meaning: figure out what is wrong with our girl.

With that, I took the scripts and headed toward the pharmacy.

When I got back the promised twenty minutes later, Rome was on the bed beside Elsie, his hand on her knee. She was curled slightly into herself, but had rested her head on his arm. When she looked up, she seemed almost shocked to see me. Feeling unsure, and not liking it one bit, I held up the bag, shaking it slightly so the pills jiggled in their containers.

"They discharged her," Roman provided, releasing her knee and moving to stand. "Talk to you for a minute?" he asked, but it was a demand seeing as he moved past me and out the door.

"Here, baby," I said, handing her the bag before following Roman out.

"What's up?" I asked as the door clicked closed.

He moved a couple steps down the hall so, presumably, Elsie wouldn't hear us. "She thinks you're going to dump her."

"What?" I said, a little too loudly seeing as two nurses across from us at the desk jumped. I gave them an apologetic smile then turned back to Roman. "Say that again."

"She said you're being weird and she thinks this was too much, too soon for your relationship and she was pretty sure that when you left to go get her meds that you were just saying that and weren't going to come back."

"Fuck," I sighed, running a hand down my face. That explained it. She was being distant and quiet because she didn't want to lean on someone she thought was going to try to shrug her off. "Did she tell you everything that happened tonight?"

"Pretty much word-for-word. Can't believe Elana stole from me."

"Elana stole from you?" I asked, brows drawing together.

Roman snorted a little. "Guess she hasn't filled you in on all the juicy details yet. I had a shipment of cold medicine go missing a little while..."

"Got it," I said, nodding. Didn't need more than that. Any idiot could see they were cooking meth in that warehouse. And everyone knew the main ingredient in meth was pseudoephedrine which was what you found in cold medicine. "Christ..."

"Yeah. So you need to get your ass back in there and make it clear you aren't leaving her. If I get so much as a whiff of you not doing what you should be doing to get her through this, I have no problem stepping back in. She deserves someone who will treat her right."

"I feel you," I said, nodding. Maybe a lesser man would have been pissed. He had outright just declared that if I slipped up, he planned on stealing my woman out from under me. But, that being said, no woman could be stolen if she was being treated right. So if I ever lost Elsie to Roman or any other man for that matter, it was my own fault. I had no right to be angry that someone else picked up what I had put down.

"Good. Now go get her home. She won't say it, but she's hurting and she needs sleep."

"You're a good man, Rome. I'm glad she has you in her life," I said. And I was. I hoped to fuck there were more men like him out there, men my sisters could come across and settle down with, men who would do the right thing even when there was nothing in it for them.

Rome nodded and turned away and I felt a small stab of regret for being a dick to him that night he admitted he loved Elsie.

But I didn't have time for that.

I had to get my woman home and show her that I had no intentions of going anywhere anytime soon.

NINETEEN

Elsie

"Really, I can undress myself," I said, wiggling out of his hands.

Okay.

I didn't know if it was something Roman said to him or what, but the second he stepped back into my hospital room, whatever tension and distance I had sensed in him was gone. Evaporated. I almost started to question if it had ever been there at all, if it was just a figment of my over-fried brain.

He'd sat down on the bed beside me, slipping an arm around my lower back, then one under my legs, pulling them gently until they went over his thighs and the good side of my face rested against his chest. His lips pressed down on the top of my head and his arms wrapped me up.

"They probably want this room emptied," I said a couple of minutes later of us doing nothing but sitting there cuddling in silence.

"They can wait, baby," he said softly and I felt a shiver run through my insides.

"My ribs hurt," I said next when I couldn't take the silence.

To that, I felt him nod as he slowly released me. "Okay. Let's get you home then," he said and then proceeded to do just that.

Which put us in my bedroom. I had kicked out of my shoes and used the toes of each foot to shimmy off the socks of the other. When I reached for my shirt, though, Paine's hands pushed them away and reached for it himself.

"I know," he said, then pulled the material gently up, waiting for me to lift my hands so he could get it off me.

I really could undress myself. While my arms and palms were wrapped, they had left my fingers mostly uncovered so I could do basic things to take care of myself.

The air of my room made my skin prickle and when Paine's fingers whispered down the center of my belly toward my pants, well, let's just say... my libido didn't get the message that it had been the shittiest day to end all shitty days and I was hurting all over and couldn't have sex. All that horny bitch realized was how good it felt to have Paine's capable hands on me. His eyes went up to mine as he started to pull the material down, then lightened, almost as if he knew where my mind was going.

"Breathe babygirl," he said as my pants pooled around my ankles.

I sucked in a hollow breath and Paine's hand moved to rest gently over the huge purple and blue bruise covering part of my belly and side. "It's okay," I said, reading the darkness that shuttered his eyes.

"Elsie, it's not."

"Well it's not okay okay, but I'm alright. And it's not your fault," I added, needing to get it out there, despite standing in the middle of my bedroom in nothing but my bra and panties and feeling way too tired for a relationship conversation.

"Elsie..."

"It's my sister's fault. D doesn't work for you. D didn't even know I belonged to you. To him, I was just some random chick. He didn't know El was my sister either. It was just... a bad situation. Maybe if I hadn't hit him..."

"Tomorrow morning, I'm running out and getting you pepper spray, a tazer, a cat-shaped stabbing weapon for that janitor's key chain of yours and a mini expandable baton. Then as soon as you're all better, I am teaching you some basic self-defense. When you get good at that, I am dragging your ass up to Hailstorm and they are going to give you the royal treatment."

"Hailstorm?" I asked, brows drawing together. I was pretty sure Hailstorm was the name of that weird storage-container community up on a hill with their guarded gates and dogs and stuff. I was also pretty sure they were just a bunch of survivalist freaks who thought the apocalypse was imminent or something like that.

"Yeah, Hailstorm. Hard to explain. They're like a lawless military. Most of the people there are ex-military. Those who aren't, have just as good of training. They can teach you the shit you'd learn in basic, but they can also get you up to snuff on things like Krav Maga and street fighting."

"I really don't think..."

"Enzo let your sister go, baby. I know you love her and no matter what happened tonight, she's still family to you. But we can't say she's not a threat. We also can't say for absolutely certain Third Street isn't a threat. I'll be taking better care of you from this point on out, but I'll breathe easier knowing you can handle yourself when I'm not around. Besides, it's a good workout. We can spar together."

Now, as a woman who has dated men who generally showed their feelings with flowers, jewelry, or even nice vacations, I had to say, nothing... no diamond earrings, no three dozen white roses, no trips to Fiji... nothing ever gave me the warm, gushy feeling in my stomach as what Paine just offered me. Maybe because jewelry and flowers and beaches didn't mean anything. It meant something that Paine wanted to keep me safe, to teach me to protect myself, to offer to train with me toward that goal.

"What?" he asked, watching my face, his lips tipping up and I realized I was doing the goofy smile I usually reserved for looking at his drawings in the morning... alone.

"I just... I really like you, Paine," I admitted with a small shrug.

His smile softened and his hand slid up my belly, between my breasts, then landed at the side of my neck. "I like you too, babygirl," he said, leaning down and planting a chaste kiss on my split lip. Then his hand slid back down and around my back, unclasping my bra.

"Paine!" I yelped as I tried to hold the cups to my chest.

"Seriously?" he laughed, shaking his head. "You're gonna be shy now? I've seen your tits before, baby. I've had them in my hands and mouth."

"Oh my God, stop," I begged.

His smile went a little wicked as he reached out and moved the straps of my bra down my arms, tugging when I didn't release the cups, completely exposing me, my nipples hardening against the cool air. As soon as the material fell to the floor, he reached behind his back, pulling off his shirt and tossing it to the side before reaching to unfasten his jeans. And, well, his near nudity was doing nothing to help the need I felt building low in my stomach.

"Now we're even," he said, standing in front of me in nothing but black boxer briefs that were doing nothing to disguise the hard-on he was sporting that made my sex clench hard in anticipation.

"I... ah..." I mumbled, shaking my head and looking away.

"Hey," he said, putting his thumb and forefinger under my chin to make me face him again. "Baby relax. It's gonna be a while before I can fuck you again and I'm fine with that."

"Obviously," I said, waving a hand toward his crotch.

"Looking at you, being close to you, especially when you don't have anything on, baby, that's gonna happen. But nothing will be happening until your ribs at least get a couple days of rest. That being said..." he trailed off, his devilish smile spreading as his hands moved down to cover my breasts. An involuntary moan escaped me as his thumbs stroked over my nipples until they were so hard they were almost painful.

"Don't," I said, finally finding my voice.

"Why not?"

"Because it's uneven," I reasoned.

"Elsie, look at you. You got beat to hell tonight. Look at me, I'm good. So I think it's pretty much my job to try to help you... feel good too..." he said, his hands moving down my belly and sliding his fingers into the waistband of my panties, pausing for a second before pushing them off my hips.

"Paine..."

"Bed baby," he instructed, walking me backward toward it.

"You don't have to..." I said, sliding carefully up onto my spot on the bed, wincing a little before I settled on my back, Paine's body moving over me, but not touching me at all, supported by his hands and knees.

"Nope. Want to," he corrected, lifting to balance on one palm as his other hand moved lower, his finger sliding up my slit to stroke over my clit, making my legs fall open in invitation as I struggled to breathe through the mix of pleasure and the pain that prevented me from getting enough air.

His body shifted lower, kissing down one of my inner thighs before he shifted inward slightly and his lips closed over my clit, sucking it hard and making my whole body shudder. He hummed a "Mmmm," around me and it was almost enough to make me come right then and there. His finger moved downward, slipping inside me and turning to work over my G-spot as his tongue moved out to stroke over my clit.

It happened fast, faster than I ever usually got off from oral, likely due to an over-tired mind and over-wrought body. His tongue had barely started working me when the tension got tight and snapped, sending a hard pulsating orgasm through me, making me cry out as my inner thighs started to shake. Paine was unrelenting through it, working my clit and G-spot harder and faster, drawing every last drop of pleasure out of me before he removed his finger and took his tongue away. He leaned up, planting a kiss at the triangle above my sex before moving up my body.

He settled onto his side beside me, reaching down to snag the blankets and cover our bodies. Finished, he settled down with me, one arm draped low on my hips, the other under my pillows. And then he leaned slightly over me and rested his head on my chest above my breast.

"You can't sleep on your side tonight and I like being close to you when I sleep," he explained as one of my bandaged hands went across his back, the other settled on the side of his neck.

I liked being close to him when I slept too.

So even though his weight was making it even harder to breathe, I fell asleep quickly to his warm breath on my chest and my arms around his strong body.

And as I drifted off, I was all-too aware of a small little feeling that started in my chest, right under my ribcage, and spread outward until it enveloped my entire body. And that feeling was: right. Being with Paine, even after the worst night of my life, it felt right. It felt like it was where I was supposed to be.

TWENTY

Elsie

Sunday, I woke up alone like I did every morning. The only difference would be that the past two mornings I woke up alone but only because Paine was downstairs brewing coffee and making me breakfast. I learned this after waking up on Friday morning alone, achy, feeling whiny and pathetic. And when I reached for the bedside table for my sketch, it wasn't there. Now, despite the good ending to the shitty night before, my mind immediately went to the worse case scenario, making me throw the blanket over my head on a tear-less sob and wallow in my painful self-pity.

For all of, say, three minutes before I heard something clang down on the nightstand and the blanket got peeled back from my head. "You gonna come out of there to eat or am I going to have to get creative here?" he asked, moving to sit down beside me.

There was no ignoring the squeezing sensation of my heart in my chest when I looked up into those perfect light green eyes in that perfect chiseled face of his and realized he hadn't left me, that I was being a worrywart for no good reason.

"Eat?" I asked, my belly doing a painful twisting thing due to not having any dinner the night before and, no doubt, taking the prescribed pain medicine on an empty stomach.

"French toast," he offered. "And a side of fruit so you don't feel too guilty," he added with a smile as I moved as quickly as my screaming side would allow to sit up against the headboard.

"Gimme," I said, holding out my hands to him, fingers opening and closing rapidly in excitement.

Paine chuckled, grabbing the tray and putting it on my lap. Looking down at my tray stacked with four pieces of powder-coated deliciousness, a bowl of cantaloupe, strawberries, and grapes, and a cup of coffee made just how he knew I liked it, I almost felt a little teary-eyed. Almost. Okay, not almost. There was some definite glistening.

When I looked up at him to thank him, the sexy little smile he had on made the words slip away. "What?" I asked, wanting to be in on whatever was giving him that look.

"Glad we're over that bullshit shy thing," he observed and it was in that moment that I realized I had sat up in my bed completely freaking shirtless and the blanket was pooled around my waist. What can I say? I almost never went to bed naked. It hadn't even crossed my mind to cover up because I usually just... was covered up in the morning. "Don't," he said, shaking his head like he knew I was going to try to figure out how to move the tray whilst simultaneously try to cover my breasts... all with sore, wrapped hands and arms. "If it's a thing, I'll head back down..."

"No," I interrupted, my word too urgent but I didn't care. "Stay."

"That's better," he said, moving around the bed to climb in with me, planting a sweet kiss on my temple.

And, well, when I lifted up the pain medicine bottle to take one, I got my sketch. I unfolded it, trying to force my lips to stay in a straight line but when I saw a drawing of me in a karate gi with a black belt at my waist, I couldn't help it... I goofy grinned my face off.

Saturday morning I woke up alone too, but only because he had gone to grab muffins and coffee after the gym. My sketch was on my brown muffin bag- a simple picture of our hands holding each others, mine all fixed and flawless. I cut the side out of the bag and put it in my jewelry box.

Sunday, I woke up alone because, as Paine had told me the day before after an extremely long conversation on the phone with his mother, then it sounded like both of his sisters, his aunts and his grandmother, they had requested his presence to help set things up for dinner. And Paine, being the good son he was, didn't even pause to offer his help. So I sat up slowly, only wincing a little at the twinge in my ribs. They were feeling better. I didn't need the pain meds anymore and Paine had locked them up in my safe for me the night before. The picture was on a normal sheet of paper that he, I assumed, took out of the printer that I kept under the counter in the kitchen. It took up the entire page and I figured he must have gotten up super early because it was extremely intricate. He'd drawn what, I imagined, was his mother's house and he'd drawn every single person who was supposed to be present at dinner: I saw us, Shooter and Amelia, Breaker and Alex, his mother, two women his mother's age who I took to be his aunts, two younger women who I guessed were his sisters, his grandmother, and... Enzo. Enzo was going to be at dinner?

I didn't put the picture in my jewelry box mainly because it would require me folding it and I decided that I was going to take that one and get it framed as soon as I looked less like I was one of those too stupid to live chicks who somehow managed to live through the horror movie despite their aforementioned too stupid to live-ness.

I left my arms unwrapped, all of the cuts having healed over. They were still all red and ugly, some bigger than others, but there was no longer any risk for infection. Besides, the bandages thing was too much of a hassle. I was over it.

I showered, spent way too much time fiddling over my hair and makeup, using a liberal amount of the tattoo cover-up, then hemmed and hawed my clothing choices for an embarrassing amount of time. It sounded like a casual event so there was no way I was showing up in a dress and pumps. But I didn't want to show up looking like a slob when I was meeting so many people for the first time. Normally, that was something I would have run past my sister.

I felt a stab of something akin to grief pierce through me. It was a feeling I knew I would have to get used to, a feeling that would never go away. Because, for me, it wouldn't matter if Elana decided to clean her act up and want her old life back... she wasn't my sister anymore. I put up with a lot of abuse from my father and, I imagined, I would continue to do so. But my father had never raised a hand, let alone a gun, to me. And if I knew my sister, that gun was absolutely loaded. Even if she never had any intention of using it on me, she was taking a major risk. What if something scared her? What if her finger twitched on the trigger? She could have killed me because of her selfishness.

I wasn't sure if I was big enough to forgive that.

And I knew I would never forget it.

So I envisioned a lot of moments in my future where the void she left in my life by her own actions would ache, would make me wince, would make me sad.

On a sigh, I reached for a pair of gray skinny jeans, a lightweight v-neck black sweater, and black bootie heels. Simple and understated, but still classy.

With a knot the size of Texas in my stomach, I drove to the florist, picking up a simple bouquet of mixed flowers for Gina, then made my way over toward the townhouse complex where his mother lived. It was the same housing complex that I had originally planned on buying a place in. It was a nice, winding complex of modest one or two bedroom houses, green

243

lawns, and tons of kids. Even in the dead of the winter, they were out in force, on their bikes, on skateboards, playing hopscotch. It was so quaint that it belonged on some campaign commercial for a politician.

I spotted the cars before I spotted the people: Paine's Challenger, Breaker's SUV, Shooter's expensive sports car. The men were all standing in the driveway talking to another man in a leather jacket with a Henchmen logo on the back, his blond hair long on one side and shaved to a buzzcut on the other. His arm was thrown around a blond woman, tall, leggy. I couldn't see either of their faces as I tentatively parked my car behind all the others which would give me a second to think about what it meant that Paine, Breaker, and Shooter were friends with a member of a lawless bike gang. I grabbed the flowers and got out, deciding it probably made a lot of sense. They were all presently, or had at one time, been criminals. I guess they all ran together. Or at least got along.

"Hey babygirl," Paine said, reaching out to sling an arm around my hips as I moved in beside him.

Up close, I finally got a good look at the biker and his woman. And, well, he was hot. Fantastic features, deep green eyes, tattoos, cocky grin. His woman was a little older than him and freaking gorgeous in a way that said she could disarm you with a smile then slit your throat before you could see it coming kind of way. Her brown eyes focused on me for a second, taking in my arms and lingering on my cheek like maybe she knew what was underneath the makeup.

"This is Cash and Lo," Paine explained, nodding at the couple.

"Heya sweetheart," Cash said with a smile that would make any woman's (who didn't belong to Paine) knees wobble.

"Cash is Mom's neighbor. And a friend. Lo runs Hailstorm."

Lo runs Hailstorm? Lo? The pretty blond-haired, brown-eyed bombshell with boobs that made my sister's look minuscule actually ran what Paine had referred to as a "lawless military"?

"So are you the one who is going to turn me into a badass?" I asked, meaning it as a joke.

Lo smiled. "Damn straight. Between me and Janie, you're going to be a force to be reckoned with."

"Janie?"

"Her husband refers to her as 'hell and headaches' when she gets on a tear," Breaker explained with a smile that said he agreed with Janie's husband's comment. "She makes all the rest of us look like teddy bears."

Lo rolled her eyes. "Don't listen to them. She's only like that when you piss her off. In which case," she said, looking back at Breaker, "you deserve all the piss and vinegar." I felt myself smiling. When Lo looked back at me, she smiled back. "Don't worry. The girls club will take care of you."

"The girls club?" I repeated.

"Yeah. When you get yourself wrapped up with one of these," she said, waving a hand to the group of guys as a whole, "you automatically get pulled into the fold. Me, Janie, Amelia, Alex, Summer..."

All the names I recognized but one. "Summer?"

"My brother's wife," Cash supplied.

"How is she?" a short, curvy woman with long, dark hair and dark eyes asked as she walked up. There was a hint of Spanish ancestry in her skin tone and features, giving her an exotic and understated sexy look. She wore light wash skinny jeans and a roomy pale pink cardigan over a white tee, assuring me that I hadn't made a mistake with my wardrobe. Judging by Paine's sketch, she was Shooter's girl, Amelia. This was verified a couple of seconds later when she joined him and he reached out and wrapped up her pinkie with his. I repeat: he held pinkies with her. Pinkies.

"Tired. Ferryn seems to have taken after her father. She's been a handful," Cash said with a smile.

"Are we serving dinner on the front lawn?" a voice called from the steps and I turned to see a tall, thin woman on the steps. She was all legs and torso with Paine's perfect skin tone and a mass of curly black hair that she had in a loose ponytail at the nape of her neck. A few tendrils had escaped to frame her face. Needless to say, she was the product of Gina who was an attractive woman, and the sister to both Paine and Enzo... so yeah... she was extremely good looking.

"Kenzi," I heard myself say, looking up at Paine. "The ball-buster."

"That'd be her," he agreed, with a happy sparkle in his eye, like he was pleased I remembered what he'd said about his sisters.

"Sugar, honey, darlin'," Shooter said, sending her a charming smile.

"Don't 'sugar, honey, darlin' me, Johnnie Walker Allen. I have food to serve and an empty table. You don't get your asses in here in two minutes, I am locking this front door and you can all starve. Hey, Elsie," she called to me, giving me a warm smile despite her firm words.

"Hey," I called back, but she was already turning back into the house.

"You guys better go," Cash advised. "She means business."

"No shit," Breaker agreed, already moving back toward the front door.

"So that was Kenzi," Paine said as we trailed behind all the others.

"I like her," I decided immediately. How couldn't you like a woman who could open her mouth and make a group of big, scary, badass dudes fall in line?

"She's a pain in the ass, but she had to grow up dealing with me and Enzo so..."

"Speaking of," I said, stopping at the top step. "He'll be here today, right?"

"I should have run that by you first..."

"No. Of course not. He saved me. He's your brother. I'm happy to get to know him better. I was just wondering if things would be... tense here with your family."

"Nah, baby. They've all kept in touch on and off. Not super close, but Ma felt like she owed it to Annie to keep an eye on him no matter what he got himself into."

"That's sweet of her. Oh, this is probably none of my business but..."

"It's all your business," he brushed away my worry.

"Was it Kenzi?"

"Was who Kenzi?"

"The one who Enzo gave..."

"Yeah, it was Kenz. She had a wild streak until she got her life on track. But just to clarify, Enzo wasn't the one who gave her the shit. But his guys never should have either. They should have known she was off-limits just like they knew when I was running things."

"Got it," I agreed just when another new face popped into the doorway.

This woman was long and leggy like Kenzi, but not related to Paine in any way. She had pale, perfect skin over her delicate features. Her brown hair brushed her shoulders and her brown eyes gave her an almost doe-eyed look. She, like Amelia, had on jeans. But she had a black long-sleeved tee on with it. And flats. Because she was already tall. From the picture, she was Alex. Paine had told me that she was some kind of hacker and that she was, a lot like Kenzi and apparently Janie, a real ball-buster. It was what Breaker liked best about her.

"Your sister is driving me up a fucking wall," she declared, shaking her head. "I apparently didn't wash the lettuce correctly. Who knew there was a wrong way to wash lettuce? Seriously..."

"Hey Alex. This is Elsie."

"Hey Else," she said easily, shrugging off her anger at Kenzi. "I hope you know how to properly wash lettuce."

"I have never washed lettuce in my life. Maybe you could... spread that around. Let everyone know not to expect much of anything from me when it comes to the kitchen stuff..."

"Don't count on it. I can't cook for shit either but they still have me in there slaving away. You're screwed," she declared, taking off down the hall that I knew from my house tours, led to the kitchen. The majority of the commotion was coming from that direction.

"Ready?" Paine asked, giving me a little squeeze.

"Yep," I agreed, feeling reasonably better. Everything seemed casual, familiar, easy-going.

Besides, I'd already met Gina and, sort-of, Kenzi. Plus Amelia and Alex. All that was left was the aunts and grandmother and the other sister.

We rounded the dining room, a huge table with a ton of chairs taking over the entire space, all the places set and I got the impression that Gina entertained on this scale often. There was a passway into the kitchen and I could see all the women except Alex inside, moving about. Alex was standing next to Breaker who handed her a beer. "I'm banned," she explained, tipping her beer up at me before taking a sip.

"I should go offer a hand at... um... something," I declared, moving out of Paine's hold and making my way into the kitchen, looking for Gina. She was standing at the stove, scooping something out of a pot and into a piece of serving ware for the table.

"Hey Gina," I greeted and her head popped in my direction, giving me a genuinely warm smile.

"Elsie! So glad he didn't fuck things up," she declared, making me choke on a small laugh.

"These are for you," I told her, holding out the flowers. She put the bowl down, wiped her hand on her half-apron, and took them from me.

"You're so sweet," she said, giving me a hug with a back rub that gave me flashbacks to my own mother. "Steer clear of

Kenz. She's like a Nazi in the kitchen. Tell her you burn everything you put your hands on," she warned close to my ear.

"Good plan," I agreed and she gave me a small squeeze before moving back to her task.

"Mom," she called to the older woman who was putting rolls into a basket. "This is Paine's girl, Elsie. Elsie, that's Cora. And those are my sisters," she added, gesturing with her spoon toward the two women who looked like slightly older versions of herself who were picking up trays to carry to the table, "Geri and Georgie. You've met Amelia and the recently excommunicated Alex, I assume."

Technically I hadn't met Amelia but she gave me a sweet smile as she lifted a huge jug of sweet tea. "Hey, Elsie," she said. "Welcome aboard."

"You," Kenzi said, pointing at me. "What's your specialty?"

"In the kitchen? Um... handing someone the take-away menu?" I offered and everyone chuckled.

Kenzi smiled. "Good to know. Reese, where the hell are you?" she yelled.

Reese. She was the other sister. The shy librarian.

"Hiding from your bossy ass, no doubt," Gina said in a motherly way.

"Excuse me for handing out drinks to our guests," a quiet voice said from behind me in a way that was both sweet and firm, like she was used to dealing with her outspoken sister and was not about to get run over by her all the time.

"Well... fine. Grab a bowl and help us serve. The men are going to start barking if we don't feed them soon."

"You know, in case it hasn't escaped you all with your nineteen-fifties sensibilities," Alex called from the doorway, "I know for a fact that at least two of those men cook better than some of us."

"We get it, you're not a 'waiting on a man' type," Kenzi said, handing her a bowl. "Now help us set the damn table," she added with a smirk.

I grabbed a plate full of roasted vegetables before I could be yelled at and high-tailed it out of there.

I had just put the plate on the table when another big figure made his way into the room. His face was less swollen than it had been a few days before, but he was still bruised and favoring his ribs. Enzo nodded at his brother, Breaker, and Shoot before making a beeline for me.

"Hey honey, how you holding up?"

"Better than you, I imagine," I said, tilting my head to look up at him. "How are your ribs?"

"Busted. Will continue to be for a good while still. Yours?"

"Oh they're real pretty," I said dryly. "But they're feeling a lot better."

"Good. I'm glad."

"Enzy!" Reese's voice went high and girly as she slammed a plate down on the table and ran around the table, hitting him bodily, apparently completely unaware of his injuries. He grunted and winced hard, but wrapped his arms around his half-sister and squeezed tight. "You never come by anymore!" she accused into his chest. "I miss you."

"I miss you too, Re," he said and there was a sadness in his tone that said he truly did.

"Alright. We can do the reunion shit later," Kenzi declared, making Reese untangle herself from her brother's arms. "Asses in seats if you want to eat. You know where you all belong."

With that, everyone moved to find their seats. It didn't escape me that, when she passed him, Kenzi gave Enzo a one-armed hug and whispered, "I missed you too, you know."

"You're with me," Paine declared, grabbing my hand and pulling me toward our seats.

Once all seated, everyone just dug in. Literally everyone was grabbing for food at once. I sat back a little shell shocked, not used to casual family gatherings. Luckily for me, Paine to my left and Enzo to my right simply dropped piles of whatever they reached for onto my plate until there wasn't a sliver of the plate visible beneath all the food.

Then commenced the loudest, craziest, friendliest, most entertaining dinner I had ever been a part of in my life. By dessert, my cheeks hurt from smiling.

Catching Paine's eye, I whispered quietly, "I love them all."

Under the table, his hand squeezed my knee as his eyes went soft.

Yeah, I loved them all.

And, in that moment, I was starting to think I might have loved him too.

EPILOGUE

Elsie - 1 Day

I was shaking when I hung up the temporary cell phone I bought at the pharmacy on the way to work that morning. I hadn't talked about my decision with Paine. I would tell him when I got home, but I hadn't been sure what I was going to do until I did it so I didn't want to make a big deal out of it for no good reason.

I tossed the phone in the garbage outside my favorite coffee spot, went in to grab coffee, then headed home with the weight of the knowledge that I just brought down a raid upon the warehouse on Kennedy.

It had been something weighing on my mind since the morning after all that craziness. I had knowledge of a federal crime. Not only that, I had a means to help Rhett and Roman save face. On top of all of that, I had the chance to keep God-knew how many drugs out of the hands of countless people.

So I bought the burner. I made the call I needed to. And I drove home feeling a thousand pounds lighter.

My sister may have been caught up in the sweep, but that was the choice she had made. I wasn't taking that guilt on as my own.

Paine, when I told him as we sipped our coffee on the couch, understood and supported my decision.

And whereas the day before I had been pretty sure I was in love with him, as he absentmindedly rubbed one of my feet with one hand as he brought his coffee up to his lips, I knew it.

Paine - 1 Week

"Enz," I said as he sidled in beside me at the bar at Chaz's. "Looking better," I said, nodding at his face. There was a scar running up his cheek that he would always have to remind him of the life he had led. Had. Past tense. He was out. And it was my plan to make sure he stayed out.

"Paine," he nodded, reaching for the beer I had already ordered for him. "Why all the secrecy?"

"I got a job for you."

"A job?" he asked, a hint of both hope and concern. Enzo needed money. He had a savings like I had a savings when I got out. But it wouldn't last forever. He had no college education, no work experience but the shit places he had worked at before he came to work for me. And I knew he'd rather rip off his own arm than go back to one of those shit jobs.

So I stuck my neck out; I put out feelers; I found an out for him, one that could give him the adrenaline fix he needed, would utilize some of his hard-earned street skills, pay a fair amount of money, let him generally work for himself, but still be relatively legal. Relatively.

"Ever hear of Xander Rhodes?"

"PI in the city?"

"Yeah. He's been expanding his operation. He needs a couple new good men with skills and a willingness to operate just under the law."

"Doing what? Taking pictures of cheating husbands?"

"Won't lie to you, sometimes it will be that boring. But he does other jobs too, ones that get more interesting, dangerous. It's not ideal, Enz, but it's a way out of here. You can start new there. No one will know your past unless you want them to."

"I'm feeling like there's a catch here."

"A small one."

"Spit it out, bro."

"I need to see your face at Ma's Sunday dinner. Once a month. It's not asking too much. Kenz and Re need you around. Ma too. And me. We got some mending bridges to do still."

Enzo looked toward the mirror behind the bar, both of us reflected, as he peeled the label off his beer. "Alright."

"Alright?"

"Yeah, alright. I think it will be good for me to get out of here."

"So long as you come back."

"Fucked up my life for a lot of years. It's about time I start fixing it. Starting with you and the girls. But to do that, I need to get my shit together, get my head in a better place. I appreciate the opportunity." He was quiet for a long minute before finally turning to me. "I owe you a..."

"You don't owe me shit," I said, shaking my head. "The only reason you got into that life in the first place was because I let you in. I could have turned my back, told you to keep yourself out of the streets. You ended up where you ended up because of me. If anyone should be apologizing, it's me."

"We both have done shit. We don't need to harp on it. Let's just move on. Sound good?"

"Sounds good," I agreed, tipping my beer to him.

For that Sunday and every Sunday dinner my mother held for the next fifteen years, he was always there.

Elsie - 3 Months

I got a sketch every morning. Every single morning for three months. Over a hundred pictures that I had finally started adding to a scrapbook. The one he had made me of his family was in a gorgeous silver frame on a shelf in our living room.

Yes, our.

He'd pretty much moved in. He still kept some of his stuff at his apartment in his store, but that was more for convenience in case he needed them when he was working. There was half a closet full of his clothes next to mine. There was a bathroom cabinet with his shaving cream and straight razor that butted up against my perfume and nail polish remover, and a nightstand covered in sketchpads and pencils that used to house my notepad that I really never needed to use in the first place.

See though, as I learned one night when I came home to Paine sitting at the dining room table with all my sealed bills spread across the surface, I realized something else about Paine. He might be willing to live in a house that technically did not have his name on it, sleep on sheets he didn't buy and put his feet up on a coffee table he didn't pick out, but he was not willing to do all those things without contributing.

"Don't even bother trying to argue about this," he said as I set my purse down. "You agree to letting me pay half or I'll pay all of them fully behind your back."

I had no doubt he would do just that so we sat down and we figured out what half of all the bills were. Every month, cash for half of each bill would appear on the kitchen counter.

"Now that's settled," Paine said, giving me a devilish little smile that made my sex clench in anticipation.

"Is there... other business to attend to?" I asked with a smirk as I lifted my ass up to sit on the edge of the table, crossing my legs in a way that made my skirt slide up my thigh.

Paine stood slowly, eyes trailing down my body. "Very serious matters, actually."

"Will we be in a good... position once we get it handled?" I asked, arching my head up as he came to stand in front of me.

"Great fucking position, but there's going to be a lot of handling first," he promised.

"We should probably get started then, huh?" I asked, making a show of wetting my lips. "What do you need from me?"

His hands went to the button of his pants, pushing it through. "First I need you on your knees."

"Hmm," I said as I slid off the table and moved to kneel in front of him. "This seems like an unusual way to conduct business," I mused as he reached inside his boxers and pulled out his hard cock.

"Are you questioning my methods, Miss Bay?" he asked, stroking himself twice before settling his hand at the base.

I felt my lips twitch. "No... sir," I said, mostly keeping a straight face.

His hand slid to the back of my neck and I opened my mouth. "Good, then get to fucking work already," he demanded with a smirk before jerking my head forward and burying deep into my mouth, making my throat clench hard once before my gag reflex settled.

Paine liked rough the vast majority of the time.

There were times he could be unexpectedly sweet and soft and gentle, like the first time we'd had sex after I'd been beaten up. He'd slid inside me slowly from behind as we spooned and made sweet, gentle love to me until an orgasm moved through me with enough intensity to make me cry.

But, that wasn't the usual.

The usual was fast, rough, uninhibited, spanking, hair-pulling, demanding sex.

And I was greedy for every bit of it.

Even when he had me on my knees, holding my head still by the back of my neck as he fucked my mouth fast and rough as he pleased, taking every bit of control from me, which was exactly what he was doing until he released my head.

I sat back on my ankles, wiping my face of spit and pre-cum for a second before his hand sank into the hair at the nape of my neck, curled, and dragged me upward.

"On the table," he growled, reaching behind his back to pull off his shirt as I got up and sat at the edge of the table. He moved in to stand at my knees, my skirt too tight to allow me to spread my legs for him. His hands grabbed the front of my shirt, jerking it out of my skirt, holding it at each side, and pulling hard, making the buttons open. And by open, I mean pop off, scattering noisily around the room. I sucked in my breath at the carefully contained violence of it, my pussy clenching hard in excitement, as his hands grabbed the cups of my bra and dragged them roughly down, exposing my breasts. His thumbs and forefingers took my hardened nipples, squeezing and twisting them hard, making a half-groan, half-gasp escape me as my system sparked with the erotic twinge of pain and pleasure. "How hard are you willing to work on this, Miss Bay?" he asked, doing another twist.

I sucked in a slow breath. "I can be worked as hard as you need to work me, sir."

"God damn right you can," he growled, releasing my nipples, grabbing me behind the knees, and jerking hard, sending me flying backward as my hips left the table. As soon as my back was on the table, his hands grabbed the hem of my skirt and tugged it upward, reaching between my thighs and ripping off my lacy panties. He wasn't in a teasing mood and the second after I was exposed to him, his cock slammed into me hard and deep, making me arch up off the table and try to plant my heels to allow me to thrust up into him. "No," he snapped, grabbing my ankles as my feet finally hit the table and pulling my legs upward, settling them both onto his left shoulder. One hand held them there, the other pressed down hard on my lower stomach, making me feel him deeper, more intensely.

Then he was thrusting, fast and deep, his pace the manic, unrelenting, predictable pace that made my orgasm build strong and fast, leaving me panting for breath as he pistoned inside me, demanding the kind of climax that threatened to make me dumb.

"Come babygirl," he demanded as his hand released my ankles and closed around my throat, just hard enough to make my head start to get fuzzy as he thrust in and jerked up, hitting that spot deep inside that pinched in the most delicious way.

Then I came, my legs jerking so hard that my shoes smacked into the side of his face, which in no way slowed him as he slammed inside me through it, dragging it out as I cried out his name. As I collapsed back onto the table, he slammed deep, growling out my name as he came inside me.

He pulled my legs off his shoulders so he could press forward over my chest, claiming my lips with none of the demands or violence of his fucking, kissing me sweet and deep, before pulling back. "Never gets old," he said when I opened my eyes.

"Never will," I agreed, wrapping my legs around his hips and my arms around his shoulders, knowing deep down in my soul that that was the absolute truth.

Elsie- 6 Years

"Mom!" I heard bellowed as the front door crashed into the wall, footsteps running toward me in the kitchen, completely unconcerned with the loud bleeping of the alarm system. "Mom, guess what?" I heard as the alarm stopped beeping just as four year old Jackson barreled into the room, his muddy sneakers dropping dirt everywhere as he came to a skidding stop right in front of me. He was an exact, perfect, tiny replica of his father (and Uncle Enzo) with his tan skin, light green eyes, and uncharacteristic height and shoulder-width for his age.

"What?" I asked, turning from the spaghetti on the stove. It was the only real dish I had in any way mastered. I was still pretty handy with a take-away menu when Paine wasn't in the mood to cook.

"Uncle Roman is taking me on his sailboat!" he declared, eyes huge, mouth open like it was the most amazingly shocking thing that had ever been uttered. To say Jack was an extrovert would be putting it mildly. He was an endless bundle of energy attached to a tongue that never struggled for words, and a brain that was way too curious and mischievous for any of our good.

"Oh he is, is he?" I asked, looking up over my son to Rome who stood in the doorway of the kitchen, his hair more mussed than usual, his pristine white shirt with the unmistakable splattered stain of a fruit juice box. I couldn't tell you how many times I had warned him to stick the straw in out of reach of Jack who was way too impatient to wait for you to finish and had a tendency to grab the box and squeeze, ruining one too many nice shirts with bright red stains in the process.

Rome gave me a smile, soft, familiar. "Come on, Mom," he drawled in a little-kid voice. "Don't say no!"

"Yeah, Mom! Don't say no!" Jackson chorused and I felt myself laughing.

"You know you stand no chance," Paine said, coming up behind Roman with eight-month old Willow (named after Lo), head to toe in pink, propped up on his hip. Whereas Paine's genes were strong in Jack, my genes were prominent in our daughter. She got my face shape, my nose, and my blue eyes. Her hair was just a whisp of a dark brown, unlike her brother's black.

"Come on. You guys could use a day off. Ship off Wills to Kenzi or Reese. Let me have Jack. You guys can have a whole day to yourselves."

"What a novel concept," I mused, smiling at Paine. It wasn't that we were ever short on babysitters. Between Roman, Enzo, Kenzi, Reese, Gina, Amelia and Shoot, Breaker and Alex, and even Cash and Lo, we never had to look far for someone to give us a few hours of quiet. But since the very unexpected appearance of Willow, we truly hadn't had more than an hour away from both Jack and her at a time. I had been breastfeeding and it was just too much of a hassle to pump and worry about leaking to leave for any extended amount of time. But since Wills started eating food a few months ago and my milk started slowly but surely drying up from disuse, a date night was looking more and more like a possibility.

"Okay, but listen, Jack... you do not, under any circumstances lean over the side of the boat. Do you understand me?"

"Man overboard!" Jack yelled, squatting, jumping, and pretending to crash down into the water.

"I hope you know what you're getting yourself into," I said to Rome with a smile.

"He'll have a life jacket and I know better than to take my eyes off him."

"Still mentally scarred from that time you lost him at the park?" Paine asked, moving into the kitchen to deposit Willow into my arms and take over at the stove to save the food I had already forgotten about.

"I didn't lose him," Rome objected, shaking his head. "He was hiding behind the water fountain."

"Don't let him fool you," I smiled. "He lost him in a clothing rack at the store. Twice."

"You staying for dinner, Rome?" Paine asked and Rome nodded, moving toward the fridge to grab a drink.

I stood back, kissing the side of my daughter's head as I watched Rome pop the top on a beer as Jack prattled on endlessly to whichever man would listen about his plans to be a pirate when he grew up. With a parrot and everything!

The goofy smile spread across my face, a smile I had found on my lips every single day for six years, a smile I knew I would never lose. Not when I had Paine and the evidence of our love in the form of a rambunctious almost-kindergartner and the, hopefully a sight less rambunctious, almost-toddler as well as the strong supporting cast of characters Paine had brought into my life. New friends in his guy friends, men I could always count on lounging around in the living room on game nights, pretending to watch the kids: Jackson and Wills, along with Shooter and Amelia's two little girls, Bri and Alexis (who got their names from Breaker and Alex), and Breaker and Alex's one and only blond-haired giant, Junior. His name was actually Johnnie, named after Shooter's birth name, but everyone called him Junior, though there was nothing junior about him. He was the only kid around the same age as Jackson who could give him a run for his money.

There were also the women who Paine had given to me: Gina, the mother who replaced the one I had lost years ago as well as Kenzi and Reese who stepped into the position of my sisters when Elana disappeared.

Of course, that said nothing of the girls club too. Suddenly, I found myself surrounded not only by Amelia and Alex, but Lo, Janie, Summer, and eventually, Maze. We were an odd, mismatched group of women from uncommonly different backgrounds who had all somehow come together thanks to the men we had invited into our lives. There was the badass side of our friendship, the training Paine had insisted on that brought me to Hailstorm where Lo and Janie and even the highly trained Maze kicked my, Amelia's, Summer's, and Alex's asses. But there was the normal side to us as well, the coffee clatch where we talked about our kids, our men, our lives in general.

And, as always, Roman was there.

It had been awkward for the first six or eight months as we struggled to find the right balance for our friendship. But once we found the swing of things, we continued on, close as ever. Paine had welcomed him into our lives, shown absolutely no signs of any distrust or discomfort about his presence and Roman had become an amazing support system with the kids.

Enzo repaired the bridges he burned with his family and had become a good uncle to our kids. He wasn't ever-present, his job in the city keeping him busy, but when he did show up, it was always with some dangerous-looking contraption for Jack to learn to ride or drive or shoot and something for Wills that, invariably, came with a really annoying sound-making aspect to it and I just knew that when they were old enough, he would start bringing over rabbits and hamsters and hermit crabs for them. Without consulting me. But that was Uncle Enzo. That was just what he would do and we all loved him enough to not pitch a fit about it. Well, the love and the fact that even if we did pitch a fit, we knew there would be no changing his behavior.

As for the last remaining part of my family, my father, well... he had shown himself to be a much better grandfather than he was a father. He would come over and patiently listen to Jack's unending ramblings and kiss Willow's head. He would bring Jack to work with him when Jack insisted occasionally that he was going to be a businessman like Grandpa, wearing some suit we had bought him for a holiday and waiting anxiously by the door for my father to show up and show him his "corner office" that was "just waiting for him to get old enough to work there".

"Babygirl," Paine's voice said, close to me, making me jump slightly because I had been so zoned out that I hadn't seen him move across the room to me.

"Yeah?" I asked, lifting my head to look at my husband.

"What are you smiling about?"

To that, I smiled wider, stepping forward to rest the side of my face to his chest, feeling his arm close around me.

"Never gets old," I told him.

"Never will," he agreed, squeezing me tight.

XX

DON'T FORGET

ALSO BY JESSICA GADZIALA

If you liked this book, check out these other series and titles in the NAVESINK BANK UNIVERSE:

The Henchmen MC
Reign
Cash
Wolf
Repo
Duke
Renny
Lazarus
Pagan
Cyrus
Edison
Reeve
Sugar
The Fall of V
Adler
Roderick
Virgin

The Savages
Monster

Killer
Savior

Mallick Brothers
For A Good Time, Call
Shane
Ryan
Mark
Eli
Charlie & Helen: Back to the Beginning

Investigators
367 Days
14 Weeks

Dark
Dark Mysteries
Dark Secrets
Dark Horse

Professionals
The Fixer
The Ghost
The Messenger
The General

STANDALONES WITHIN NAVESINK BANK:
Vigilante
Grudge Match

OTHER SERIES AND STANDALONES:

Stars Landing
What The Heart Needs
What The Heart Wants
What The Heart Finds
What The Heart Knows
The Stars Landing Deviant
What The Heart Learns

Surrogate
The Sex Surrogate
Dr. Chase Hudson

The Green Series
Into the Green
Escape from the Green

DEBT
Dissent
Stuffed: A Thanksgiving Romance
Unwrapped
Peace, Love, & Macarons
A Navesink Bank Christmas
Don't Come
Fix It Up
N.Y.E.

ABOUT THE AUTHOR

Jessica Gadziala is a full-time writer, parrot enthusiast, and coffee drinker from New Jersey. She enjoys short rides to the book store, sad songs, and cold weather.

She is very active on Goodreads, Facebook, as well as her personal groups on those sites. Join in. She's friendly.

STALK HER!

Connect with Jessica:

Facebook: https://www.facebook.com/JessicaGadziala/
Facebook Group:
https://www.facebook.com/groups/314540025563403/

Goodreads:
https://www.goodreads.com/author/show/13800950.Jessica_Gadziala
Goodreads Group:
https://www.goodreads.com/group/show/177944-jessica-gadziala-books-and-bullsh

Twitter: @JessicaGadziala

JessicaGadziala.com

<3/ Jessica